3° BATCH
(AFTER RED & ROBIN)

OMNILOGOS
EXTENDED EDITION

MICHELE AMITRANI

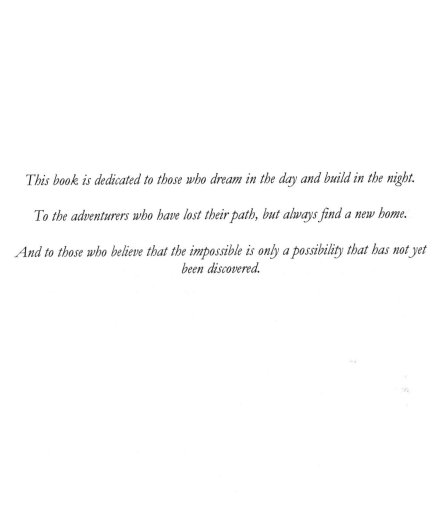

This book is dedicated to those who dream in the day and build in the night.

To the adventurers who have lost their path, but always find a new home.

And to those who believe that the impossible is only a possibility that has not yet been discovered.

CONTENTS

FIRST PART

WEI

PROLOGUE

"HAVE YOU HEARD? The Wangs moved to Florida."

"Who?"

"The Wangs."

"Yan Wang?"

"No, not Yan. William, William Wang. He took his wife and his son with him. The son … you know, right?" He tapped his index finger over his temple.

"Oh! *That* Wang. Moved you say? Why?"

"It seems William has found a job in Orlando."

"Remind me what the guy does for a living."

"He's a rope technician."

"Oh, yeah, that's right. He's the Mr. Clean of the skyscrapers."

They both laughed uproariously.

"It must've been a sudden departure. They left a lot of stuff behind."

A long moment of silence followed.

"You think… Well, you think all of this has something to do with their little pest?"

"What do you think? After what he did to that poor bastard…"

More silence.

"Yes, an awful mess. Neighbours I will not miss."

"Hmm," agreed the other.

There was the tinkling of a spoon in a cup.

"You know what? It looks like my Jenny is the only one who

seems to care. She didn't want them to leave."

"Jenny? Jenny is your little girl, right?"

"No, no. She's my eldest. She's a couple of years away from college."

"That's right. Well? What's her problem?"

"It seems she got close to Wangs' little Satan. He often wandered into the library where she studies, you know."

"Who? The kid? At that age? Shouldn't he be spending his days drooling on a napkin, or something?"

The other shrugged.

"Well, looks like Jenny found him there often, staring at books."

"He was probably messing them up with his crayons."

There was a murmur of approval.

"I understand. Your daughter babysat him when he was there, right?"

"No, it's not that."

"Then, what is it? She helped him color Mickey Mouse?"

The other shook his head, chuckling.

"No, it's quite the contrary. If you listened to Jenny, it seems *he* helped her with her chemistry."

A long pause followed with no one breathing. Then both laughed heartily.

ATLANTIS

2011

THAT DAY THE roof of the world was covered by a thick blanket of clouds. The light, dimmed by the greyness dominating the sky, weakly illuminated earth, sand and ocean.

Wei quickened his pace while greedily biting into a hot dog. On the third bite, an abundant dose of ketchup slid down his arm.

"Wei! Look what you've done!" The man who was holding him by the hand suddenly stopped, pointing at the mess. He took a paper napkin from his pocket and hastily wiped the child's arm. "Come on now, or we'll lose the best spots."

The child followed his father, still eating and splashing ketchup all over his clothes, as if nothing had happened. To their left, the cars kept coming. The long line of people who were walking on the side of the road trailed behind them chairs, umbrellas and boxes packed with food.

Wei finished his snack and licked his fingers while they were passing under the big billboard near the road where they had parked the car. *401 North Cape Canaveral A. F. Station* was written on it. A boy was pointing to the billboard as he asked a friend to take a picture.

They walked for a little while. Finally, his father decided to stop. He then looked at a distant point on the horizon, scratching his head thoughtfully.

"Yeah, should be fine here," he finally said, hands resting on his hips. His son was not listening. He was busy taking the cookie and the can of Coke that a lady nearby was offering him. Wei loved sodas.

"Thank you." The father smiled, nodding toward the woman as the child began to eat the edges of the cookie with methodical precision.

Both sat on the towels they had brought with them and waited.

Fifteen minutes passed. Just when Wei was starting to get bored, people around him began speaking louder, smiling at each other and pointing to a specific point in front of them. His father stood up and began to talk with the people nearby. Wei paid little attention to the growing frenzy and continued to focus on the stretch of water just a few dozen meters away, busy counting the waves.

"Come here." Wei felt two strong arms around his waist. His father gently lifted the boy from the ground and put him on his shoulders. "Can you see?"

"No," cried the child, complaining more than answering the question.

"Look over there, then. It's good to go! Can you see?"

The child didn't answer, he just folded his arms across his chest and snorted. Meanwhile, the line of people who besieged the edges of the road was growing.

"Twenty-five seconds," a voice suddenly cried to their right. Another two or three voices echoed the first, as the excitement grew.

Wei put aside his grudge and started to pay attention to the excited murmurs that saturated the atmosphere. Ever more intrigued by what was happening, he finally turned to the horizon where everyone was focused. He narrowed his eyes, eager for details, but he couldn't see anything.

An old man turned to him with a toothy smile and raised the volume of his radio to allow everybody around to hear.

"Go for main engine start. T minus 10, 9, 8, 7, 6 … all three engines up and burning." The crowd stopped talking, captured by the message on the radio.

Wei looked around him, puzzled. People were smiling with excitement. Many were nudging at friends or family members with their elbows. Wei saw a couple of kids jump like crazy rabbits. Somehow he felt part of that incredible family of strangers, bonded by an inexplicable sense of participation he couldn't really explain. Time seemed to stop for everything except the voice on the radio that continued its countdown.

"… 2, 1, 0 … and lift off! The final lift off of Atlantis! On the shoulders of the Space Shuttle …"

The voice got lost in the sea of cheers and celebrations as a powerful spark ignited on the horizon. The little boy, completely taken aback, stared breathlessly at the light lifting from the ground like a powerful firework that quickly became lost in the cloudy sky.

The crowd continued to cheer at the light for a few seconds.

When it was clear that the show was over, people started to gather their things and leave.

"Come on, Wei. Pick up your things and thank the lady here," said his father, nodding to the woman who had offered the snack to the child.

Wei didn't obey. He simply remained still, deep in his thoughts. It was as if he was trying to catch the last glimpse of the light, now completely gone from the world.

"Dad. Can we see it again?" he asked.

"Again?" repeated his father, confused.

"Yes, again. Can we see the light again?"

"This was the last time, Wei. I told you that. Don't you remember? This was the Space Shuttle's last departure."

The little boy seemed disappointed, almost annoyed. He looked at his father with a puzzled expression. "The last departure," he echoed his father's last sentence. "Why is that?"

The man opened his mouth, but didn't say anything. He had no real answer to the question.

"I want to see the light again!" The child's eyes shone with a magical fire as he pointed to the sky with his hand. "It was beautiful … No. It was awesome! Where will it go now? What was it made of? How come it was that fast? It'll be back, right?"

His father smiled. It was the very first time he'd seen his son, usually quiet and introverted, so interested and passionate about something. He covered the distance between them in a few steps then he knelt in front of him.

"You really want to know all these things?"

"Yes," the little boy immediately answered, "and I also want to see that light again."

"You will then, I promise," his father said with his hand over his heart. "Now let's go." He gently took his son's hand and together they walked back to their car.

Wei obeyed, letting the man guide him, but continued to stare at the legacy left by the tall column of smoke in the fading light.

Unknown Song

ANURADHA

2013

THE SOFT GLOW of the laptop faintly illuminated the room otherwise shrouded in darkness. Miss Gloria Powell settled back in her chair as she finished filling out a form full of graphics, letters and numbers.

After a few minutes, she snorted with disgust and pushed aside a stack of papers so huge it took up one third of the desk.

The woman absently moved her hand to grasp the cup on the table.

"Jesus Christ!" Miss Powell cursed after spitting out hot coffee. The brown liquid went all over the monitor. She cursed again and looked around in search of a paper napkin to sop up the spreading liquid. She found none.

After looking through her pockets, she decided to use one of the sheets on the table.

When she was done drying the last keyboard button, she threw the dirty paper in the trash bin. She then stood and turned to go to the restroom -- when the alarm she had set a few hours before began to ring.

"What time is it?" she asked, as if expecting an answer from someone. She scratched her frizzy hair, recovered the alarm clock shaped like a hamburger from the ocean of paper on her desk, and turned it off.

She moved the mouse and typed a password.

After a few moments, an icon on the desktop began to glow. Miss

Powell checked the time on her laptop. She shook her head, cursed once more, then clicked the left mouse button with a sigh.

The face of a woman with dark skin, grey eyes and an aquiline nose appeared on the monitor. She had long, dark hair tied back in an incredibly long braid that stretched beyond the borders of the screen. Her skin was rough, porous and hazel brown, as if she had worked for years under the hot midday sun.

"Miss Powell, can you hear me?" the newcomer asked as she adjusted her webcam.

"Y-yes, I hear you loud and clear," Miss Powell confirmed while clearing her throat.

"I'm Dr. Anuradha Galacta, from the Jet Propulsion Laboratory," the woman continued. "Thank you for your time, I really appreciate it."

"Of course. No problem," Miss Powell said as she fidgeted in her chair to find a more comfortable position. "I read your e-mail last night and I must say I didn't expect to see you personally, today. I mean, after checking your profile, I was expecting a call from your secretary or something like that."

"A secretary?" Anuradha repeated, grinning. "Well, I can't say it wouldn't be nice to have one, but I assure you that NASA's funds don't justify such a luxury." She waited a few seconds and then added, indicating the stack of papers, "Judging from what I see there, though, it seems you could definitely use one. Did I catch you at a bad moment?"

"Not at all." Miss Powell shook her head while awkwardly moving a stack of papers. "So," she continued once she had created enough space to rest her elbows on the desk, "to what do we owe the honour? Your e-mail mentioned my kids' letters, if I'm not mistaken."

"Exactly," Anuradha confirmed while fiddling with a pencil, moving it back and forth from one finger to another.

Miss Powell absently scratched her cheek as she stared blankly at the screen. "I remember when I was ten, I sent you guys a letter with my ideas on how to colonize Venus: get to the planet's surface with a huge umbrella made of diamonds to protect us from the acid rain."

"It looks like a promising start to me," Anuradha said, nodding briskly. "Your suggestion has been noted. If you come up with similar solutions to overcome the lack of oxygen, the atmospheric pressure and the impossibly high temperature, I see no reason why you should not send us your résumé. We are in constant need of original ideas here."

Miss Powell laughed heartily as she got rid of another stack of papers, pushing them into a drawer. "So they say," she answered showing a white, toothy grin. "I never knew who he or she was, but a few days after sending the letter I received a huge picture book with a description of all the planets of the Solar System. I think I still have it tucked away somewhere in my basement. That book literally blew me away. I believe I've never written back to you guys to thank you for the gift."

"Don't mention it." Anuradha leaned forward on her chair. "What an interesting story. I guess that's why you ask your kids to send us their ideas."

"Exactly, and some of your colleagues always send us something. You know - stickers, calendars, star charts, pamphlets, magazines - that sort of thing. It's nice to have that kind of attention, especially in places like this, if you get what I mean." Miss Powell looked around her, as if that gesture explained what she meant better than any words.

"However, this is the very first time we've received a call from a PhD at MIT."

Anuradha absently rubbed her eyebrow. "Actually this call is the result of a … well, I guess 'misplacement' is the correct word," she said as she kept her pencil moving between her fingers. "You see, the package with your letters arrived on my desk due to a misplacement. Imagine my surprise when I found what was inside: a dozen proposals suggesting how to boldly go where no man has gone before."

"Are you serious? By chance?" asked Miss Powell surprised. "Well, maybe at the JPL someone *really* thought that you needed new perspectives, 'original ideas' as you said. Don't you think?"

Both of them laughed, but Anuradha's face seemed to tense. Her smile was the first to fade.

"It may well be, yes," she said drumming her nails on the arm of the chair, "and honestly I've called you because of one of these ideas. I hope … well, I hope you can help me figure this … issue out. To tell you the truth, this thing is giving me a headache."

"You're still talking about the kids' letters?" Ms. Powell looked nonplussed.

"Absolutely."

"I have no idea what you're referring to, but if I can be of any help—"

"Thanks, I really appreciate it," Anuradha cut her off, suddenly becoming serious. "Well, to start off, I seem to understand that your institution sends the letters without the supervision of an adult. I mean, none of your staff usually puts his or her ideas in one of the kids' letters, right?"

"Dr. Galacta, my 'staff' is composed of my sisters and I. And we're not included in the senders list in any way whatsoever."

"No one else corrects or checks their work?"

"Well, no. The letter is an assignment the kids complete in class in a couple of hours. When they are done, we collect the letters and send them to you guys."

"I understand," said Anuradha, suddenly thoughtful. "If what you say is true, you've just made this conversation a lot more interesting."

"What do you mean?" Miss Powell asked while pulling her chair toward the desk in order to look more closely at the caller on her terminal.

"You see, most of the letters you sent us were ... well, normal. One portrayed a banana-shaped spacecraft powered by flatulence, while another mentioned a bunch of astronauts riding comets. The bolder among them suggested hitting a spaceship with a giant base-ball bat to allow them to exceed the speed of light. All stuff that one expects to hear from kids, nothing strange in this, and yet ... there is one letter I just can't explain."

"Which letter is that?"

Anuradha Galacta took a sheet near her and read, "It's signed Wei."

"Wei?" Miss Powell repeated thoughtfully, then she suddenly said, "Oh, yes! Wei Wang. He arrived a few weeks ago here at the Institute. What's so interesting about his letter?"

"First, let me ask you a question," Anuradha said, raising her hand. "The kids were supposed to send their proposals on how to travel among the stars. Is that right?"

"Well ... Yes, that was the point."

"I understand. You see, this Wei sent us ten reasons why we *can't* do it."

Miss Powell looked puzzled for a moment then she said, "Let me get this straight. You called because an eight-year-old boy didn't do his homework properly?"

Anuradha shook her head. "Of course not. That's not the point. What I wanted ... Wait a second! You said eight-year-old?"

"Yes, eight-year-old."

"I thought your institute takes care of only ten-year-old boys or older."

"That is correct, but we are temporarily entrusted with some younger cases if the circumstances require it."

"I understand," whispered Anuradha as she kept her pencil moving from one finger to another. Miss Powell realized that was her habit when she was thinking of something.

"But I don't," said Miss Powell, folding her arms across her chest and studying the now silent woman, "I don't understand what is—"

"Is it possible to see this boy, Wei?" Anuradha interrupted her.

"To see Wei?" slowly repeated the other woman, perplexed by the question. "I don't understand ..."

"I'd like to see him. Can you arrange a meeting with the child, tomorrow, maybe?"

"What? I ... no, I'm afraid it's not possible. Wei will leave the Institute tomorrow morning. I've already said that his staying here was temporary. But why do you ..."

"Excuse me, do you know where he'll be transferred?"

"Well ... yes, actually." She paused. Anuradha's questions and pushy tone were starting to make her uncomfortable. "The procedure in these cases is clear," continued Miss Powell, massaging her elbow. "Wei will be transferred to an institution equipped to meet his special needs."

"What special needs?"

"Dr. Galacta, with all due respect, I think I've already said more than enough. Excuse me, but we are dealing with confidential information here." Powell's face was irritated.

"My apologies. I've been too pushy," Anuradha said, looking a bit embarrassed. "This situation has sparked my curiosity and annoyed me at the same time."

"Never mind," said Miss Powell with a dismissive wave of her hand. "Just tell me why you're so interested in this damned letter."

Anuradha nodded. "I'll show you why. Open the file I've just sent you. It's Wei's letter."

Miss Powell did as she was told and started reading. After thirty seconds of silence, she said, "I don't understand."

"That makes two of us," said the other, spreading her arms.

Another minute passed. Anuradha waited.

Miss Powell continued to read the document without saying anything. When she emerged from reading, her expression was somewhere between surprise and disappointment.

"So, what do you think?" asked Anuradha. Her pencil was now dancing between her fingers.

"I think the kid's spelling is a disaster."

Anuradha's eyes widened. "That's it? What about the content?"

"I'd say that today's kids can give a whole new dimension to the term 'plagiarism'. Isn't it obvious? He clearly copied sentences here and there and tried to make some sense out of them."

Anuradha shook her head vigorously.

"No, that's not it. This is an original piece of work, with an introduction, a development and a conclusion that complete each part of the paper. Despite the text's appearance, whoever wrote it shows remarkable knowledge and impressive analytic capabilities."

"What? Are you kidding me?" Miss Powell laughed uproariously as she nervously scratched her elbow. "I mean, are you suggesting that the child actually knows what he's talking about? Don't you think you're exaggerating this whole thing? Here, I read terms like 'muscle atrophy', 'microgravity', 'ion thruster', and 'nuclear fission.' Do you realize that? Eight-year-old children have difficulty understanding the concept of a hot air balloon, for God's sake."

"Fine. Then tell me what to make of it."

"I don't know! Maybe ... maybe he was helped by one of the older boys."

"Have some of them taken courses in astrophysics or nuclear engineering recently?"

Miss Powell snorted. "And I thought I was the funny one."

"Are you beginning to understand my dilemma? I'm reading an essay of six pages filled with specialist terminology. This is clearly an unfamiliar subject for the average adult and still, at the end is the signature of an eight-year-old kid. Try to put yourself in my shoes. What would you do?"

"Look," said Miss Powell, shifting uncomfortably on her chair. "I understand the situation you've found yourself in, but I assure you that Wei simply couldn't have written that stuff. I have repeatedly tried to talk to him since he arrived, but he has been as talkative as a fish. Not a single word. He isolates himself from the others, looking for solitary and quiet spots. He doesn't want to stick with the other boys and ... well, we had a couple of incidents a few days ago involving him and two other kids ..." Miss Powell closed her eyes for a second and massaged her temples. She waved her hand, as if dismissing a disturbing thought. Then she added, "Plus ... to say it all, he didn't seem to me to be particularly clever, either."

"Don't you understand that this makes the whole thing even more fascinating? Just think. What if Wei really wrote that letter?"

Miss Powell remained silent for a few seconds while checking the file sent by Anuradha again, then nodded.

"Well, if nothing else, I now understand why you're so interested in seeing the boy. There is obviously something weird in this whole thing. If I were in your place I can't deny that I would like an answer; a damn good answer."

Anuradha sensed the hesitation in her voice. She stopped playing with her pencil and took a closer look at the screen.

"Look, I know I'm definitely not in a position to make such a request. I know that you have your rules to follow and I realize I'm only acting out of curiosity here, but please try to look at the bigger picture, try to do the right thing. Miss Powell ... Gloria ... I really just need to talk with Wei for a few minutes and—"

"I'm sorry, I can't," Miss Powell cut her off, standing up from her chair with a strange expression on her face.

Anuradha clenched her fists, unsure of what to say.

"I can't just ignore the Institute's rules," Miss Powell continued as she grabbed the cup of cold coffee and walked away from her desk toward the exit of the room.

Anuradha started to say something but the other interrupted her suddenly. "What I *can* do is get another cup of coffee from the kitchen downstairs and leave the door open to get some fresh air in the room. We will continue this conversation in exactly ten minutes." She blinked. "See you in ten, Doctor."

Amazed, Anuradha stared at the open door for half a minute. When she roused herself from her surprise, she couldn't suppress a grin. "Good," she muttered triumphantly while unconsciously continuing to fiddle with her pencil.

A minute passed that seemed like an eternity. Then she heard footsteps approaching hesitantly, followed by silence.

A figure appeared in the doorway, impossible to identify due to the dim light.

"Come on in." Anuradha's heart was slamming against her sternum and sweat was gathering on her palms.

The figure crossed the threshold of the room with a small jump, as if to avoid something on the floor. Anuradha leaned forward, almost touching the screen with her nose, then smiled a wide grin.

"Hello. You're Wei, right?"

The little boy signified assent with a single long vertical movement of his head.

"It's nice to meet you. I am Anu." She waved both hands and greeted the boy in front of her. "How about you sit down here and have a little chat with me?"

Wei didn't answer. He simply walked gingerly toward the laptop that was displaying Anuradha's smiling face. He stared for a few seconds at the woman's face with his small amber eyes, then tilted his head to the right, until it rested nearly on his shoulder.

"I'm Miss Powell's friend," she said, deliberately stressing each word. "I have read your letter, the one you sent to JPL a few days ago and I wanted to let you …"

The child looked away from the monitor and started staring curiously at the sheets spread all over the desk. He picked up a couple of them and began to read, apparently no longer interested in the speaking laptop.

"Wei? Can you hear me?"

The boy put the papers down, looked around, took the burger-shaped alarm clock from the table and put it in his pocket. Anuradha started to speak, but the kid had noticed something on the other side of the room that attracted his attention.

"Wei, where are you going? Wei?"

The boy disappeared from the screen, heedless of the woman's calls. She tried to lean forward to follow his movements but without success. The boy had vanished.

For a few seconds she heard noises coming from an unknown corner of the room. Then something fell on the floor followed by a sharp noise.

"Wei!" called Anuradha, unsure of what to do. The child, on the other hand, continued rummaging through Miss Powell's things, deaf to the increasingly desperate voice that kept calling him.

Suddenly the woman's cell phone came to life, filling the air with the bright notes of 'La donna è mobile'. Anuradha jumped off her chair, taken aback, and began to look around for the source of the sound. When she found the cell phone, she turned it off, annoyed. She then looked back at the screen. Surprisingly, Wei was returning her gaze. The boy cocked his head and stared at the woman, as if he was seeing her for the very first time. He sat down on the chair left by Miss Powell and started typing on the keyboard.

Anuradha read the message but it took her several seconds to understand it. In a small window the sentence *I love Verdi* appeared.

The woman repeated the three words to herself several times.

Finally a spark lit up in her mind. Eventually she was able to connect it with the ringing of her cell phone.

"You love Verdi?" she asked, hesitantly.

The child nodded briskly.

Anuradha read the message again but her thoughts were suddenly interrupted. Another message appeared.

Do you like him?

From her laptop a powerful, magnificent, vibrant and completely unexpected music broke out. Without even thinking Anuradha whispered incredulously, "Richard Wagner?"

The child clapped his hands, visibly pleased. A new message said: *Your turn.*

The woman was speechless. Willy-nilly she found herself in the midst of a musical competition against an eight-year-old child. If nothing else had done so before, she was convinced that Wei was nothing like the average eight-year-old boy. She decided to treat him as the special person he had proved to be. From that moment on, she put aside his physical appearance and focused on his uniqueness.

"OK, listen up. If you can't guess the next tune I'll win and you'll answer all my questions. What do you say?"

The boy covered his ears with both hands, closed his mouth and eyes and stood for a few moments without moving. A smirk appeared on his face then he typed on the keyboard: *OK*.

Anuradha fumbled for a moment with the mouse and keyboard. After a few seconds, she finally found what she was looking for.

Wei waited anxiously, as if someone was about to serve him a giant piece of chocolate cake.

Sweet, relaxed and poetic notes flooded the room like a slow but inevitable magma of gentle sounds intertwining with each other. Wei held his breath. He was concentrating now, two deep vertical lines grooving his forehead just above his eyes. The child was soon captured by the unique melody, devoid of logic, mathematics, foreign to anything he had ever heard.

After two and a half intense minutes, the melody uttered its last note and Wei found himself wiping his eyes with his sleeve. He didn't know who had composed the music but he felt his heart pounding in his chest. It was so beautiful, he thought.

You won. Who made it? the boy wrote.

"Ennio Morricone, an Italian composer. The melody has appeared in my favorite movie: The Legend of 1900."

The child nodded with a serious look on his face, as if he was storing a fundamental notion. He settled back in his chair and waited.

Anuradha knew that it was now her turn. "You know, you really have quite specific interests for a boy your age. Music seems to be only one of these. I imagine that on the list of things that you like there's also a place for astronomy, isn't there?"

Wei placed his forefinger on his right cheek then nodded.

"Did you write that letter yourself?" Anuradha noticed that her hands were shaking.

The boy nodded again.

"Well, if that's so, I'm really curious to know why you seem to believe that we can't travel to the stars."

Wei cocked his head to one side then slowly tapped on the keyboard: *We can, but we don't want to.*

Anuradha seemed puzzled. "I don't understand. Why are you saying that? I work with thousands of people who devote their lives to this purpose. You should know this, everyone knows it. You know what NASA is? The people who work for it? What they've done? Miss Powell didn't explain all of this to you?"

The child looked at her straight in the eye. The woman looked back at him without blinking. The only sound now was Anuradha's pencil, passing from one finger to the other at an ever increasing speed.

After a few moments the child leaned toward the keyboard and started typing.

The woman watched the words forming quickly one after the other. Without realizing it, she began holding her breath. Once she finished reading the answer, the pencil fell from her hand with a clatter. She didn't bother to pick it up.

"Well, well, well. Look who we have here!"

Anuradha shook herself out of her trance as she watched Miss Powell darting into the room, speaking to Wei.

"You should not be here, you rascal!" she said, shaking her head and smiling. "Come on, let's go back to your room."

Anuradha watched Miss Powell trying to hold Wei's hand, but the child pulled away, screaming.

"All right, all right." Miss Powell held up her hands. "Walk by yourself, then. Come on."

Wei walked toward the door, as silent as a tomb. Miss Powell sighed and followed him at a distance.

When she came back, she closed the door behind her. "So, what happened? Did you do it? Did he talk? That alone would be a miracle."

"Not a word," said Anuradha absently as she kept staring at the last message written by Wei.

Miss Powell crossed her arms and shook her head. "Come on, don't be too hard on yourself," she said, misunderstanding Anuradha's expression. "It was predictable. I told you that the child clearly has issues. So I guess that the mystery surrounding the letter has been solved."

"I guess so," whispered Anuradha.

"So ... he didn't write it, right?"

Anuradha looked at the other woman. Then she swallowed and shook her head to clear it. "On the contrary," she said, her eyes now bright with excitement. "Now I'm sure it *was* him who wrote it."

Miss Powell listened in round-eyed silence. "What?" she finally burst, clearly taken aback. "And how do you know that? You just said he didn't speak at all!"

"You're right. Wei doesn't seem very inclined to talk. But I assure you that I managed to establish some sort of contact. I'm not sure I can explain it, but believe it or not, there's no doubt: the kid is special, though I don't believe he needs the kind of attention you spoke of. He's extremely knowledgeable and incredibly smart."

Miss Powell put both hands behind her neck, shaking her head repeatedly. "All right, all right... Let's say you've established a contact.

What are you saying, that the kid's good with equations?"

Dr. Anuradha Galacta bent down and picked her pencil up from the floor, again moving it from one finger to another, an enigmatic smile on her face.

"No, Miss Powell. What I'm saying is that with all probability, I've just met the Einstein of the twenty-first century."

EVANGELINE

2015

WEI WAS SIPPING his hot chocolate while his fingers moved at the speed of light over his tablet.

After he finished drinking, he took a pen from the backpack at his right, then a flashlight and a handful of white sheets. Although the restaurant was very well lit, Wei turned the flashlight on, pointed it at one of the sheets and began to write.

After about half an hour, he put his pen and the flashlight down and rummaged once more in his backpack.

Eventually he found what he was looking for: a vanilla-colored cap. He quickly put it on.

Around him the few customers inside the restaurant were busy talking about the weather, the government and everything that the big TV over the bar showed on its flat screen.

The TV was now broadcasting a documentary that attracted his attention. The boy put down the tablet, moved the sheets aside and folded his arms across his chest, his head resting nearly on one shoulder and his almond-shaped eyes wide open with sharp curiosity.

"… created with the intent of warning the public about the harmful impact that space exploration has had on human civilization. LAND is a fierce organization backed by politicians, journalists, scientists and simple volunteers scattered throughout the territory."

Wei's attention was captured by the symbol of the organization that the reporter was speaking about: a man and a woman kneeling on opposite sides of a sphere enclosing the symbols of the four elements. The boy pulled a sheet toward him and began to write something as he continued to follow the news.

"When Spine Woodside founded LAND in the financial district of Pasadena, he felt as though he was called to fulfill a mission. Born in Dallas Texas in November 1979, Woodside has spent much of his youth volunteering for the elderly and caring for disabled people. After completing his Masters in Public Relations and a PhD in Advanced Strategies of Communication, he decided to dedicate his time to those whom he called 'the forgotten'. He has since been involved in numerous projects around the world supported by FAO, Amnesty International and Doctors Without Borders. After living for some time on the five continents, comparing poverty and hardship in the most diverse peoples and cultures, Woodside began to develop the idea that humanity was at a crossroads, a moment in which our civilization as a whole must decide what is really important for its survival and what needs to be abandoned."

The face of a handsome man with big green eyes, high cheekbones, dark hair and an intriguing smile appeared on the screen. Spine Woodside seemed comfortable under the light of the studio that made him shine like the most prestigious piece of a diamond collection.

"Mr. Woodside, your organization -- which some refer to as a movement -- has lately grown larger and more powerful," a beautiful journalist sitting in front of him was saying, "...and your message seems to gather more and more supporters and sympathizers every day. On the other hand, you have also made many enemies. Many of them call LAND the 'anti-NASA'. These people find your message, the message of LAND, limited and wrong, or simply not making any sense at all. A few days ago, the astrophysicist Neil Tyson called you, and I quote: 'a well-dressed snake oil salesman', end quote. How do you feel about that?"

Spine Woodside crossed his arms and put on a condescending smile. "Wendy, I think the contempt these people show toward me and my organization is reassuring. It means that my message has reached their homes, their families, and that it has become part of their lives. The first step in solving any problem is awareness. The second step is admission."

"I guess the problem you're referring to Mr. Woodside, and the main reason why LAND exists, is space exploration?"

"What I'm referring to, Wendy," Woodside answered with a smile so wide that Wei could see the back row of his teeth, "is a dream that became a nightmare. A toxic fantasy that has clouded the intentions of some of our best minds and that has required the diversion of billions of dollars that could have been used for more constructive purposes. Things we really need."

"Such as?" Wendy pressed him.

Woodside licked his dried lips. He then breathed in and looked at the journalist right in her eye. "What about homes, tractors, water wells, hospitals, a school in the Congo, a research center to cure cancer in California, a highway in Bangladesh, a pair of jeans that don't fade, automatic hair clips or a longer and more resistant toilet roll?" Woodside looked up pleadingly. "For God's sake," he went on, spreading his arms, "any of these things is more valuable than giving a blank check to an imbecile with a white coat and asking him to build a twelve million dollar spacesuit for another imbecile who'll be satisfied when he looks like a giant snowman."

The reporter nodded. "So, what you're basically saying is that if we had not gone to the moon, we could have solved world poverty."

"It's never that simple," Woodside replied calmly, with a wave of his hand. "The money invested for the Apollo program wouldn't have met the food needs of Zimbabwe, let alone those of the hundreds of millions of people who still eat only once a day and will continue to do so for the rest of their lives."

Woodside paused for a few seconds. Then he looked straight at the camera lens that had a flashing red light, as though that object was his last friend left on earth. "And yet, try to think of the energy, the tenacity and the resources of the thousands of people that have made this project, an undeniably massive undertaking, albeit completely useless and expensive. Try to re-invest these resources in everyday problems, problems that we face here on earth, and I'm sure that today we would have a lot more than a handful of useless lunar rocks."

Wendy, the journalist, took her glasses off and looked directly at Woodside. "Is it possible that for you there's nothing to be salvaged from what many believe to be mankind's greatest achievement?"

"My grandma used to say that the meat that fell on the floor should not be trashed, but given to the dog. I think it was her way of saying that we can see the bright side in every situation, if one tries to look carefully enough," Woodside said, smiling seductively into the camera. "Let me think. You first mentioned NASA. Well, I feel compelled to admit that if, up to this point, we hadn't spent around six hundred billion dollars to finance it -- that is, more or less Saudi Arabia's annual GDP -- surely we would not have microwave ovens."

Those who were following the interview burst out laughing. Wei, on the other hand, was frowning. While listening to the television, he took an object that looked like a large walnut out of his backpack. He turned it in his hands for a while and then put it back with a strange grimace on his face. When he turned to continue watching the interview, his view was obstructed by a tall woman with broad shoulders, massive cheeks and eyes as big as ripe cherries.

"Would you like another glass of chocolate, honey?"

A waitress had appeared at his right. She had a wide and bright smile on her face, the dull expression that people use with small, helpless and cute creatures in the zoo; the ones that win more applauses and sighs from the public.

The boy touched his tablet a few times and showed the stranger the screen without making a sound.

"No," she read loudly, frowning.

The waitress shook her head slightly, then placed the coffee pot she was carrying on the table and looked closely at Wei, further widening her already generous smile. "Are you sure, honey?" she asked, in a shrilly voice. "The next one is on the house."

Wei gave up trying to follow the interview. He glanced at the big woman with annoyance and then turned his attention back to the tablet, touching it occasionally.

"Are you all alone?" the woman asked suddenly, not noticing Wei's attempt to completely ignore her. She looked around warily, her expression a mix between concern and curiosity.

Wei did not answer. He just continued what he was doing while hoping the waitress would eventually leave him alone.

"Where is your mother, honey?" In an unexpectedly bold act, the woman moved with the clear intention of sitting down in front of him. It was in that very moment that the boy couldn't take anymore. He quickly wrote something on his tablet and showed it to the woman before she could sit down.

"She's six feet underground ..." she murmured. She didn't immediately grasp the meaning of the sentence. Then she gaped at him.

The waitress stood for a moment in a strange position, her bottom almost on the seat with her knees already bent but her back still straight. She seemed bewildered by the boy's answer, too surprised to be able to decide what to do next.

Wei was staring at her with a severe, almost disgusted expression, as though she were the biggest cockroach on the planet. He waved his hand, pointing insistently at another table.

After seconds of complete silence, the waitress finally grabbed the coffee pot and began moving away from the seat with a dazed expression, like someone looking for a quick way to get out of an embarrassing situation.

Wei was happy to help her out. He pulled a ten dollar bill from his pocket and quickly put it in her apron. She watched without saying a word as the boy nodded and gave her a pat on the butt that made her squeak.

Keep the change, honey, read the speechless waitress before quickly leaving his table, looking around embarrassed and confused.

Wei smiled a wicked smile. He turned to watch the TV but disappointedly noted that the interview was over. The screen was now showing what seemed like a huge construction yard, with countless cranes that crowded the horizon and an army of hardhats swarming around everywhere.

"... and the Korean government decided earlier this year to speed up the construction plan. We spoke with several engineers here and most of them are confident that Saemangeum City will welcome its first family long before ..."

Suddenly, the restaurant's door slammed open and a slender teenage girl with long, straw-colored hair appeared in the doorway, panting heavily and trying to catch her breath. Heads turned to watch the newcomer. She looked around with urgency, pointed to a guy sitting at a nearby table and darted toward him.

Wei, distracted by the frenzy, saw her speaking to first one customer and then another. But none of them seemed interested in what she was saying.

After a few minutes, the boy lost interest in the strange girl and turned to the tablet screen. The report about the city in construction was over, replaced by news describing a new foundation that was acquiring legions of teenage members in Japan. Wei shook his head, closed his eyes and returned to his reading, deaf to everything that surrounded him.

Meanwhile, the girl kept walking around, her face tense and impatient. Whatever she was trying to do, she didn't seem to have any luck. After speaking with half a dozen people, she finally found someone who nodded with a smile, and pointed to Wei.

The girl thanked the costumer and quickly headed toward the table where the boy was reading. Wei was so concentrated that he didn't even notice her sit down with a sigh in front of him.

"Hey. What's up? You're the climber guy, right?"

Wei nearly jumped out of his skin. It took him a couple of seconds to control his accelerated breathing. Then their eyes met.

She was looking at him with two giant, shiny, light blue eyes.

Wei's throat felt swollen. He swallowed hard. He opened and closed his eyes, his mouth half open. He found himself carefully studying the girl's freckles, a constellation of small brownish spots gracing her nose and cheeks. Her hair was a shiny waterfall of pale yellow lines flowing over her shoulders.

Wei swallowed again. His ears were red and itchy as though an invisible needle was piercing them repeatedly. Without really understanding why, his stomach felt weird -- somehow heavy -- and his mouth was dry. He cleared his throat and scratched his ears, looking away from the stranger.

"Look, I really need your help!" the girl quickly went on, gesturing with her hands and looking at him with a pleading expression.

"I'm Evangeline. Kruscha was following that stupid bird and ... Oh, I'm sorry! Kruscha is my chinchilla, you know, a very stupid chinchilla, but still ... Well, that moron followed the damned bird up a tree. I don't even know how the hell he got there on his own, short and fat as he is ... Anyway, as I said, now he's over there on that branch. He can't get off on his own and he's scared to death. I'm afraid he'll fall if we don't do something quickly! Nobody wants to help me! Please, please, you're my only hope!"

Wei realized that the buzz coming from Evangeline's mouth was probably some sort of a request for help, but other than that, he didn't understand a single word of what she had said. And he didn't care at all.

After pulling himself together from the initial surprise, his brain worked hard and fast to get rid of what he believed to be some kind of nutcase.

He touched his tablet and showed it to the girl without a word, waiting for a response.

"I'm deaf and dumb... What does that mean?" Evangeline asked, puzzled and pointing to the screen.

Wei shrugged and went back to his reading.

The girl didn't move.

"Look, he told me you'd listen to me! Aren't you Wei?"

The boy stopped reading, his eyes wide open.

Who told you my name? immediately appeared on his tablet.

"I thought you were deaf. I hate liars!" Evangeline angrily exclaimed, pointing at him with both forefingers. "It doesn't matter. I'll forgive you if you get up on that branch and save Kruscha. That's all I want."

Wei bit the inside of his cheek, then took a deep breath, picked up his pen and began to write fast, his forehead almost touching the paper.

"Well?" Evangeline said, impatient. "At least say something!"

I'm busy, typed Wei waving the tablet under her nose.

"It's a matter of five minutes. Kruscha is right outside ..."

Get lost!

"He needs you, don't you understand?"

Not listening.

Evangeline shouted his name in frustration. She jumped up, took off one of her shoes and began to beat it on the table.

Wei and everyone around turned to look at her.

STOP IT! The boy gestured harshly to his tablet, his face both angry and embarrassed.

Evangeline stopped, took off the other shoe and slammed both of them on the table.

"Hey, what the hell is going on over there?" asked the waitress who was serving a nearby table.

"It's a matter between me and my boyfriend. Stay out of it!" Evangeline shouted in reply, indicating Wei with a shoe.

Wei's face and neck went completely red, his jaw wide open. He couldn't believe what the crazy girl had just said.

However, it seemed to the costumers a normal enough reason. They turned away and went on with their own conversations.

"I can go on forever, you know?" Evangeline said with a triumphant smile.

Wei could have just picked up his things and left the place, but he didn't want to be forced out by the girl's nonsense. It would have been like giving up. He decided to cover his ears, close his eyes and wait for the girl to go away to bother someone else.

He remained still for a minute and a half. After a while, he no longer felt the girl's presence.

He waited a couple more minutes and then slowly opened his eyes.

Wei smiled, satisfied. There was no one in front of him. He was finally alone.

The boy breathed a sigh of relief and settled back in his chair to go back to his reading, but then he suddenly realized that there was nothing on the table. His tablet had disappeared.

"The Pheno-phenomenology of Spirit? What the hell is this?"

Wei turned his head and saw Evangeline holding his tablet, absorbed in the reading.

"Hey!" shouted the boy angrily, without even realizing it.

"Mute, is it? You're the worst liar I've ever met!" Evangeline said looking at him with contempt.

Wei immediately stood up and tried to grab the tablet back, but he stumbled on something and fell hard to the ground.

Evangeline laughed. "If you want it back, you'll have to help me, asshole!" and she quickly left.

Wei, his cheek on the floor, realized that the strings of his shoes had been laced together. Evangeline had kept herself busy while his eyes were shut.

Creeping like a worm he slowly got back to his seat, grabbed his backpack and pulled out a pair of scissors that he used to quickly snip the knot.

Once he was on his feet, Wei collected his things and hastily rushed out of the restaurant, stumbling a couple of times on his way.

It was late afternoon outside and the streets were almost empty. Evangeline was waiting for him near one of the trees that lined the sidewalk.

"Hurry up! He's here!" said the girl, the stolen tablet clasped tightly in her arms.

Wei clenched his teeth and charged toward the thief, trying to grab his tablet, but Evangeline dodged him just in time, causing the boy to lose his balance. For the second time in five minutes, he found himself with his face on the ground. He grunted and spat.

"Don't get smart with me, moron!" the girl warned him, batting at his head. "Now come on and save Kruscha if you don't want me to destroy this damn thing."

Wei rubbed his aching head, wiped his mouth and sat up. The girl was too tall, too fast and too determined. He couldn't hope to take the tablet away from her by using force. Frustrated and helpless, he pushed himself up to look where she was pointing.

On one of the branches of the tree, more than ten feet above the ground, a small rodent with long ears and thick greyish fur was watching them, immobile and scared.

"Looks like you need a ladder," Wei said slowly, considering the distance that separated them from the frightened thing.

"Kruscha is dying of fear, can't you see? I don't have time to look for a ladder! Come on, climb up. And be quick about it!"

"Are you kidding me? How am I supposed to get up there? It must be more than twelve feet high! You think I've been bitten by a radioactive spider or something?"

"You're just a liar. I know you can do it! Come on, now! Otherwise I'll break your stuff!"

Wei stood up and dusted off his pants. Clearly the girl had issues. It was impossible to reason with her, he thought, looking at her intently. But he really wanted his tablet back in one piece.

For a few seconds he seemed to estimate the distance that separated them from the chinchilla. Then he licked his forefinger, exposing it to the wind.

"What's its favorite food?" the boy suddenly asked.

Evangeline looked at him, confused. "Its favorite ..."

"What does the damn rat like to eat?"

"You mean, Kruscha?" Evangeline asked, taken aback by the question. "Well, raisins but—"

"Have you got any with you?" Wei cut her off.

"Well, s-sure, but what—?"

"Just shut up and give me some if you want my help!"

Evangeline considered the boy for a moment, his hand held out toward her. Eventually, she reached into her pocket and gave a little bag to Wei.

The boy turned it over in his hands, considering its weight. He tossed it in the air and caught it. He mumbled something that

Evangeline couldn't catch, then threw the bag up in the air again, this time higher. Wei knelt down, took off his cap and with the scissors from his backpack, made four holes equally spaced on each side of the hat. After that, he took a long string out of his pocket, made a couple of knots to secure it with the four holes in the cap and put the half-opened bag full of raisins in the middle of it.

"What are you doing?"

Wei didn't answer. He fumbled for a few more seconds with the string and made sure it was tied to the four sides of the cap.

Meanwhile, the chinchilla seemed to show signs of restlessness. Perhaps because it had noticed Evangeline, it began to turn on itself, almost falling half a dozen times.

"Kruscha! Stay still, you idiot!" Evangeline, her eyes bright and wide open, looked as though she was about to burst into tears.

"Go under that branch and be ready to catch your rat," Wei said, urging the girl to move.

Evangeline opened her mouth, but Wei stopped her by raising his hand.

"Get under that branch. *Now.*"

Evangeline did as she was told.

Wei stood motionless for a couple of seconds. Then he suddenly threw his cap toward the tree and over the branch with the chinchilla.

"What the hell are you doing? You almost hit him! Do you want to kill him?"

"Just look!" Wei silenced her while pointing to the branch.

Evangeline saw the boy's cap dangling in the air, held up by the twine that he firmly held from the other end.

The chinchilla stopped moving and sniffed the air, its head dodging back and forth, looking for something. Soon it noticed the cap a few inches away and in no time, the little thing dived in, lured by its content. The boy felt the weight of the rodent on the twine.

Slowly and steadily, the cap came closer and closer to the ground. When the rodent was finally within Evangeline's reach, Wei tied the string to a light pole nearby. While the girl was busy rescuing Kruscha, he was finally able to get his tablet back.

"Kruscha! Gosh, are you OK?" Evangeline was ecstatic, her eyes swollen with tears.

The rodent was happily eating one of the raisins scattered inside the hat. It raised its head for a second then went back to eating.

Wei snorted and quickly shoved the tablet inside his backpack. After closing it, he immediately put it on his shoulders. Then the boy started to untie the string, eager to put more distance between him and the crazy girl, but something grasped his shoulders, forcing him to turn around. Before he could realize what was happening, Evangeline pulled him toward her and kissed him on the lips. Wei was petrified, unable even to blink.

When she was done with him, she put her arms around his neck.

"You saved ... you saved Kruscha! Thank you!"

Wei started breathing again, his face as red as a tomato. He recoiled, spitting on the ground. "Disgusting!"

"Thanks, thanks, thanks," Evangeline chanted happily, staying as close as she could to Wei and grasping his hands.

"I ..." Wei stopped, searching for something better to say that would shut her mouth and get rid of her. "My ... my plan was to hit that stupid thing with my cap on the first try... but I failed."

Evangeline laughed out loud -- a laugh that seemed to Wei as fresh and crisp as a sweet melody. Again he felt that strange heaviness at the bottom of his stomach. All of a sudden, the psychopathic thief was surrounded by inexplicable charm.

"Come on, you moron, today's dinner is on me. You're officially my guest. I'll show you my home after—"

"Your guest?" Wei looked around, bewildered. "Are you kidding me? You don't even know who the hell I am!"

"Who cares?" the girl answered, humming happily while spinning into a strange dance. "You have green light."

"I have green light?" the boy echoed genuinely confused. "Listen: you're totally nuts! You hear me? I'm not going to—"

"Oh, shut up, brat, or we'll start all over again. We have to celebrate Kruscha's adventure!"

Wei found out soon enough that Evangeline was incredibly strong for a girl her age. His attempts to free himself were useless and painful. Tired, he finally gave up, letting the girl guide him.

The boy touched his head with a simple gesture that was evidently a habit, and suddenly realized that he had left his cap behind him, still hanging in mid-air.

"Wait, I've left ..."

"You're a smart boy for your age, you know? Weird, but smart," Evangeline said while patting Kruscha with one finger. "How on earth did you come up with that idea? I mean, the elevator thing back there. It was brilliant!"

Wei remained silent for a few seconds, looking absently at his cap lolling lazily in the breeze that spoke of the quickly approaching sunset.

Wei looked at Evangeline, and then at the little thing she was holding in her hands.

Again he watched silently with a blank expression as his cap dangled lazily at the side of the tree, swinging in the warm wind.

"I ..." Wei said absently, while studying the chinchilla and the cap; first one then the other, over and over again.

Finally, before completely losing sight of it, he looked at the string that was holding his cap in the air for the last time. His eyes lit up for a moment, as if he had caught the last spark of a firework.

"Yes," he whispered. "That really was a brilliant idea."

TIAGO

2017

"2360 QUEENSBERRY RD. Destination is fifty-eight feet North-east. Estimated time to …" Tiago turned off the device and put it in his pocket.

With a slow and deliberate pace, he continued walking along the road, carefully looking at the numbers painted on the sidewalk's edge.

After a few minutes, he stopped in front of a house, similar to the others that faced the street. The number 2360 was partially covered by a dry and twisted plant.

Thirty or so people were waiting in line in the driveway, frantically speaking with each other and occasionally glancing around. Tiago followed their gaze and saw a tall, burly man opening the door and coming out of the house. He carried a wooden table and two chairs. The man set the table down at the beginning of the driveway and the two chairs on opposite sides of the table, facing each other.

Without further ado, Tiago walked briskly toward the man.

"Hey you! The damn line starts here!" someone shouted at him.

Tiago paid no attention to the shouting man and simply continued on his way.

When he reached the big man, he held out his hand and put on his best smile.

"It's a pleasure to meet you, sir. My name is Tiago Melo and—"

"Max Lewis," the other cut short without shaking his hand. "Now do us all a favor, boy. Turn your ass around and move to the back of the line."

31

Max moved toward the house but Tiago quickly blocked his way standing in front of him.

"Excuse me, Mr. Lewis. I'm from L.A. I study at USC Annenberg. I just wanted to make sure that this is the right place ..."

"Yes, this is the place," Max said unceremoniously, his eyes glaring with menace. Tiago stepped back, intimidated by the man's look. "The 'magic' will start shortly," he continued. "I suggest you find yourself a nice spot. This place will be crowded in no time. Now get the hell out of my way."

"Hey, Max! The line starts—"

"Oh, shut up, Josh!"

"But that asshole skipped—"

"He's just a parrot, goddammit!" Max called back to the bald man who kept complaining. "He only came to sniff around, like all the others."

"Parrot?" Tiago muttered to himself as he watched the big man quickly going back into the house, cursing under his breath.

He noticed that in a brief interval of minutes, the line had grown in length and a few dozen people had already occupied the garden that surrounded the driveway. All eyes were staring at the bare table that Max had carried out earlier.

Tiago decided it would be wise to follow the man's advice and found himself a good spot by the garden.

Five minutes later, Max came out of the house with a big sign that he put up in front of the door so that everybody could see it.

Tiago leaned forward to read it.

Straight questions, straight answers in 10 seconds.
$10 against $1,000.
Complaints are not accepted. No refunds.

The student took his smartphone from his pocket, ready to take a picture, but a growing racket forced him to turn around.

The people waiting in line gradually fell silent. Tiago craned his neck to see what was happening.

"OK, guys, make way. Move! Let him through!"

A couple of men in yellow T-shirts were yelling at the crowd gathered around the house and in the garden. People slowly moved aside. From the passage, a kid emerged who could not have been more than twelve years old. He wore a red cap and a large pair of dark sunglasses that hid a third of his face. He was very short and thin. Tiago looked at him with interest.

The kid was not walking; he was swaying, as if he was staggering on the deck of a ship caught in a storm. His hands were clasped tightly behind his back and he seemed completely uninterested in the crowd of people watching and pointing at him with growing excitement.

Tiago watched the short figure slowly approaching from the street. The kid took a seat on the chair that Max had earlier prepared, and waited in silence. The other chair in front of him was empty.

"That kid is the Omnilogos?" whispered Tiago, bewildered.

He closed his mouth and looked around. The two men in the yellow T-shirts had taken places on both sides of the line of waiting people, looking around them to make sure everything was going smoothly. People had meanwhile resumed their excited chatter, insistently pointing to the kid with the red cap.

Tiago decided to take a picture of the boy.

It was then that he noticed something strange. His smartphone no longer responded to his commands. He shook it, turned it over and repeatedly touched the screen, but nothing happened. The device was dead.

"Outstanding." Tiago huffed. He tried to reboot it. Nothing happened. "This is just awesome."

Meanwhile Max Lewis came out of the house carrying a small box. He walked toward the kid and reached to shake his hand, a warm smile on his bearded face.

The two talked for a few moments. Max laughed heartily as the boy said something that Tiago could not catch because of the increasing noise from the crowd. After a while the big man took some bills out of the box, placing them on the table.

"One thousand dollars!" Max called out loudly, while showing the money to the crowd. He then put the bills on the table, on the right hand side of the kid.

"Who's first?"

Tiago turned his head toward the voice. He noticed that Josh, the bald man who had yelled at him, was talking with someone else, indicating the very first man waiting in line.

"Dunno. Some new guy, I think. They told me he camped around here a day ago, the poor bastard. He's probably just a junkie who smelled easy money."

"Yeah, and what about you?" asked Josh, showing a line of yellow teeth. "You've come prepared today? Got any surprises for Mr. Genius there?"

"You bet. This time I'm going to squeeze that little shit. Oh, yeah. I've spent an hour on the damn question. You'll see."

Max clapped his hands three times and everyone fell silent.

"OK, folks, let's start!" He pointed. "You. Yes, you! Don't be shy. Come on."

Tiago tried to turn on his smartphone again but it was pointless. He cursed, realizing he could do nothing but watch in silence as the first in line sat in the empty chair with his back turned to the audience.

The first man in line waited a few seconds. Then he reached into his pocket and put ten dollars in front of Max's one thousand. The little box was laid open and empty in the midst of the two contenders.

Max took something from his jacket and while watching it closely he chanted, "Three … two … one. Start!"

The first competitor cleared his throat and asked with a wry smile, "What is the square root of 857,965,847?"

Immediately after he spoke, the majority of the people waiting in line broke out into laughter.

"29,291.05404385441," the boy replied, dead serious.

Max took the ten dollars and put them in the box.

"Next!"

A young woman with long hair sat in front of the Omnilogos.

"How to lose ten dollars in two seconds," said Josh, the bald man, looking at the first contender who was leaving quietly, losing himself in the crowd. "Idiot," he added, looking at him with contempt.

Everything happened so fast that Tiago's brain had no way of explaining it.

Max's voice, inviting the second contender to start, suddenly interrupted Tiago's thoughts.

With a honeyed and persuasive voice, the woman asked, "What was the name of the second vessel of the Kaiser class of battleships built by the German Imperial Navy?"

Two seconds of absolute silence.

"SMS *Friedrich der Grosse*," was the answer.

"Thank you, thank you. OK. Come on! Next!" Max bellowed to overcome the indistinct noise from the crowd.

An old man in his eighties stepped forward. Max nodded. "Go on," he said.

"What is the name of the fifth book of the Jewish Torah?"

"Deuteronomy."

Max took a step forward. "Thank you. Next?"

The chair creaked dangerously under the weight of the fourth participant, a short but incredibly fat man whose face was covered in sweat.

"To which animal family does the Western Capercaillie belong?" asked the contender, swinging his fat cheeks while speaking.

"The Western Capercaillie is a bird belonging to the grouse group, which is a subfamily Tetraoninae in the family Phasianidae."

Max invited yet another competitor to come forward.

Tiago watched speechlessly as dozens of people, one by one, challenged the Omnilogos with their questions and inevitably lost.

Tiago had heard of what some called the 'human database' or 'Omnilogos', but nothing could have prepared him for this. Omnilogos was a compound word made up from the Latin word 'omnis', meaning 'all' and the Greek word 'logos', meaning 'a principle of order and knowledge' or 'word'. Although it was unclear who crafted that word, it immediately became the most widely used to describe the genius boy.

"Next in line!"

Tiago snapped to attention and returned to focus on the competition. It was Josh's friend's turn.

"How was the chemical element lawrencium synthetized for the first time?"

The Omnilogos absently scratched his nose. "The first atoms of lawrencium were produced by a team led by the nuclear scientist Albert Ghiorso. They bombarded a three-milligram target consisting of three isotopes of the element californium with boron-10 and boron-11 nuclei."

Max took the ten dollars and put them in the box.

"Come on, Josh. It's your turn."

The bald man rubbed his hands as he sat on the chair.

Looking menacingly at the boy he asked with a malicious smile,

"What is the perihelion of the dwarf planet called Haumea?"

"The perihelion of Haumea, or 136108 Haumea, is about 35.164 AU."

Josh looked at a notebook he had in his hand. When he finished reading, he slammed his fist on the table. "Goddammit! That's impossible!"

"Next!" Max yelled, angrily staring at the bald man still sitting on the chair. "Get out of the way, Josh. I won't say it again."

Josh cursed as he reluctantly got up. After throwing a look of animosity at the boy, he left without saying another word, rudely moving aside everyone who was in his way.

Time passed quickly, and with question after question, the money in Max's box never stopped increasing.

While studying the Omnilogos, Tiago's brain was working to figure out how he could possibly answer all of those questions. For the people around him, cheering and chit-chatting, it was nothing more than an exciting show to enjoy and to have fun with. For Tiago, however, it became a challenge -- a puzzle to solve.

He turned toward a group of people who were muttering to each other and asked, "Excuse me. Is this your first time here?"

A girl quickly shook her head. "Oh no," she said. "This is the third time, actually."

"Look, I'm new here," Tiago said, tapping his chest with a finger. "Doesn't it seem a bit odd to you all? I mean, come on! There must be something going on. That kid is clearly cheating, somehow. Someone or something is giving him all the answers. It's probably a buddy somewhere around here, or maybe a portable device. I don't know ... *something*. Couldn't it be?"

"Oh, well ... yes, that's what I thought too the first time I came here to see. But I assure you it's not like that."

"How can you be so sure?"

Another girl from the group answered, "Try to turn on your cell phone."

"Beg your pardon?"

"I said, try to turn on your cell phone or any other device you have with you."

Tiago shook his head.

"Well, I'd like to do that, but my—" Tiago cut himself off. He stared at the girl, his eyes wide open. Alarm bells rang in Tiago's head.

"Got it?" said the girl, noticing Tiago's expression. "Calling, taking pictures, videos, getting information or anything that involves the use of technology is impossible during the competition. We think there could be some sort of electromagnetic field or something like that that blocks any device around here. The only thing that works is the stopwatch Max is using, and a couple of guys have already checked it several times. There's no weird stuff in it."

Tiago looked at his smartphone, baffled, and then at the girls, who looked back with a grin.

"But how can …?"

He never finished the sentence. The audience was pointing out the last participant in the line who was about to sit down. The excitement in the air seemed to grow exponentially.

"Who is he?" Tiago asked the girls, forgetting the last question.

"That's Professor Otto Von Bauer, from the University of California, Los Angeles. He's what we call a regular competitor. The professor is always one of the last and usually his questions are the most … entertaining."

Professor Otto Von Bauer was a short, middle aged man with a long, thick moustache that made him look like an old walrus. Before sitting, he held out his hand. The Omnilogos shook it.

"Make yourself comfortable, Professor," Max said respectfully, ready to push the stopwatch's button.

Professor Von Bauer crossed his arms and asked, "When did Albert-Pierre Sarraut hold the office of Prime Minister in the French Third Republic?"

One, two, three, four seconds. There was no answer. The audience held its breath while mentally counting the handful of seconds left to the Omnilogos.

The boy settled back in his chair and slightly cocked his head, almost touching his shoulder.

"The question has been poorly worded," he said after what appeared to be a seemingly endless time. "The correct question should have been: in what periods did Albert-Pierre Sarraut hold the office of Prime Minister of France. This is because he was Prime Minister twice, the first time from October 26, 1933 to November 26, 1933, the second time from January 24, 1936 to June 4, 1936."

The professor smiled and nodded, his moustache resembled a coal colored broom. "That is correct," he said.

An ovation shattered the heavy silence that had prevailed. In the uproar that surrounded him, Tiago could hear the professor ask the Omnilogos, "Have you had time to think of what I told you?"

"Professor, your persistence is admirable, but the answer is the same." The boy stood up and outstretched his hand. "Have a safe journey."

Von Bauer shook the boy's hand and said something else that Tiago wasn't able to grasp. Then the professor quickly disappeared somewhere in the crowd.

Tiago turned to watch the short man walk away, and for a moment he had the distinct feeling that the Omnilogos was watching him from behind his glasses.

"You're not from here, are you?"

Tiago turned and saw one of the girls who'd asked the question.

"N-no, I'm from L.A.," Tiago replied absently. "I am ... I study at USC Annenberg."

"Oh, you're a parrot!"

Tiago sighed. "Apparently I am."

"Pleasure, I'm Sonia."

Tiago introduced himself and offered his hand as he restlessly looked around. The Omnilogos was talking to Max and the two were heading together toward the house. Before the door closed, Tiago was almost certain that the boy had pointed to him.

"Hey, are you listening?"

Tiago, completely uninterested in what the girl was saying, took his leave abruptly and tried to make his way amidst the crowd that was quickly dispersing. He reached into his pocket and made sure that his smartphone was working again. The device turned on without any problem. Unfortunately for him, the table, the chairs and the big board with the rules of the game were all gone.

When he finally reached the door of the house, all that remained of the competition were a couple of beverage cans left on the ground by the crowd.

He closed his eyes, took a deep breath and knocked. No one answered.

"Mr. Lewis!" he called out in a loud voice, "It's Tiago Melo. Remember?"

There was still no answer. He waited a minute then knocked again and again.

"Mr. Lewis? Can you hear me?"

At that point it was impossible that no one could hear him. Tiago thought that they were deliberately trying to ignore him. He didn't give up and knocked on the door with both fists.

"I just want to ask the Omnilogos a few questions! Mr. Lewis?"

When the door opened Tiago almost fell forward.

Max Lewis loomed in the doorway, his jaw clenched, his hands clasped tightly and anger clearly showing on his face.

"Listen to me, jackass. Back away. Keep backing away till you're off my property. Then back away some more," said Max slowly, calm and as menacing as a nest of giant hornets.

"Look, I just want to ask him some questions."

"What?"

"I just want to ask the Omnilogos—"

"What are you blabbing about?" Max cut him off, raising a big hand. "What the hell is an *only goes?*"

"The Omnilogos," Tiago repeated, "the boy that was ..."

"Boy? What the hell are you talking about?" Max said, rubbing his knuckles. "There's no *werdy goes* or boy, here. You understand?"

"I ... I saw him ... I saw him going into this house a few minutes ago."

"Fine. Listen. Listen very carefully." Max hit Tiago with a rapid kick to the knee. Before the student even realized it, he was kneeling on the ground, with Max's strong arm around his neck.

"This won't end up well if you don't pay attention. Now, this is Terry." Max showed him a Colt Anaconda, a double action revolver that he kept hidden behind his back. Tiago hadn't noticed that detail. "She's specialized in keeping stubborn parrots like you in line. Now, do as I said, and be quick about it."

Max pushed him away. Tiago coughed then he took a step away from the porch.

He gazed at the mountain of muscles in front of him and swallowed hard but he didn't go anywhere.

"This ... this would be a threat?" he said, touching his neck. "I wonder what the police would say if ..."

Max sighed, annoyed, and spat on the ground. He put a hand on his hip and showed him a sparkling police badge.

"I am the police, asshole. Now get lost."

Tiago looked surprised, but he didn't move a finger. He remained as still as a stone, exactly where he was.

"I get it, you really prefer the hard way, don't you?" Max started moving toward him but all of a sudden he stopped. He searched in his pocket and came up with a cell phone. He looked at Tiago while answering the phone.

"What?" Max said after ten seconds. He touched his gun.

Tiago stepped back and stopped breathing.

"No … no. Yes, I understand. I do." Max spat on the ground again while putting his cell phone back in his pocket.

"Your guardian angel must have been working overtime today." He got closer to Tiago, who could now smell his heavy breath. "Do what you want, scum, but if you touch my door again, I'll tear you apart with my bare hands! Got it?"

Max turned away from Tiago, moved up the steps to his porch and vehemently shut the door without waiting for an answer.

"Tell the Omnilogos I'll be out here waiting for him," the student stubbornly insisted, talking to the door.

There was no answer. Tiago moved away from the door and wandered around the porch for a few minutes while massaging his sore neck. He realized his hands were shaking only when he looked at his smartphone to check the time. He breathed in, then looked around to make sure that the house didn't have any back doors.

Once he had done that, he sat on the grass and waited, legs and arms crossed.

Ten minutes passed and nothing happened.

Tiago took a few pictures of the house and of the neighbourhood. He checked the street occasionally to see if anybody was around to ask some questions. In fact, the place now seemed deserted, completely empty. No one would have said that fifteen minutes before there were dozens of people swarming around.

After more than an hour, no audible noise had come from the house. The place seemed to him silent and still, as if everybody inside had gone to sleep, waiting for him to go away. He stubbornly refused to give up, and remained planted on the grass.

His mind was stormed by a legion of questions he couldn't even begin to answer.

Discouraged and bored, he grabbed a thin blade of grass and began to chew on it while lying on his back with his hands behind his head, watching the clouds lazily dance in the sky.

Another half an hour passed in boredom and silence.

Tiago took his smartphone from his pocket and played a hip hop tune.

After a few minutes, he picked another blade of grass as he reached up to stretch, and it was at that moment his hand struck against something.

"Ow!"

Tiago, surprised, quickly drew his arm back and looked to his right, eyes wide open.

"What the hell ...?"

A little boy with a crew-cut was rolling on the grass, rubbing his head with both hands. "Geez! You hurt me!" he muttered with tears in his eyes.

"What? I ... I'm ... sorry," Tiago said, hesitantly edging the boy. "I didn't see you. Who ... who are you? Where did you come from?"

The boy suddenly stopped complaining and jumped to his feet.

"Never mind, my name is Wei Wang, nice to meet you." He held out a hand that was covered with grass and dirt.

Tiago looked at the boy's smiling face and then at the filthy hand.

"Yes, well. Pleasure ... kid," said Tiago, without shaking his hand.

"You're not introducing yourself," the boy said, looking both surprised and annoyed.

"OK, my name is Tiago," he answered scratching his head. "Now, could you ..."

"Tiago? Tiago ... T-I-A-G-O," repeated Wei, as though he was memorizing a nursery rhyme. "Gosh, that's quite a name, isn't it? Short, easy to remember ... Sounds like a fruit, or a flower. Yeah. Well, what other names do you have?"

Tiago looked carefully around, searching for parents desperate to find their lost child.

"I've just got this one. Listen, are you lost?"

"Let me guess," said Wei, without answering the question. "Tiago Bernardes. Is it?"

"No. Listen ..."

"Cardoso."

"No."

"Conceição."

"All right, all right! Tiago Melo, my name is Tiago Melo. OK?

Now, would you just—"

"I bet you've also got a Tavares somewhere in between."

"NO!"

"Vasconcelos."

"I said no! Can't you just shut—"

"Vila Lobos."

"Tiago Silva Abreu Melo!" Tiago burst out. "Are you happy now?"

Wei nodded, paying no attention to the annoyance on Tiago's face. "I wish I had a name like that. With such a name you can do whatever you want. When you show up, you must leave everybody speechless, right? Of course, if someone was in urgent need of you, he or she would be really fuc—"

"OK, listen kid," said Tiago while he kept looking around, "I'm busy here, OK? Why don't you just go home and—"

"What are you doing here all alone?" Wei interrupted him, pointing to the garden.

"I'm busy!" repeated Tiago, clearly annoyed.

"Busy? Busy doing what? Digesting the grass?" he said pointing to the blade of grass Tiago was holding in his hand.

"What?" the student answered, letting the grass slip away from his fingers. "No, I'm … I'm waiting for someone."

"Really? Who are you waiting for?"

"It's none of your business! Now get lost!"

"How can I?"

"How can you *what?*"

"How do I get lost? I know this neighbourhood like I know—"

"Damn! Has anyone ever told you that you're weird?"

"Speak for yourself! I don't say my name in bits and pieces."

Tiago spread his arms, not knowing what else to say.

"Fine, stay, but stop talking!"

Tiago sat back on the grass and began to stare at the door. Wei sat down beside him.

After a few moments of silence, Wei began to hum.

"What did I say?" barked Tiago.

"Fine, stay, but stop talking," Wei repeated, mimicking Tiago's annoyed tone. Then he went back to humming.

Tiago jumped up and yelled with all the breath in his body, "Officer! Open the door!"

Wei looked at Tiago, who kept on yelling. When he saw him start walking toward the door, the boy said, "Hey, who are you yelling at?"

"I'm yelling at a cop with issues. Now would you just …"

"You mean, Max?"

Tiago whirled on the spot and turned toward the boy. "You know him?"

"Sure. He's one of my best friends."

"Yeah, sure," Tiago said, shaking his head. "All right, one of your best friends. If that's so, then maybe if you ask him to—"

"Nobody's home."

Tiago looked at him, puzzled. "Say that again."

"Max went out an hour ago. He had some errands to run."

"What? Gone? Where? How? No one left this house."

"He didn't use the door, you moron."

"Yeah? And how on earth could he possibly have left this house? Using a secret passage?"

"Precisely." Wei nodded, dead serious.

Tiago was speechless for a good half a minute.

"You're kidding me, right?"

"No. But if you wanna laugh I know a—"

"You're saying … you're saying that the house really has a secret passage? I mean … a *real* secret passage?"

"Yes, you know? Like those castles in the Middle Ages …"

"And how could you possibly know that?"

"I do because I used it ten minutes ago."

Tiago stared at the boy, as if he was seeing him for the very first time.

"You used a secret passage to get out there?" he finally asked, pointing to him with both hands.

"Stop repeating what I say! It makes you look retarded, you know?"

Now that Tiago was paying attention, Wei was not much taller or shorter than the Omnilogos but on the other hand he was wearing completely different clothes. He had dark hair, sure, but that alone didn't really mean anything. It could have just been some kid who was making fun of him, he thought.

"So you're the Omnilogos."

"Omnilogos?" the boy repeated confused. "No idea what that is supposed to mean."

43

"Forget it … OK, listen, if you're the kid who answered those questions, prove it."

Wei shrugged. "OK, ask me a question. Any question. I have ten seconds to answer."

Tiago had already prepared a question that came to his mind while looking at the row of competitors dwindling before his eyes.

Years before, he was challenged by his grandfather to finish the most boring and difficult novel he'd ever laid his eyes upon. He never finished the book, but he exactly remembered one of its sentences. The book was a classic but not an easy read, nor particularly popular, and almost a century old. There was no way a kid like that could have ever heard about it.

"OK. Can you tell me in which book appears the sentence: Because no battle is ever won, they are not even fought. The field only reveals to man his own folly and despair, and victory is an illusion of philosophers and fools."

"Easy," Wei said, scratching his buttock. *"The Sound and the Fury,* written by William Faulkner."

It was as if someone had hit Tiago's face with a baseball bat.

"No way," he murmured, almost without realizing it. "Is this really you?"

"Are you happy now? Good. It's time to pay up, buddy."

Tiago immediately recovered from his surprise. "I'm sorry?"

"You heard me right, Tiago Silva Abreu Melo. You owe me ten dollars." Wei outstretched his hand.

"Are you serious? You asked me to ask you a question," Tiago said.

"I never said it was for free. Now pay up, if you don't want me to start screaming that you're harassing me."

"What? No! I will never …"

"Now, now, don't be a smartass," Wei warned him, smiling a wicked smile. "Do you have any idea what could happen if a kid like me started shouting the word 'pedophile' in the middle of a street?"

"I … I … I don't believe this!" Tiago said, clasping his hands behind his head. "Is this really happening?"

Wei moved his fingers, impatiently. "Come on. I don't have all day."

Tiago looked at Wei. Wei looked back at him. Finally Tiago spread out his arms and put his hand in his pocket. "I don't even know if I have enough cash ..."

His hand finally came up with a pair of crumpled five-dollar bills. Wei grabbed them before Tiago could add anything else.

"Well, now that we have solved this financial transaction—"

"This robbery," Tiago corrected him, his face red with anger.

"May I ask, Mr. Melo, what business brings you here?" Wei continued, paying no attention to the guy's expression.

Tiago's heart was pounding. He took deep breaths. He forced himself to think. After all, he thought, ten dollars was a reasonable price to pay for what he came for.

The Omnilogos was in front of him, at his mercy. He just had to play the part of the friend, ask the right questions and he would go back home with a story with a capital 'S'.

Tiago smiled, trying to sound less hostile. "I am a student at USC Annenberg and—"

"Ah! So, you're a—"

"Yes, I know, a parrot," Tiago anticipated him, closing his eyes in frustration.

"I was going to say, a wannabe journalist."

"Oh, well ... yes, exactly," Tiago said, taken aback by the kid's answer. "I came ... well, I think you know exactly why I came here."

"You're not the first and certainly will not be the last," said Wei, touching Tiago's shoulder. "The only difference between you and everyone else is that you, my friend, will get exactly what you came for."

"Really?" Tiago asked with shining eyes.

"Really," Wei confirmed. "Even better, you'll have the unique opportunity to follow me minute by minute on my typical day. What do you say? Sounds good?"

"Well, I say that's fantastic." He waited a moment then alarm bells rang in his head. "Wait a minute. How much will it cost me this time?"

"Not a penny," Wei said, smiling innocently.

"You mean, you'll do it for nothing, without asking anything in return?"

Wei laughed. "Now, don't be naive, my friend. Nothing is free in this world. At the end of our day, you'll return the favor. Don't bother," Wei said, raising a hand, "you'll know exactly what it is at the right time."

Tiago closed his mouth. He didn't like the idea of being held hostage by this twisted little boy, but he would have done anything and everything to unravel the mystery surrounding the Omnilogos.

"Agreed," the student finally said.

"Good, because we've already lost too much time chit-chatting. We have a long day ahead."

Wei picked up a small backpack from the ground that Tiago hadn't noticed before, and together they set off.

"Do you have a car or something else we can use to reach the city center?" Wei asked, staring at his wristwatch. "I've left my bike at home."

"Yeah, of course, I came with that." Tiago pointed to an old motorcycle parked a few meters away.

"Curious and courageous," Wei said when they were in front of the motorcycle. He touched the tank and the wheels. "This thing would make the fortune of a museum."

"This *jewel*," Tiago pointed out, patting the seat, "works just fine. It's convenient, considering its age, and it consumes close to nothing. A great motorcycle."

"If we don't get blown up on our way, it'd be more than enough for me. OK, then. Let's go!"

The two climbed on.

"Where are we going?" Tiago asked as he started the engine.

"Go straight. When I tell you, turn left. We'll go down Allen Avenue for a while till we get to Colorado Boulevard. Our destination is the Old Town."

∞∞∞∞

The trip lasted less than fifteen minutes. Neither of them spoke on the way, except for Wei who gave some pointers. When they arrived at their destination, Tiago parked his motorcycle and examined the landscape: they were surrounded by strong smells, horns, beggars and passers-by who swarmed around the shops which lined the main street.

"Come on. This way." Wei motioned vigorously to Tiago to follow him.

For a few seconds, they walked in silence.

"So," Tiago finally began, going over in his head the speech he

46

made up on the ride. "No doubt about it, that question-answer show you performed in Queensberry was ... remarkable, truly remarkable, wasn't it?"

Wei didn't answer. He kept walking, occasionally looking around.

"I'd like to know how you did it," concluded Tiago in a neutral tone, trying not to betray any emotion.

Wei's face suddenly brightened. "And I'd like to eat chocolate grapefruit," he said, looking straight at Tiago and putting a finger on his lips. "Of course it would have to be dark chocolate, not milk, obviously. That would ruin the contrast between the bitter of the fruit and the flavor of the cocoa."

Tiago frowned. "This ... what is that supposed to mean?"

Wei shrugged. He looked confused.

"I thought we were playing 'I wish I could'. You know, when you start talking hypothetically and the one who wins imagines the most absurd thing. Don't you guys play this in L.A.?"

"What?"

Wei waved his hand to dismiss the matter. "You parrots just don't know how to have fun."

"How did you know all of that stuff?" Tiago asked, ignoring his comment. "Are you ... like ... some kind of genius?"

Wei shook his head. "Don't think so," he said, thoughtfully. "It's the rest of you who are stupid."

Tiago started to reply but Wei suddenly raised a hand. "That's it. This is our first stop."

Wei stopped in front of a store with a big black sign shaped like a vortex.

Before Tiago could say anything, the Omnilogos took off his backpack. After a moment of rummaging around inside it, he came up with a small mirror. He handed it over to Tiago.

"Take this."

Tiago grabbed the mirror without understanding.

"What are you doing?"

Wei wasn't listening. He took a small case out of the backpack. When he opened it, Tiago found himself staring at what appeared to be two contact lenses.

"Hold the mirror. Yes, like this," he said to Tiago. "I need to put these in."

Tiago reluctantly did as he was told while watching the boy moisten both contact lenses and put them in his eyes.

"Well, now let's try."

"Try what?"

Wei approached the shop window. He put his face close to a zone marked by a black and orange rectangle and waited.

A beam of light erupted from the window and surrounded Wei's face, as motionless and impassive as a stone in the desert. All of a sudden a voice from both everywhere and nowhere announced: "Welcome to the Dark Matter Store 54 West Colorado Boulevard. By accessing the Matter-Quick service you authorize us to process your personal data contained in the government's database. Your data will be used for marketing purposes. Please wait."

Tiago crossed his arms, impatiently waiting. He didn't understand what they were doing.

The automated voice suddenly resumed talking. "Welcome back Mr. Bernard Pascal. We are pleased to inform you that you have accumulated a total of one hundred and twelve Matter-Trust points. Selec—"

Wei moved away from the window and the beam of light instantly turned off. The boy had a huge smile on his face.

"Done and done. Let's go."

"Wait a minute!" Tiago was indicating the window. "Didn't the voice call you Bernard Pascal?"

"Yes it did, so what?"

"And what's Wei Wang, hmm? An alias? Is Bernard Pascal your real name?"

"Are you stupid? Does this seem to you the face of a Bernard Pascal?" Wei pointed out his almond-shaped eyes. "Of course it isn't, genius. That's the name that belongs to its rightful owner in France."

Tiago looked at the boy who was pointing to the contact lenses.

"Two plus two?" Wei said, putting the mirror and lenses back in his backpack.

"Whoa, whoa, wait a minute! You mean you have impressed on those contact lenses the reticular imprint of a guy who lives in France?"

Wei pointed with his thumb and index finger to the sky, simulating a machine gun that hits an enemy aircraft.

"Hit and crashed," he said triumphantly.

Tiago was speechless. He couldn't understand how such a thing could be possible. What some called the reticular information industry had only very recently started up. The services and the technology related to it were still poorly developed. A few days earlier, his university discussed the possibility of creating a course focused on this fascinating but still largely unknown subject. Yet Tiago realized as he watched the Omnilogos in awe, that he had just witnessed a real robbery perpetrated with that very experimental technology. Wei didn't steal money, sure. But he did steal something valuable: information.

Tiago rubbed his forehead and then looked at his hand, which had come away wet.

He still couldn't believe what had happened. He wanted to express his amazement, ask Wei how on earth he did it, but all of a sudden he realized other major implications of what he had just witnessed.

"This is illegal," Tiago finally said, lowering his voice and looking around visibly uncomfortable, as if he expected the police to show up any minute now.

"Illegal," Wei repeated, dismissing Tiago's worried tone with a quick flick of his hand. "The right word is *awesome*."

"Do you ... do you even realize you've just committed a crime?"

"Try not to shit your pants, Heidi."

Tiago got closer to the Omnilogos. "A security camera could have recorded you ... recorded us."

"Relax."

"It's not funny, not funny at all."

"I don't believe it." Wei looked straight into Tiago's eyes as he continued walking. He seemed surprised and annoyed at the same time. "What kind of journalist are you? Oh, sorry, wannabe journalist."

"What's that supposed to mean?"

"Do you think you'll get your best stories legally? Blackmail, deception, theft, extortion, stalking, these are all essential tools for any Pulitzer Prize winner."

Tiago felt humiliated. How dare this suckling little prick talk to him like that?

"You don't even know what you're talking about," he said, looking at the boy with an outraged expression. "A journalist is a respected, independent and decent person."

"As was a money-lender in ancient Rome. You know, the kind of guy who asked fifteen per cent interest on loans? These days, they call him a loan shark."

"Journalists are socially useful and above all *legitimate*," Tiago insisted, emphasizing the last word.

"So too were hangmen," Wei threw back, speeding up his gait.

Tiago felt as though he was in the middle of a virtual tennis match where he invariably lost, set after set. The boy always seemed to be one step ahead of him.

"So, is this the strategy you've used with the other 'parrots'?" Tiago asked, not willing to give up. "Did you just send them all to the local nuthouse?"

"Are you kidding me? You are the first one who has the honor of speaking to me. I remind you that if I hadn't approached you, you'd still be grazing grass. Now stop whining. We have to get into that restaurant."

Wei stopped. On the sign in front of them, *Sapori & Sentimenti* was written in beautifully crafted letters.

"What does it mean?" asked Tiago, looking at the foreign words.

"It's Italian. It means Flavors and Feelings."

Tiago nodded.

"Are you hungry?" Wei asked.

Tiago hadn't eaten in a long time. An unmistakable growl erupted from his stomach.

"You want to stop to eat here?" Tiago looked puzzled.

"I have some matters to discuss with the owner," Wei said, checking his watch. "In the meantime, I'll ask the chef to cook something for you."

"Really?" Tiago put his hands on his hips. "*You* will ask the chef? Sounds like you own this place."

"Don't be ridiculous," Wei said, smiling a toothy smile, "I'm only twelve."

He grabbed the handle and then stopped, lingering in front of the restaurant door. "Oh, yeah," Wei said, scratching his forehead, "I almost forgot. The chef here, Tonio, is a bit like … hmm … particular. Keep that in mind, please."

"What do you mean by 'particular'?"

"Well, don't get me wrong, he's a genius. Personally I think he's the best chef I've ever met, but … you know, he's one of those 'compassionate' Italians." Wei said, looking for the right words. "There have been some misunderstandings where he worked before.

And there are stories ... you know." Wei stopped.

Tiago shook his head. "What? What stories?"

"Let's just say that his former boss didn't appreciate some of Tonio's recipes. It seems that Tonio didn't take it very well."

"Come on, don't tease me. Spit it out. What happened?"

"It looks like ... well, it seems he filled the owner's car with tar." Wei looked straight at Tiago. "With the owner inside."

Tiago opened his mouth but no sound came out.

"Well, anyway, you keep a low profile. Promise me?"

Before Tiago could answer, Wei opened the door and took a couple of steps forward, spreading his arms as if he was waiting to catch a huge ball.

"Uncle Matthew!" the Omnilogos cried out at the top of his voice.

Tiago winced. He entered just in time to see a fifty-year-old man wearing a suit and tie -- and running like a hurricane toward them.

"Disgraziato! Ma tu mi fai penare!"

The man, a giant six and a half feet tall, embraced Wei like a son, lifting him off the ground with one arm. The boy laughed and laughed.

Every head in the place turned to watch the scene.

Once he was back on the ground, Wei pointed to Tiago. "Uncle Matthew, this is a very dear friend of mine who has come to visit. He's hungry. Can we give him something to eat?"

Tiago didn't say a thing. He just put on a weird grin that he hoped looked like a smile.

The restaurant owner studied him very carefully. Finally he made a half bow and held out his hand.

"Matthew Bonati, here to serve you. Wei's friends are my friends."

"Tiago Melo, sir. It's a pleasure," he said, nodding at the giant.

Matthew Bonati snapped his fingers. "Rodolfo!" he called, looking around the room.

One of the servers hurried to him immediately. The owner indicated Tiago.

"Prepare the twenty-four for our special guest," ordered Matthew, putting a hand on the server's shoulder. "Also, ask Tonio to prepare something appropriate for our friend Tango, here."

Tiago held up a finger and opened his mouth, about to say something. He looked at Wei, who was shaking his head. Tiago lowered his finger and closed his mouth, resigning himself to the Italianization of his name.

Matthew smiled at Tiago and Wei. Then he lowered his voice a little and continued giving Rodolfo instructions. "After that, you go straight to table forty-one and clean up the mess under it, all right? Dai, dai! Go on, quickly now. I pay you by the hour, not by the minute."

Rodolfo nodded meekly and invited Tiago to follow him.

"I'll see you in an hour," Wei said, as he walked into the kitchen with the owner. "Buon appetito!"

Tiago was sitting at the table with the best view of the whole restaurant. The place was very well maintained, clean and elegant. He realized only then that he was in a very fancy restaurant.

"Mr. Tango," Rodolfo said with a strong Castilian accent. "Do you have any allergies that I should be aware of?"

"Tiago. The name is Tiago. No, no allergies. Thanks for asking."

Rodolfo nodded as he picked up a basket of bread and a saucer of oil from a nearby table, setting them to his right.

"Sir, would you like a bit of bread with caramelized onions and tomato bruschetta with olive oil?"

"Wow, thanks, Rodolfo." Tiago sniffed and smiled.

"It's my pleasure, sir. This is our wine list. Our sommelier ..."

Tiago shook his head. "No, thank you, Rodolfo. I don't drink alcohol."

"I'm sorry, sir? Say it again."

"Oh ... I said ... I'm a teetotaller. I don't drink alcohol."

Rodolfo repeated the word 'teetotaller' as though he had never heard it before.

"Just ... just water?" he asked slowly.

"Yes, please."

Tiago started to eat while the server filled his glass with some sparkling water.

"Sir, chef Tonio wanted to know if you prefer a vegetarian, fish or meat based menu."

"Whatever he decides is fine."

Rodolfo nodded and disappeared into the kitchen. While he waited, Tiago read the menu on the nearby table. He could not find anything priced less than thirty dollars, except bread and water.

"Here you are, sir. Squid and shrimp meatballs covered in a sweet cheese sauce. Would you like some fresh pepper?"

"That'd be great, thanks."

What followed was probably the best meal of his life. He could not even pronounce half the things that Rodolfo served him, but they were all masterpieces. Wei was right, after all. The chef might have been a psychopath, but he knew his stuff in the kitchen.

Rodolfo was wiping some crumbs from his table. "In a moment, chef Tonio will come over to make sure everything was of your liking."

Tiago spat out the water he was drinking.

"Sir, are you OK?"

"Fine … fine, thanks, Rodolfo," said Tiago coughing, as he wiped his mouth with a napkin. Mr. Tar was coming? Sweat was gathering on the palms of his hands.

Soon after, a man came out of the kitchen. He was very thin, in his forties, with no hair and no beard. He had huge bulging eyes, a sharp chin and a nose so long that it would have been disqualified in a fencing match.

"I'm Tonio. Glad you're here."

"Ta … Tiago! Tiago Melo," the student said, wiping his sweaty hand on his jeans and shaking Tonio's. "It's a pleasure, sir."

"Tonio will work fine," said the chef with a wink.

"Tonio, of course," repeated Tiago.

"So, how did you like—"

"I've never eaten so well in my whole life," Tiago cut him off, indicating the table. "Your dishes … your dishes are masterpieces. They are truly works of art. If there was a Nobel Prize for the cuisine … I mean …"

Tonio put his hands on his hips and looked at Tiago. "I got it, boy. Wei told you the story, right?"

"Wha—? No, no … It's just … Wei said … Look, I don't …"

Tiago stopped. "I think I'm going to throw up," he admitted finally, rubbing his stomach.

Tonio exploded in laughter.

When he finished, he wiped his eyes and said, "Yes, it's typical of that rascal. Look, I've never done anything like that I swear." The chef put his hand over his heart. He was still smiling.

"You mean you've never drowned your boss in tar?" Only after he finished the sentence did Tiago realize how incredibly ludicrous it sounded.

Tonio laughed again. "This time it was tar? Geez, that little criminal always finds new ways to tell it."

The chef sat at his left while describing the dessert that Rodolfo was carrying toward them. "Lemon sorbet with mint and slivers of candied orange."

Tiago thanked him. He picked up the spoon and let the flavors linger for a few seconds in his mouth before swallowing. It was as if his taste buds were screaming with joy. Once again, the dish surpassed all his expectations.

"Outstanding," Tiago murmured, complimenting the chef. "I guarantee you every bite is a blessing, really. If I may ask, how do you make things so ... well, exceptional?"

"I have no idea," Tonio said with a shrug.

"I mean," continued Tiago watching the man with interest, "where did you study? How long have you been doing this?"

"To tell you the truth," said Tonio, "I started this job nine months ago."

Tiago wiped his mouth. "You mean you started working *here* nine months ago."

"Oh, no, you got it right. Before working for Matthew I was a simple government employee. That is the only work I've done over the last fifteen years."

Tiago looked at the chef. He couldn't tell whether he was serious or simply joking.

"Are you saying you've never practiced this profession ... I mean, cooking, before?"

"I finished my evening course exactly one year ago. Before that, the only kitchen in which I was allowed to set foot in was the one in my house."

Tiago felt uncomfortable. He shifted in his chair. "Sorry, I don't think I actually got this. I mean, your dishes are truly exceptional ... seriously. I thought that to make these kinds of things it would take years, if not decades of practice, you know."

"So they say," Tonio answered, absently rubbing his chin.

There was a moment of silence. Tiago finished his dessert and put the spoon down.

"You said you were a simple employee, right? Before, I mean," Tiago said, thumbing over his shoulder. "What convinced you to wear your apron?"

"Wei," Tonio answered without hesitation. "It was that sweet, little rowdy kid who convinced me to turn what I thought was a hobby into the dream of my life. Before then, I never even thought I was cut out for the job."

"Wei convinced you? Wait a second. You quit your job on a twelve-year-old kid's say-so?"

Tonio looked him straight in the eyes, without blinking. "Damn straight. He convinced me to quit that awful job and get my diploma. He even introduced me to Matthew who hired me on the spot, thanks to his recommendation."

Tiago nodded thoughtfully. The chef looked like the kind of person who loved to talk, if he could just ask him the right questions.

"How long has this restaurant been open?" he asked, trying to keep a neutral tone.

"Sapori and Sentimenti? It's quite new. Not even three years old." Tonio crossed his legs and looked around. "Matthew told me that on day one, it was a little more than an inn. Then of course Wei came with his advice."

"Advice?" repeated Tiago, craning his neck.

"Well, from what I've heard here at the restaurant, Sapori and Sentimenti would not be what it is today without him. Don't ask me how, but Wei introduced Matthew to the right people, counselled him on what to invest in and what to save on. He literally revolutionized this place."

Tiago frowned. "Really? You're still talking about the twelve-year-old kid in the T-shirt and sneakers?"

Tonio nodded. "The one and only."

"Look, I'm not saying ... OK, the truth? I really have a hard time believing that. Come on, put yourself in my shoes. It looks like you're talking about a super manager, not a kid whose idea of transportation is a bicycle. Wei is smart and clever, nothing to say about that, but you know ..." With a sceptical smile, he left the sentence hanging in the air.

Tonio drew his chair closer to Tiago's.

"Let's not play games, young man. If Wei introduced you here it means that he trusts you and that you know him as much as I do."

Tiago nodded, dead serious, even if he had known Wei for only a few hours. He felt his heartbeat accelerating. Beads of sweat dotted his forehead. This conversation was heating up. He smelled the distinct fragrance of revelations in the air.

"That kid's got something special, if you ask me," the chef continued in a low voice looking into his eyes. "It's something you understand as soon as you start speaking to him, it's no secret. But that's just the tip of the iceberg, trust me. That kid is not just damn precocious, erudite and monstrously clever. It's the way he literally reads people, as if they were an open book. That is unique. Sometimes, when I see him talking to other people, well … a chill creeps up my spine. It's almost scary. You should see the way people seem to drink up what he says as if it were pure nectar."

Tonio looked around. He crossed his arms and nodded toward the kitchen.

"My opinion?" Tonio continued, planting both feet on the ground. "That kid has a gift."

"Yes, I know," replied Tiago. "I've seen what he can do with …"

Tonio held up a hand and shook his head. "Forget his brain. There are others out there younger, smarter, more precise and faster than him. No, Wei's special for another reason … something less visible. That kid has a gift for finding talent. For me, it seems he feels compelled to find special people, people who can make a difference. His gift is in finding these people and … I don't know how to explain it with words, but, well, once he finds them, his magic is to empower them."

"Honestly, it seems to me that Wei also feels compelled to make a lot of money," Tiago said without losing sight of his interlocutor's eyes. "I saw what he did in one of his 'morning shows', you know, up at Queensberry. You know what I'm talking about, right? Do you have an opinion on that too?"

"You mean, his 'ten-against-a-grand' contest?"

Tiago nodded.

"Yeah, that's one of his favorite pastimes, from what he tells me."

"A rewarding pastime," Tiago said, rubbing his thumb against his forefinger. "He made ten dollars every ten seconds for an hour. Call me stupid, but I see no interest in helping anyone but himself in that case."

Tonio shook his head as he wiped some crumbs from the tablecloth.

"Trust me, young man. That show, as you called it, has little to do with money. The little thug has a dozen other ways to make more money in less time."

Tiago didn't reply to that. He felt that the conversation was taking an interesting turn. He let the chef go on talking. Meanwhile he unobtrusively searched in one of his own pockets.

"Take Sapori and Sentimenti, for example. Each week, Matthew puts an envelope in a safe box here at the restaurant. A pay check destined to a certain Mr. 'No one'. He and Wei are the only ones with the key for that box."

"And what would the amount in this safe box be?"

"Well, I don't know how much there could be in a pay check that doesn't exist," Tonio said, waving a hand as if to ward off invisible smoke, "but I'm sure you've had a look at our menu."

"I understand," Tiago said, scratching his head. "I wonder why Mr. 'No one' is using all his skills to help those who need it, as you said, and at the same time making a considerable amount of money."

"Don't let appearances mislead you, boy. Money is only a means to achieving a goal. Wei has a goal, that's as certain as death and taxes, but money is only a part of the answer. That kid likes to surround himself with useful people, people with potential, but at the same time in need of help. Look at me and Matthew. Matthew was on the verge of bankruptcy before Wei arrived, and I was unhappy with a life that didn't give me anything important. I'm going to return the favor when he asks me to do so. I owe him, as Matthew does."

"He said something like that to me too," Tiago said, looking at the chef, "but I haven't the slightest idea what he wants from me. I have nothing special to offer him."

Tonio shook his head. "If today you're here, it means he can use you. That makes you a special person in some—"

"Tiago Silva Abreu Melo!" a shrill voice interrupted their conversation. "Time's up. Gotta go. Now!"

Tiago saw Wei open the restaurant's door and leave without another word. The young man jumped up from his chair and stretched out his hand to the chef, who shook it.

"Thanks for everything."

"You got it." Then Tonio added, "You're not from around here, are you?"

"L.A.," Tiago answered.

"Enjoying the tourist's tour?"

"Let's just say that more than a tourist, I feel like a taxi driver at the moment. I'm beginning to suspect that he only needed a cheap means of transportation."

"It's a good thing, my friend. It's a good thing," said the chef, nodding.

"Really?" Tiago said, leaving his napkin on the table. "Surely it's a good thing for him. He got a driver for the rest of the day."

"No." Tonio grinned. "It means he really likes you."

"Move your ass, motor boy," Wei shouted from a nearby window.

"Yeah, I agree," Tiago said, making a face. After thanking Rodolfo, Tiago walked quickly toward the exit.

"Finally!" Wei said when the restaurant's door closed behind Tiago. "We're late, you know? Chop-chop!"

Tiago quickly joined him.

"You know, I had a very interesting conversation with Tonio," he said, indicating the restaurant.

"I'm sure," the boy replied. "That spaghetti-eater is a motor-mouth."

"I'd like to ask you some questions."

"By all means, my friend."

"Oh, really? All right. Tonio told me a bit about yourself ... your interests, what you have done for him and Matthew, for the restaurant and many other people. It looks like you're using your skills to create a kind of ... network of people you trust. Is that so?"

Wei crossed the street as he checked his watch.

"Is that so?" Tiago repeated.

The Omnilogos just kept walking without even looking at him.

"Are you deaf all of a sudden? You don't have any answer to that?"

"Answer?" Wei asked, suddenly turning toward the student. "I thought you were talking about questions. You can ask me as many questions as you want."

"You mean you're not going to answer them?"

"No," Wei said, smiling. "See? I answered."

Tiago suddenly stopped just before they reached his motorcycle. Wei stared at him blankly.

"I have no reason to continue this charade if you don't give me something back. Do you understand?" Tiago said, pushing his hands deep into his pockets.

Wei approached the student and looked at him straight in the eye.

"I understand that, since you came out of that restaurant, you know more about me than you knew starting out this morning in Los Angeles, chasing mere rumors. I understand that by continuing to follow me you could keep sniffing around -- and figure out some answers to your questions. But I also understand that you don't like the idea of being the chauffeur of a twelve-year-old kid and that you probably have much better things to do than trying to unravel the mystery of the Omnilogos." Wei paused and raised a hand indicating the motorcycle parked nearby. "Now you have a choice. Either you decide to go back home or you keep collecting material for your Pulitzer. What do you say?"

Tiago knew his bluff had been called even before Wei finished speaking. The student shook his head and grinned so wide Wei could see the back row of his teeth.

"Come on, boss. We're late," Tiago said, starting the engine.

Wei smiled and followed him on the motorcycle. "Go straight and turn left when I tell you."

∞∞∞∞

Five minutes later, they were in front of a four-story building in the middle of the financial district.

As soon as they got in, Wei asked for information at the reception desk.

"Fourth floor," he said to Tiago, pointing to the stairs.

When they reached the fourth floor, Wei stopped in front of the men's room.

"Wait here, I'll be back in no time." He pulled out a plastic bag from his backpack and went in.

A few minutes later, the Omnilogos came back wearing new clothes: shirt, jacket, tie and black shoes. He put the old clothes in his backpack. Tiago studied his new outfit.

"Don't ask," Wei said, putting his finger to his lips.

"Asking questions is my job," Tiago said, "and an answer doesn't cost anything. I'd appreciate even a lie. A lie is something I can work on."

"Some answers need to be earned."

Tiago huffed in frustration. Then he indicated the green and yellow tie that the Omnilogos was wearing. It was a very particular tie:

59

smooth, shiny, small and very colorful. Like Roger Rabbit's bow tie. Not exactly the best style choice of the century.

"Ken won't be happy to know you've been sacking his wardrobe."

"A Barbie fan," Wei announced, putting his hands on his cheeks and looking around as if he was talking to an imaginary audience. "Now I understand many things." The boy put his hand on his hips. He then twisted a finger in his dark hair and walked away from the student, waddling like a model on a catwalk.

Tiago closed his eyes and murmured something that never went beyond his ears.

They soon found themselves in front of a wooden door. Wei knocked. The door opened almost immediately. A middle-aged woman with big glasses and sagging cheeks greeted them and invited them in.

The two were escorted into an empty waiting room with a television fixed on the wall.

"Mr. Banks will see you in a moment."

"Thank you," they said in unison.

When the secretary left them alone, Tiago asked, "Can I at least ask what we're doing here?"

"I have stuff to do," Wei answered, smoothing his tie.

"What stuff?"

"If I tell you, then I'll have to kill you," Wei said.

"Well, I tried," Tiago said, raising his eyebrows. "For the sake of conversation, I think you should know that the jacket should be unbuttoned when sitting. Since you want to look like an adult, you might as well act like one."

Wei looked at his jacket. "This is my style, Barbie-boy," Wei said with a wink.

Tiago started to reply, but the secretary entered the room in that very moment.

"Mr. Banks will receive you now. Come this way."

Wei followed the secretary, and the door closed behind him.

Tiago found himself staring at the wall of the room.

The television was broadcasting a documentary about the recent expansion of an organization called LAND. A reporter was interviewing a certain Spine Woodside, a tall and handsome man with a hell of a smile, Tiago thought. On his chest the 'Landist', as the reporter called him, had a pin that showed a man and a woman kneeling on either side of a sphere containing the four elements. Tiago imagined that the sphere represented the earth.

With nothing better to do for the following half hour, Tiago listened to the reporter describing the proselytizing that the Landists were carrying out in California, Texas, Washington, D.C. and Florida. The last scene showed a dozen Landists shouting slogans inside the Kennedy Space Center, at Cape Canaveral, as they were being taken away by security.

Wei left Mr. Banks' office just when the documentary was starting to get interesting.

"Done and done." The boy snorted, apparently exhausted. He took off his tie. "Let's get out of here."

Tiago reluctantly followed the Omnilogos as he looked at the screen one last time.

Once in the hallway, Wei stopped again in the men's room to change clothes. He came back after a couple of minutes, half naked and still putting on his shirt.

"Nice," Tiago said pointing to the odd-shaped pendant that Wei had around his neck. "Why eight?"

Wei looked at the student as if he did not understand what he was talking about. Then he saw the pendant. His face paled instantly. He put it hastily under his shirt.

"It's not an eight, you moron." He walked away without looking at him.

Tiago smiled. The Omnilogos was embarrassed, he thought, intrigued. He would want to find out more about the pendant.

When they were both out of the building, Tiago noticed that the shadows were beginning to lengthen as the afternoon wore on.

"Next stop?" the student asked, mounting on his motorcycle.

"Wait here," Wei said. "I'll be right back."

Tiago turned off the engine and waited, looking at his smartphone.

Wei came back shortly, holding a large bouquet of flowers.

"Look at these," Tiago said, smelling the aroma. "Any point asking for whom ..."

"For my girlfriend," Wei answered, scratching his ear.

"Oh ... you have a girlfriend?"

"Is something wrong with that?"

"No," Tiago said, spreading his arms, "and no comments on the matter."

Wei climbed on and placed the bouquet of flowers under his arm, careful not to squeeze it.

"We're late," Wei said, looking at his wristwatch and placing a finger in his mouth. "Vámonos."

Tiago started the engine and drove off. "So," he said, stopping at a traffic light. "Has your girlfriend got a name?"

"Evangeline," Wei immediately answered. The tone of his voice, Tiago noticed, had radically changed from acid and contemptuous to soft and slow.

"What is she like?" Tiago asked, while passing a car.

The Omnilogos watched a cloud then he smiled. "She's tall and lean, fair hair and fair skin, eyes the color of the sea," Wei started in a passionate voice. "She is witty, intelligent, cheerful, charming and incredibly sweet. She loves cheeseburgers, starry skies, hearty breakfasts, the scent of Pelargoniums, Monet's paintings and nights with a full moon. You know, she has a natural talent for ...."

Tiago smiled as he listened to the Omnilogos describing Evangeline in every detail with growing excitement. For the very first time, he remembered that, after all, Wei was only a teen, and when it came to girls, he was not very different from the majority of his peers.

He seemed almost normal.

∞∞∞∞

"That's it," Wei said, nudging Tiago with his elbow and pointing to a small house painted in white.

Wei climbed off the vehicle and looked in the side view mirror, fixing his hair. "How do I look?" he asked, visibly nervous.

"Insecure and damn funny," Tiago said, teasing.

Wei made a face and then looked at the house.

Tiago was contemplating a completely different person from the sharp, brilliant and ruthless Omnilogos that he had come to know. At that moment, Wei seemed to him just a clumsy little boy, eager to make a good impression.

When they were in front of the door, Wei took a deep breath and put his bouquet of flowers in plain view. He knocked three times.

"Michelle will skin me alive," Wei said in a low voice, ignoring Tiago's questioning look.

The door wasn't opened; it was almost thrown off its hinges.

A black woman with long, frizzy hair, with large, full breasts and two hands as big as baseball mitts stared at them with bloodshot eyes. "*You*," she said with a hiss, pointing to the Omnilogos with her finger. A large bluish vein protruded from her forehead. "You're late."

"Geez, I know Michelle, I'm so, so sorry!" Wei seemed about to kneel and beg forgiveness. "I had some unexpected ... I tried to get things done as soon as possible, but ... look, I got these for ..."

"Let me see," she said, snatching the bouquet of flowers.

"Roses, tulips, daisies, lilacs ..." Michelle chanted, inspecting the Omnilogos' gift. "... and red geraniums."

There was a long moment of silence. Tiago was sure that the woman would have thrown the bouquet of flowers on the ground, trampling it without mercy.

"At least you know your flowers," said Michelle instead, showing a row of white teeth. The vein in her forehead narrowed and her gaze became gentler. "Hurry up and step inside, you punk, before I change my mind."

Wei sighed then indicated Tiago. "This is my friend. Tiago, Michelle. Michelle, Tiago."

The two shook hands.

"This would be the guy you were talking about?" she asked, eyeing Tiago from head to foot.

He answered with a shy wave of his hand.

"Yes he is."

"All right," said Michelle moving from the door and letting them in.

"Is she awake?" Wei asked, passing by a small living room full of flowers, paintings and books before heading up the stairs.

"The last time I checked, she was sleeping," Michelle said, staring at the young man from L.A. and indicating the stairs.

Tiago approached Wei, trying not to be heard by Michelle. "The guy you talked to her about?" he whispered in his ear.

Wei didn't answer and kept walking. At the top of the stairs, they found themselves in front of a simple yellow door. Wei pushed his hair back. He breathed deeply.

Tiago didn't understand what was happening. Rather than going to meet his girlfriend, Wei seemed about to start a marathon.

Swallowing hard, Wei put his hand on the knob and opened the door. Tiago crossed the threshold followed by Michelle.

The dark room they found themselves in pulsed with red, blue and yellow lights. Holoposters were scattered all around, on the ceiling as well as on the walls, creating images and sounds that made the room look like an ancient sanctuary.

Tiago needed a few seconds before he was able to distinguish the forms that surrounded him. Eventually he recognized some of the evanescent objects that swirled about: planets, comets, asteroids, nebulae and bright stars. The young man had the feeling of being at a show offered by a planetarium, if not better. These three-dimensional projections had the best resolution that he had ever seen.

Tiago walked through what seemed a reproduction of Saturn, and moved quickly to follow the kid's fast pace. There were so many of the three-dimensional reproductions that sometimes they overlapped each other, mingling with the shapes and profiles of real objects. As he followed the Omnilogos, Tiago nearly stumbled twice.

"Watch out," Michelle warned him just in time.

"Thank you," said the student, dodging the edge of a table at the last moment. He also instinctively avoided a comet that appeared to his right.

Tiago watched the comet cross the room and bounce off the wall. He shook his head, confused.

Surely he had just imagined that. Holoposters were decorations often used at parties and receptions or large gatherings. They were three-dimensional projections of objects that moved within a room, created by a projector that could be programmed at will. They were very expensive items, the latest rave of the entertainment industry -- but they could not possibly bounce off the walls.

"What are you doing?" Michelle said, gesturing to him to move ahead. "Wei is waiting."

Tiago roused himself from his thoughts and kept walking.

Wei was putting his flowers in a vase surrounded by a small asteroid belt. He was humming the tune of a song that Tiago didn't recognize.

The sudden explosion of a supernova brightened the pale face of the girl lying on the bed, silent and motionless. Tiago closed his hand over his mouth as he looked at the girl, studying the details that until then had remained hidden by the wonderful and misleading holographic shapes and lights.

Evangeline was sick. Wei did not include that detail in his rich and passionate description. The tiny body, the small veins that wandered up her neck like an intricate network of cables, and the face beset by shadows gave Tiago the impression of weakness, sadness and resignation. She was so pale that her lips were bloodless.

He carefully scrutinized her from top to bottom. The shape of the thin white sheets suggested an amputated leg just above her knee.

On the bedside table, a prosthesis covered by dust made him realize that Evangeline hadn't left that room for quite a while.

Tiago's initial surprise, soon replaced by annoyance due to the Omnilogos' omission, turned into bitter anger. Why hadn't Wei said anything? he thought.

"What's wrong with her?" Tiago whispered to Michelle.

"Oste ... osteosarcoma," Michelle managed to say, sniffling.

"What is that?" Tiago had never heard that word before but he suspected it was not good.

"It's a cancer, a ... a common form of childhood cancer."

"A cancer? Why ... I mean, what is the cause?"

"No one knows."

"Good God," Tiago murmured, watching the diminished figure lying before their eyes. "And she's ... Evangeline, I mean ... She'll recover?"

Michelle had no time to answer. At that very moment Evangeline's eyes opened.

Wei smiled at her.

"Don't you ever get tired of sleeping?"

The girl licked her dry lips and cleared her throat. She seemed confused and disoriented. Her eyes caught another small explosion, caused by the clash of two comets. A smile enlightened her face. "Hmm ..." Evangeline tried to get up, leaning on her elbow, but Wei gently placed a hand on her chest.

"Some water first," he suggested.

Evangeline nodded and let Wei help her drink. When she finished, the Omnilogos took a handkerchief from her bedside table and wiped her chin.

"As a nurse, you suck," Evangeline managed to whisper, pointing to him with a bony finger as white as milk.

Tiago noticed that the girl was shaking.

Wei took her hand in his. "I know, I'm hopeless," Wei said,

shrugging. "I'm still stuck with First Aid. Mouth-to-mouth, you know." He blinked.

Evangeline smiled. "You moron."

Wei continued to hold the girl's hand, then pointed to Tiago. "Look, I brought you a guest."

Evangeline saw the student, who was trying to look as natural as possible. After a long silence, she beckoned him to come closer.

Cursing Wei under his breath, he walked slowly to the bedside, unsure of what to do. No one had told him what to expect or how to behave.

Just smile? Maybe shake her hand? Smile and shake her hand? Tiago glanced at Wei for help. He found none.

"You don't look in great shape," said Evangeline watching Tiago approach.

It sounded like an odd joke coming from someone without a leg, as pale as death and with trouble breathing,

"Tiago Melo," he introduced himself. Then, fearing that was not enough, he lowered his head and bent his knees slightly.

"A bow," Evangeline said, turning to Wei. "Here's someone who knows good manners."

"A bow? You're kidding me? I thought he was going to stumble on something," Wei said, genuinely surprised.

From where he now stood, Tiago could see the girl's clouded face. Although lean and altered by the disease, she could not be older than sixteen and was much more mature than he expected. A bandana covered her head, so he couldn't see her hair. Although clearly ill and undernourished, Evangeline was a girl who suggested a kind of simple and universal beauty, like dawn's first light.

"So you're the chosen one," Evangeline said with a strange finality in her tone.

Wei started to say something but she raised a hand to stop him.

"Leave us. I want to talk with him for a while. Alone."

"Honey," Michelle immediately replied. "I don't think ..."

"Michelle, I'll be fine. I promise."

Wei stood up from the stool where he was sitting, and without another word he left the room. Michelle looked to Evangeline first, then to Tiago. She finally followed Wei, reluctantly closing the door behind her.

"Make yourself comfortable," Evangeline said, gesturing to the stool near her bed.

Tiago obeyed. Another sudden light, due to some kind of clash between projections, lit up the room again. Evangeline smiled. Sparks of scarlet light brightened her blue eyes.

Only then did Tiago fully realize that he was alone with a girl who was fighting death in front of him, surrounded by the wonders of the galaxy that moved, glowed and exploded all around them.

Something inside told him he was going through one of those special moments that one often reads about. One of those rare situations where you feel you are in a place you know you shouldn't be, with a person you thought you'd never meet and without the slightest idea of what is going to happen next.

"I was sure that he would have chosen a woman," Evangeline said, looking at the ceiling. "He always says that they tell the best stories, the richest, the ones that make you want to read them all over again."

Tiago shook his head. "I'm sorry, I don't understand."

Evangeline turned and looked at him in the eyes.

"Never mind. Tell me about yourself. Do you study or do you work?"

"I'm a student of USC Annenberg."

"No way," Evangeline interrupted him, surprised. "You're a parrot?"

"I am afraid so," Tiago said, apologetically. "I have no idea what it means or why they call me that, but it's my second name since I came here."

Evangeline shrugged. "You know, it's the word we use for guys like you. Let's see ... Journalists, paparazzi, etc., etc."

"I see."

"Wei always comes up with new ways to avoid them, especially since he decided to ... well, to go public, I guess."

"Yes, clearly we are unworthy parasites, the scum of society," Tiago admitted, putting a hand on his heart. "Extortionists, criminals, liars ..."

Evangeline laughed a sweet, crystalline laugh. A bad cough forced her to stop. She leaned forward, as to throw up.

"Are you OK?" Tiago asked, nervous and worried at the same time. He looked around. The door was closed. No one came running. He was really alone.

"No, not at all," replied the girl, wiping her mouth with a hand-kerchief. "Could you pass me that glass, please?"

Tiago whirled around and almost brought down the glass full of water that was on the bedside table. Cursing silently, he took the glass with both hands and gave it to her.

A long moment of silence followed.

"Are you here for him?" Evangeline asked, handing him back the half-empty glass.

Tiago nodded. "Yeah, just out of curiosity, I guess. I wanted ... I just wanted to know."

Evangeline stared at him. "What do you think of Wei? Tell me the truth."

"The truth?" asked Tiago, raising an eyebrow.

Evangeline pursed her lips, looking at Tiago's conflicted expression. "Don't worry. I know the guy. Go ahead, shoot."

"If you insist." Tiago crossed his arms and stared at the white sheet covering Evangeline. He thought about what he saw and of Wei's omission regarding Evangeline's situation.

"The first impression I had was that of a greedy, conceited, manipulative little prick. Now I think he's also a criminal, an opportunist and a liar."

There was another long moment of silence.

"It's much better than I expected," Evangeline said, absently touching her bandana, as if making sure it was still there. She cleared her throat. "Wei hasn't always been like that, you know? Before ... before we met, he was a very different person. He was an isolated child, quiet, full of anger. He never spoke to anyone. He was closed in on himself in a way that I would call dangerous, trapped in a world different from ours. A person limited and frightened. But things have changed."

"Changed? In what way have they changed?"

Evangeline thought before answering the question. Finally she said, "I guess it all started with a mouse."

"What?"

Evangeline shook her head. She smiled. "Forget it, it's a long story. Let's say that over time we have discovered a common passion that helped us get to know each other better. I like to think that our relationship has transformed him. Slowly, Wei has learned to trust people, or at least some people. And he stopped being afraid."

The girl seemed to have recovered. After yet another long moment of silence, Tiago leaned toward her. "Before, you told me that he has chosen me. Chosen to do what?"

"It's not up to me to answer that question. If he hasn't said it yet, it means it's not the right time for you to know."

"He also said that I'll owe him a favor."

"You bet. It's the way he thinks. He does nothing for nothing, but he's very picky when it comes to choosing the people he believes useful."

"Useful for what?" Tiago said, unable to conceal his impatience. "Look, it's been all day that I've been following him and it seems I know less and less. I need help. That kid … he's driving me crazy. I don't even know how to say it. It's like an enigma wrapped in a puzzle hidden in the most intricate maze of the world. The quirks I saw today have been enough to make me sleepless for the next decade. I need to know more. What does he want? What is he trying to achieve?"

Evangeline looked into Tiago's hazel eyes. The face in front of her was handsome. Tiago had amber-colored skin, very dark hair and a very short beard, shaved with an almost maniacal neatness. He had broad shoulders, muscular arms and a narrow waist. And he was tall; very tall. Evangeline focused again on his eyes. She felt kindness and curiosity, passion and determination. She began to understand what Wei saw in the guy from L.A.

Evangeline didn't answer his questions. Instead, she let the stellar show surrounding them lull her senses. What seemed like a small galaxy was flying over her bed. A pair of planets shaped like tiny rugby balls were following the concentration of stardust and lights a short distance away.

"Wei is a gift," Evangeline said finally, drowning her eyes in the light show. "I think he was born to amaze people. Look around you. Isn't it amazing?"

Tiago looked at the stellar objects swirling around the room. "Are you talking about the holoposters?" he asked, a little surprised by the sudden change of subject. "Well, yes, I guess," he answered, following Evangeline's gaze. "I don't think I've ever seen such vivid projections. But what does all this have to do with Wei?"

Evangeline smiled. "These are not holoposters."

Tiago stood motionless for a few seconds, trying to grasp what he thought was a joke. Then he turned abruptly. Understanding dawned upon him.

He looked around for a minute, bewildered by the revelation: there was no projector in the room, no energy source that nourished the stellar shapes, no device that would explain their fluid and hypnotic dance.

"He made them for me, for my birthday," she said, pointing all around her, as though hugging the entire room. "The best analgesic I've ever been prescribed."

Tiago followed the downward spiral of an arrow-shaped asteroid, unable to look away. Whatever those forms were, he now knew that they were not sold in stores, they were unique, personal gifts crafted by a visionary mind.

"I'm weak. I'm afraid our conversation ends here," Evangeline said suddenly, touching Tiago's hand. "It was a pleasure to meet you, Tiago Melo. Before calling the others, I want you to do me a favor. Wei may seem only like a big mouth with a brain above average but know this: behind him there is a huge project, something that involves us all. Please, have an open mind, be patient, but above all have faith. I think he made a good choice with you. Show him that he was right. Promise that you will take care of his dream, that you will become part of it."

Tiago didn't know what to answer. In fact he didn't even understand what Evangeline was talking about. He remained silent for a few seconds, trying to grasp the meaning of those words.

"Are you putting a dying girl on hold?"

Tiago snapped to attention, caught staring at the amputated leg. Without further hesitation he nodded. "I promise," he finally said, gently shaking his head.

"Thank you."

Evangeline revealed a white bracelet tucked under her pyjamas. She touched it and the door was opened by Michelle, who was the first to reach her bed.

Wei appeared at Tiago's left and looked at Evangeline. Evangeline nodded. She gave a thumbs up and smiled.

"Come with me," Wei said, gently tapping Tiago's shoulder, leading him out of the room.

Tiago followed him without questions while looking at Evangeline for the last time. The girl put her hand on her lips, made a kiss and blew it to Tiago.

When the door clicked into place behind them, Tiago had completely forgotten to be angry with the Omnilogos. He simply felt a great emptiness inside and a sense of loss that he didn't know how to explain.

Both went down the stairs, crossed the living room in silence and quickly left the house.

Outside, it was getting cold. Afternoon was quickly turning into evening and the sun was reduced to a flattened ball on the horizon. Tiago's mind was busy with thoughts, haunted by doubts and uncertainties. He felt tired -- bone-tired.

Surprisingly, he found himself in front of his motorcycle. He could not remember how he got there.

"You'll find a message in your inbox," Wei said, interrupting his thoughts. "Inside there is the information you came for, plus a small gift."

Tiago frowned. He picked up his smartphone. In the folder inbox, there was a message that had arrived three minutes before from a certain...

"Kruscha?" Tiago asked, not understanding.

Wei put a finger on his nose.

"What does that mean?" Tiago asked, reading the e-mail. "You want me to publish in thirty days time a story of this day without mentioning the real names of the people and referring to you as ... as the Omnilogos? I don't understand."

"Well, I've decided that I like that name after all. The Omnilogos is a name like any other."

"I wasn't talking about that," Tiago said, annoyed by the answer. "I don't understand why you want me to publish an article about you under these conditions. Why ... what do you need it for? Is this also part of your big plan?"

"Big plan?" Wei repeated, puzzled. "No. No big plan. I only have many small projects."

"I still don't understand what you're talking about. What do I have to do with all of this? If you want to write today's diary, do it by yourself."

"I can't do that. I don't get along with words."

"What?"

"You heard me. I don't do words."

"Wait a minute. Are you serious? You want me to believe that a living encyclopedia, able to crack experimental technology and to build those flying things, can't write?"

"You're a champion in pointing out your lack of tact."

Tiago read the message again. "This would be the favor that I owe you?"

"Exactly."

"That's it? You're basically allowing me to do what I wanted."

"Yes, the only condition attached is that you must wait thirty days from today before publishing your piece."

"Why?"

"Because, I say so."

"Oh, yeah? And what would happen if I publish my piece tomorrow?"

"You won't."

"No? How can you be so sure?"

"Because, you've got green light, my dear Tiago Silva Abreu Melo."

Tiago tapped a foot on the asphalt, frustrated. "Enough bullshit, I want real answers. What do you expect to get from me? Why do you want me to write this story?"

"Because I read your article on the social inequalities plaguing Los Angeles ghettos and I found it mind blowing. Because I studied your research on the possible applications of the Cloud and they made me think. Because I've seen your photo exhibition on the evolution of the greeting and I was speechless, and because you demonstrated an innate talent in public relations when it came to sponsoring the Web space of your classmate. When I saw you today in front of Max's house I felt you were different ... different from the others. You've proven to be resolute and stubborn when you waited for an hour and a half until I showed up. And I saw the spontaneity in your work only by exchanging a few words with you. Does this answer your question?"

Tiago gasped, his jaw wide open. "I ... I can't believe it. How could you ... how do you know all these things? We've never seen each other before!"

"Tiago, don't be naive. In the fantastic and frightening era we live in, anyone is able to know what you had for breakfast yesterday."

"You ...?"

Wei nodded. "I surfed the Net while you were grazing in the garden."

"You knew … you knew who I was all along?"

"Of course I knew! Haven't your parents told you never to talk to strangers?"

"Shut up!" Tiago shouted, anger clearly showing on his face. "Evangeline told me that you have chosen someone to tell a story. She was referring to this? This is what you need me for?" He indicated his phone with an inquisitive look.

"No, she always thinks big. She was referring to the broader picture. The reason why I have chosen you is very selfish, you know? I chose you because in the future someone will look back and in front of a bunch of people ask the question: 'What kind of person was Wei Wang before it all started?' I want you to be the one answering that question."

∞∞∞∞

Michelle's face was lighted by a tiny comet the color of ice. The black woman bit her lips as she clasped her hands behind her back.

"I gave her hot soup and something for the pain," she murmured, gazing behind her. "She said … she said she wants to see you."

Wei nodded and started to move but Michelle grasped his arm, holding it tight.

"She's dying," she whispered, tears in her eyes. Blood was coming from her lip. "I … don't think she has …"

Wei put a hand on the woman's arm. He smiled.

Michelle let him go. The woman sniffled and continued, "She needs to rest. Five minutes. You have five minutes."

Wei nodded. "Thank you."

Michelle closed the door behind her. Silence.

The Omnilogos took a step forward. He stopped and closed his eyes. He breathed deeply, trying to slow down the uncontrolled hammering of his heart. He muttered something to himself. He kept walking forward.

As he sat on the stool near the bed, he looked at Evangeline's chest, slowly rising and falling.

"I like Tiago," Evangeline said suddenly, her eyes closed. "He's got a nice ass."

73

Wei raised an eyebrow. "I don't know if I feel like laughing or throwing up."

"Do both things, please. That'd be funny."

Evangeline coughed. Wei gave her some water.

She moistened her lips. "Think you can trust him?"

"Absolutely."

"Good." Evangeline nodded. "Very good."

They sat in silence for a few minutes. Then Evangeline turned toward him. "What did Matthew say?" she asked, opening her eyes.

Wei sighed. "He didn't take it very well."

"You mean ... you think he won't help you?"

"At the moment he's worried about the new branch in Los Angeles and the one under construction in New York. When he figures out that Sapori and Sentimenti is not on the verge of doom, he won't refuse. He'll see sense."

"He'd better," Evangeline said. She seemed annoyed. "His little Italian oasis wouldn't even exist without you."

Wei didn't answer to that.

"And how is Tonio coping with the new ... ingredients?" Evangeline sounded curious and amused at the same time.

Wei tried not to laugh. "I think his scorpion's nest in spicy sauce is improving, but he's still struggling when handling all the stuff that Nok puts in front of him. He shivers like a child. Right now, his fried grasshoppers are the only decent dish he can cook."

"How do you know that?" Evangeline asked, covering her mouth with one hand. "Have you tried it ... personally?"

"Sure." Wei shrugged.

The girl made a strange face and stuck her tongue out, as if she had just drunk a bitter medicine.

"I'll never kiss you again."

"Is that a promise?"

They both laughed.

Evangeline yawned. "Are you ... augh ... what about Banks? Did you go meet him?"

Wei nodded. "Yes. That's the reason for my delay."

"And?"

The Omnilogos rubbed his forehead. "Well, he said that it is legally possible. He'll introduce me to someone who could give me those kinds of documents. The Visa will probably be the hardest thing to get."

Another long moment of silence followed. Wei noticed that Evangeline was dozing off.

"Wei?"

"Yes?"

"Can you turn the lights off? I'd like to dream."

Wei stood up from the stool and walked toward the middle of the room.

He raised his right hand in the air and then he clenched it.

The projections stopped in unison, motionless like frozen fish in a tank.

Wei swung his arm, as if waving a lasso.

The projections moved toward him, inexorably dragged by an invisible force.

Wei stopped and opened his hand again. The projections started to lose their shapes and quickly became simple beams of light that threw themselves toward him. For a fraction of a second, Wei saw galaxies, comets, stars and planets shining in the palm of his hand. It was a tiny universe peeping through his fingers.

He touched the bracelet hidden under his sleeve and the last remnant of light disappeared at once.

The room was now dark, silent and infinitely smaller.

"Thank you," Evangeline said.

Wei took his place by her side. The girl would be asleep very soon.

He looked at her. "Eva," he called softly, brushing her hand. "I've decided on a name."

"Really?" murmured Evangeline. "Finally. Let's hear it."

The Omnilogos approached the bed. He kissed the girl on the forehead and whispered something in her ear.

Evangeline smiled with her eyes. "Polaris," she murmured, visibly happy before dropping her head on the pillow, following Morpheus' call.

That night, she dreamed of an ocean of grass that looked over an ocean of stars and two familiar shadows in the midst of that infinite.

In that place without time and space, she remembered Polaris.

SECOND PART

POLARIS

INTROLOGUE

KRUSCHA SPUN FOR a few seconds before noticing her open hand beckoning the little animal to come closer. The chinchilla sniffed at her moving fingers, then took a little hop, climbed up her arm and ended up snuggling on her shoulder.

Evangeline absently stroked the small, furry head of the rodent. After a few seconds, he raised his tail and ears and jumped to the ground, beginning to wander around her again, without ever getting more than a couple of meters away.

The evening was cool and quiet. Evangeline opened her arms and whirled a few times, as if to greet nature's beauty all around her.

A light breeze from the west washed over her. She looked at the sky and smiled. Then she closed her eyes, breathed in and stretched her arms, murmuring with pleasure.

The stars were an unending succession of bright spots that gave life to the timeless blackboard of the night sky.

Evangeline started counting them. She stopped at thirty and lost count. She began again, using a finger to keep track, but got lost again at fifty stars. She laughed heartily and laid down on the ground, folding her arms behind her head. The grass bent under her weight, turning into a soft mattress that smelled of leaves, bark, flowers and wind.

She looked to her left. "Wei, the grass is not going to bite you," she said, sighing. "I promise."

The little boy looked around, rubbing his elbow. Clearly he seemed uncomfortable. He had the look of someone who, from some unfortunate set of circumstances, found themself naked on a stage in front of a wide audience.

He took a step forward, hesitated, took two more steps, then stopped completely. First he looked at Evangeline, who was inviting him to lie down beside her. Then he noticed Kruscha, trotting around the girl, happy as a clam.

Wei snorted but approached the girl, keeping a distance of about ten feet. He looked at the ground and wrinkled his nose.

"It's wet?"

"No, it's fantastic."

"I don't want to get my pants wet."

"Then take them off and sit in your underwear."

Wei was about to reply, but in the end he said nothing. He knew it was a lost cause arguing with her.

After finding what he believed to be the least dirty piece of land, he bent his knees and slowly sat down.

He immediately felt uncomfortable. The ground was hard and gritty and the grass annoyingly tickled his buttocks. Several ants invaded his legs the very moment he touched the ground. Wei took a stick and for a few seconds fought off the little invaders.

It was a useless battle. His clothes were still besieged by platoons of ants, relentless and numerous as the stars above his head. Even the stick, he realized, was full of insects. He gave up and threw it away with a frustrated sigh, wrapped his arms around his knees and glanced at the girl beside him. She was gazing silently at the sky.

Wei swallowed hard as he watched Evangeline absently tucking her long, shiny hair behind her ears. He scratched his ears, then looked away and tried not to think of the annoying itch that was growing at the base of his stomach.

"Look! That's the constellation of the Dragon!"

Wei snapped to attention when the girl shouted, excitedly indicating the night sky.

Wei followed her finger and raised an eyebrow. "Actually, that's Cassiopeia," he replied, as dry as a desert. "The constellation of the Dragon is right there."

Evangeline looked at him with an expression that Wei could not decipher. The girl looked back at the sky, and a moment later outstretched her arm again, eagerly pointing to another group of stars.

"That's Gemini! Isn't it beautiful?"

Wei cleared his throat as he again followed the girl's index finger. "Gemini? I don't think so. It's not visible in the northern hemisphere at this time of the year."

Evangeline seemed to ignore his remark. Five seconds later, she said again, "Look, look! The constellation of the Pelargonium." The girl was beside herself with excitement.

"What?" Wei exclaimed, completely caught off guard. "There's nothing like that!"

Evangeline approached him, crawling on the grass, propping her elbows on the ground. She was looking at him very carefully, as if she was about to make one of the most important decisions of her life.

Wei instinctively drew back a few more inches. That look made him uneasy.

"Can you show me the constellation of the Radiator?"

"Wha—? No, of course not, because it doesn't exist!"

"And what about the Little Underpants?"

Wei started to reply, but was preceded by Evangeline. "And what about the constellation of the Hangman, or that of the Royal Palace, the Bill, the Sea Storm, the Flamingo, the Crucifix, the Keychain, the Avocado, the Lover and the Immortal?"

Wei shook his head without answering. He didn't know if she simply wanted to tease him or was just making fun of him. Probably both, he thought.

"You're weird," Wei said, without looking at her in the eyes.

Evangeline stared at him for a half a minute before returning to her previous spot, without saying another word.

The two remained silent and still for a long time, rocked by the simple but impressive show offered by the night sky. The wind created a subtle symphony of sounds around them, moving the grass and dry leaves as if by direction of an invisible dance conductor -- a dialog between Mother Nature and herself.

"You know, I don't think that the constellation of the Dragon looks like a dragon after all," Evangeline said, examining the roof of the world with a serious look on her face. "No. It looks more like a river. Yeah. I think I'll call it that from now on, the constellation of the River."

Wei looked at her and sighed. He'd had enough of the childish game.

"That's so stupid," he said. "You can't just change the name of a constellation."

"Why can't I?"

"The names of constellations are convention," Wei replied. "You can't possibly all of a sudden change the name of a constellation and expect people to take you seriously."

Evangeline seemed to reflect on those words. Finally she said, "Wei, what are the brightest stars in the constellation of the River?"

Wei rolled his eyes. "If you are referring to the apparent magnitude of those stars, the brightest in the constellation of the *Dragon* are Eltanin, Aldhibain, Rastaban and Altais."

Evangeline got closer while he was talking, so close now their shoulders touched. Wei could feel the heat of the girl's body and the distinct smell that she emanated -- a mixture of vanilla and peach blended with something sweet and alien, like a bouquet of exotic flowers gathered in a meadow at the edge of the world.

"Wei?"

"What?"

"Which of them is the brightest star? In the constellation of the River I mean."

Wei swallowed hard as he spied on the girl, trying not to be noticed. For a fraction of an instant he got distracted by the slow and steady dancing of her hair that moved like the hypnotic ripples of a jellyfish's tentacles, bright and beautiful in the vastness of the ocean. Wei looked away and closed his eyes. Then he cleared his throat.

"T-the brightest star in the constellation of the Riv—, of the Dragon, in the constellation of the *Dragon*, is Eltanin."

Evangeline nodded.

"Wei?"

"What?"

"If I changed the name Eltanin to Aquamarine, do you think that the constellation of the River would be less bright?"

Wei was about to reply but when he opened his mouth his eyes found Evangeline's waiting for him. They were shining like polished diamonds crafted by the world's finest artisan.

For the first time since the beginning of the conversation, those eyes forced him to be quiet. He then started to think. Something lit up in his mind.

He thought back to the strange questions that the girl asked him, and a precise pattern began to form before his eyes.

Changing the name of a star does not deprive it of its brightness, or of its position in the sky, he thought. A convention is the common way humanity interacts with itself. It does not describe the reality of things, but only the need of men to find an order, a pattern to follow; a way not to be afraid.

Despite himself, his lips slowly parted and formed a smile. Evangeline sure had her own way of explaining things, he suddenly realized.

"No, I don't think so. I don't think that would make much difference," Wei finally said, looking at the constellation of the River from a new prospective.

Another island of silence closed the conversation and they both got lost in their own thoughts.

Kruscha rolled on the ground, sniffed the air, and then responded to Evangeline's call since she was holding a small stick of willow. The chinchilla took it eagerly, put it in his mouth and began to gnaw at it.

"When did we meet for the first time?" Evangeline asked suddenly, looking at Kruscha chewing happily on his stick. "Was it last week?"

"Two weeks and two days ago," Wei answered, without hesitation. His cheeks flushed almost immediately. He cleared his throat and added, "I … I believe."

"Two weeks," Evangeline whispered, looking at him as if the kid was some sort of strange sculpture.

"Wei?"

"Yeah?"

"What are you working on?"

Wei shook his head, surprised by the sudden change of subject. "What am I … What do you mean?"

"You know what I mean. I always see you taking notes, listening to people's conversations, reading huge books with weird titles, studying things that would make Einstein puke and doing a bunch of other strange stuff for a kid your age."

"I'm not a kid!" Wei protested, realizing at once that he sounded like one of them.

"What are you working on?" Evangeline insisted, looking at him intently.

Wei hated that look. It made him feel as naked as a worm. He didn't answer, but his cheeks blushed further. Now his face looked like a ripe tomato.

A minute passed ... two. Evangeline continued to stare as Wei turned to look the other way. The boy moved slightly, as if he wanted to shake off the discomfort caused by her look.

"I think you want to change things," Evangeline said after a while, as if she finally found a way to read his thoughts. "I think you're trying to build something. Or undo something else."

Wei kept his silence, staring stubbornly at the night sky.

"Fine, keep it to yourself," Evangeline snapped, rubbing her hands against her knees. "You know what? Whatever you want to do, I don't think you're going to make it. In fact, I'm sure you won't."

The statement made Wei's head spin. He turned to face the girl. "I have no clue what you're talking about," he said, digging his nails into the earth, "but if I really wanted to build something, I could do it without any problem."

"No you couldn't."

"What ... What do you think you know? You know nothing!" Wei said. Resentment kindled in his voice.

"I know you, Wei Wang," Evangeline said, indicating him with both her thumbs. The boy had learned to recognize that pose. It was Evangeline preparing to give one of her sermons. He started to say something, but the girl interrupted him.

"Admit it. You're a stubborn kid, closed off in your little, complicated world, impossible to reach. You treat others with contempt and disgust. Don't look at me like that, you know I'm right! You insult me, Kruscha, any person around you. I'm sure that today you insulted someone before breakfast. Insulting is what you do best, your way to keep people at a distance, your way to feel yourself."

"I don't ... You are ..." Wei began, getting knotted up in his words. He was angry, outraged and frightened at the same time. He didn't know whether to hide from the girl's look or just slap her. "You know nothing about me. Nothing," he managed to say in the end, stammering, his heart pounding rapidly. He had no idea how the conversation had degenerated, but at that moment it didn't matter. He felt attacked and humiliated, treated like a stupid little kid with no brain. Wei closed his hands into fists and felt the earth between his fingers.

He started to get up. He wanted to get away from this stupid and arrogant girl.

"I know you," Evangeline repeated stubbornly, without ceasing to stare at him.

Wei stayed where he was, staring back, challenging her pretentious look.

"If you keep doing things the way you're doing them now, you'll never get anything done ... *never.*"

"How can you be so sure? You ... you don't know what I can do, the things that I know and ..."

"Everything is useless, don't you see? All your knowledge and all your confidence is worthless."

"Why do you even care? I've never asked your opinion on anything, have I? So why are we having this conversation in the first place?"

"Wei, I want you to understand."

"You don't even know what you're talking about."

"Yes, I do."

"OK, let's hear it then." Wei pushed her, pointing to himself with a thumb. "What do I need, hmm? What's so important that I don't have?"

"You'll need other people."

Wei blinked, confused. "Other people?" he repeated, shaking his head. He wasn't expecting that answer. He felt like someone who had just shown up in the middle of a conversation, without the slightest idea of what others were talking about. "What ... what do you mean?"

"You'll need people like yourself if you hope to make a difference, or to succeed in your project, or build what you want to build, or whatever you want to do. Don't you see? Only someone stupid would think they could do it alone."

Wei challenged the girl's eyes, trying not to blink. He pointed at her with his finger almost as though he was pointing a loaded gun, ready to fire.

"Other people slow me down," he finally said, releasing a flow of magma from his mouth. "People are stupid!"

"I am a person."

Wei looked at Evangeline. The burst of heat that warmed his neck disappeared instantly, becoming a shiver that ran down his spine.

"You ... you're different," Wei said at last, his voice unsteady. "You're not like the others. You're weird. I can't understand you.

You have … a sparkle. I don't know how to explain it. Sometimes … sometimes you scare me."

Evangeline laughed. "Really?"

Wei nodded. He lowered his head and stared at the grass.

The tension between the two of them slowly dissolved, like snow under the sun.

Evangeline put her hands on her hips.

"Dummy," she said, smiling.

Wei looked at her but he didn't answer.

"Listen," the girl said, getting closer to him, "you're incredibly intelligent, that's true. I've seen you do things that I've never seen anyone else do before. I admit it, you're special, but you're not all powerful. Now, try to consider the people around you. They are human beings Wei, with passions, weaknesses and strengths. They're resources. Resources you can use. If you want to change things, if you have an idea, you will need other people to make it happen."

"Why?" Wei asked stubbornly.

Evangeline's face was embellished by a spontaneous curl of her lips. "Because only people can change people."

Wei paused, reflecting on that phrase.

In the end he looked away and began to tear the grass from the ground, muttering something that never went beyond his ears.

The girl let him mull over what she had said. Although she had only known him for a little more than two weeks, Evangeline thought the kid was some kind of gift sent to her from heaven. A gift locked in a safe box. To open that safe box had become her mission; something to devote her days to. A task she accepted with joy.

Evangeline rubbed her hands. All of a sudden, she seemed uncomfortable. "Wei?"

"What do you want?"

"Sorry. I didn't mean to yell at you or … tell you that stuff."

Wei reflected on her answer. He opened and closed his mouth a few times. The third time he shrugged and simply said, "Apologies accepted."

Evangeline put her arm under the boy's, smiling a wicked smile. Wei moved away a few inches. She laughed, poking him with her elbow.

Evangeline continued to bother him for a while, tickling or trying to hug him. Wei responded with varying degrees of irritation and indifference.

After a few minutes, Evangeline lay back on the grass. There was silence for a few heartbeats.

"Wei, where's the North Star?" she asked after a while, looking blankly at the sky. "Where is Polaris?"

Wei considered a sour and sharp answer, but when his gaze lingered on the girl's dreamy face, he forgot what he wanted to spit at her.

A constellation made of tiny freckles dotting the girl's face made him swallow hard again. Eventually, he turned away and began to search the firmament.

His eyes followed a well-known pattern. He studied the sky and quickly found the constellation of the Big Dipper, bright and familiar like few others. He then focused on the two stars at the edge of the formation, Dubhe and Merak. He drew an imaginary line segment from Merak to Dubhe and multiplied the distance for five times the space between the two stars. At the end of the segment, shining and stable, was Polaris, the North Star.

Wei pointed it out to Evangeline, who nodded.

"How did you find it?" she asked, looking at him with admiration. "I would have never spotted it among so many lights."

Wei shrugged. "It's easy. You just need to rely on the constellations."

"Really?"

"Yes."

"So even you need to rely on something, sometimes."

Wei didn't answer, but he acknowledged to himself that he was the loser of that exchange. It was in times like these that he both hated and admired the girl. That was also one of the reasons why he felt so uncomfortable around her. No one could make him feel that way. So ... stupid.

The girl searched in her pocket. "I've got something for you."

Wei saw Evangeline holding an object. It was a pendant, as strange as its owner. It was silver colored, streaked in a particular shade of blue.

It had the shape of a horizontal eight.

The girl gave it to Wei.

"The symbol of infinity?" he asked, studying it carefully.

"It's a good luck charm. You'll need it."

"I don't believe in luck."

"That's why I'm giving it to you, moron," Evangeline said, chuckling.

"OK. Thank you," Wei said, finding nothing else to add.

"Do you like it?"

"It's … it's girl's stuff," he ascertained, turning it over in his hands. It was thin and bright. It caught one's eye.

"Of course it's girl's stuff, you idiot. It's mine! And if you lose it, I'll kill you. Got it?"

Wei put the pendant around his neck, without replying.

Kruscha dropped the stick of willow on the ground and sniffed around him, seeking Evangeline's hand. He found it in the end, but it seemed too busy squeezing something else …. another hand, smaller and paler, that was apparently trying to wriggle away, without much conviction.

The City of the Insects

AVALON

2022

SAEMANGEUM SKYSCRAPERS OFFERED an impressive sight, a unique mixture of frenzy and magnificence. It was the unfinished work of a newly born settlement, without a clear shape, where hundreds of soaring towers made of steel and concrete stood isolated and incomplete. The sparks that joined their metal bones shone like the heart of the Milky Way itself.

Beams, cables and titanic scaffolding dominated the skyline. They looked like a rugged and intricate spider web, ready to support the very foundation of the world.

Roads and bridges under construction linked the different parts of the city, most of them still ruled by water and mud.

The city was a beast ready to wake up, a masterpiece of human ingenuity brought to life by technology's latest wonders. Most of the buildings were naked, with profiles just hinted at, like a painter's immature sketch struggling to take on a clear shape. The scenery was chaotic and lively at the same time, and the urban environment expanded minute by minute.

The unfinished city was in constant motion, swarmed by a never ending army of hard hats in emerald green uniforms, busily adding height, texture and thickness to the many unfinished buildings.

Avalon Moon put down his fork and wiped his mouth with his sleeve as he watched the glowing city coming to life before his eyes. The smell of wet earth, wet cement, and dust mixed with humid air filled his nostrils. He breathed in deeply and closed his eyes. The city had a particular smell, like the scent of a beast, sweaty and breathless, that had just finished its hunting.

From the top floor of one completed building, Avalon realized as he looked at the scenery, how lucky he was. He could see the world below him slowly taking shape before his eyes.

The noises from the city too had their own special charm. They were swift and powerful and beautifully matched the hammering of steel against steel in the background. The echoing sounds reminded him of the heartbeat of a giant; an infinite entity as inexorable as time.

The man blinked against the sunlight, absently scratching his buttocks as he shifted his weight on the chair. A creak accompanied his movements.

He was a fat man, with short legs and short arms and a huge belly. His face was yellow and sweaty. His head, broad and misshaped, resembled a big potato, and his cheeks were two cascades of flesh that hung close to his neck. From his nostrils, a generous number of long, sturdy hairs came out.

The rest of his body was no different. Countless layers of fat rested one over the other, like a peculiar Christmas tree made by a butcher with a despicable sense of humour.

Avalon breathed heavily while clogging up one nostril with his finger. His throat produced a weird sound, like the soft cry of a wild animal.

After a couple of seconds, he spat out a gob of phlegm that joined the puddle of mucus and saliva a few inches from his feet.

He finally looked away from the city's skyline. The man grunted and breathed in one more time. It seemed as if he was about to spit again, but he changed his mind at the very last moment. Instead, he licked his hands and passed them slowly and carefully over his greasy hair.

Avalon repeated the action a couple of times before turning to the man who was watching him from behind, motionless and silent.

"An increase of those proportions in the Northeast in such a short time makes no sense," Avalon said incredulously while rubbing his wet hands.

He grasped the table with both hands and pushed up his bottom. A long and intermittent noise burst from his body, changing tone several times before dying in a low splutter. The man settled back in his chair, sniffing and nodding, visibly pleased.

"It looks like I'll need another pair of pants, Hector." Avalon grinned.

The tall, lean man behind him had straight shoulders and a severe expression. He resembled a very stiff and shiny surfboard that had never been used. His eyebrows formed a thin, dark line that marked the lower part of the wide and prominent forehead.

The man frowned and cleared his throat. Ignoring the last comment, he simply focused on keeping his frown as taut as possible.

"Our analysis of the performances of the Somsak Khon Kaen confirms our suspicion, sir," he said, his hands clasped behind his back. "I checked the data half a dozen times."

"You checked half a dozen times?" Avalon whistled and slammed his hands on the table, blasting away some bowls. "Ah! And people say you have no sense of humor."

"A careful analysis seemed simply appropriate to me, sir," replied the man, keeping his stance.

Avalon Moon shook his head and snorted, apparently disappointed with the answer.

"Long Standing Mahaverik Curve?" he asked at last, rubbing his hand over his protruding belly.

"It has an exponential growth, as in the past three months. In the province of Khon Kaen alone, they have increased their profit by thirty per cent. In other western provinces of the country, like Sakon Nakhon and Si Sa Ket, they managed a similar increase, despite all our countermeasures. Their resourcefulness is growing day by day."

Avalon's face paled further. The shadow of sarcasm that had spiced his voice a few moments before faded into a glooming face with no expression at all.

"And you say they're planning to expand in the North too," he asked, after mulling over for a few seconds.

"Yes, sir. They already have an established presence in Lampang province," answered the assistant, his posture so rigid that it looked like someone had replaced his spine with a steel rod. "According to the logistics department, the Somsak Khon Kaen has also contacted some local landowners and farmers to secure part of their production of bamboo caterpillars. We know for a fact that they have increased their demand for insects from Laos and Burma. We suspect it is a move aimed at collecting and storing a considerable quantity of the product, to treat it and then sell it in other parts of Thailand and China."

"Crickets and weaver ants in the Northeast, grasshoppers and giant water bugs in the East and now an expansion in the market of bamboo caterpillars in the North," Avalon said, visibly irritated while coughing and spitting on the ground. "This is an attack on all fronts."

"As I have already shown you, sir, our market share continues to be dominant," Hector said, as if to emphasize something important. "Our advantage over their—"

"Spare me, will you?" Avalon cut him off, raising a large, greasy finger. "I know a predator when I see one. We've made two mistakes. The first has been to allow an unknown sheep to join our flock. The second was in not recognizing that this sheep was actually a Yet Mae wolf. We underestimated this Somsak and we took too many things for granted, shielding ourselves behind our damn statistics for far too long."

Avalon kept a finger pressed on the table, moving it slowly until it outlined an imaginary circle.

"These white muzzles came out of nowhere. *Nowhere*, and in a year they have done the impossible. Now, thanks to our stupidity, they control ten per cent of the entire edible insect market of Southeast Asia."

"Fifteen, sir; fifteen per cent of the market," Hector corrected him promptly.

"Shia!" cursed Avalon, shaking his head. "How did this happen? How?"

There was a moment of silence, interrupted only by the advance of the imperious herd of bulldozers, tractors and Caterpillars orbiting nearby, intent on either demolishing or building parts of the city.

Avalon Moon slammed a hand on the table. "This Somsak Khon Kaen is a problem that must be solved. And we must solve it now!" He closed his hand in a fist. "This is my territory, dammit! I'd prefer to be eaten alive by a legion of army ants rather than allow this Yankee colony to dump their shit in my backyard."

Avalon spat on the ground again before turning to look into the assistant's eyes. "Make sure that the Q department finds out which farmers are supplying them with the product and which facilities they are using to process it. I also want to know how on earth they produced that amount of giant water bugs in such a short time. It doesn't make any sense. If we are to believe the reports, it would appear that they have increased the production of that insect one hundred and fifty per cent in four months. This is not possible and the impossible is unacceptable! I want reliable data, not fairy tales. I want answers to these questions, satisfactory answers, and I want them now. Is that clear?"

"Yes, sir."

Avalon nodded while focusing his attention on the table. On it, a dozen plates and bowls sat empty or half-empty. With a quick gesture of his arm the fat man reached out for the only plate still full of food. For a moment he considered its contents: a generous portion of fried grasshoppers, crickets, termites and ants, all mixed into a paste-like crimson sauce. He sniffed loudly, then reached into the mixture of insects and tasted a couple, chewing with gusto. He shook his head slightly and added a little pepper before taking his fork and resuming his meal.

"Well, don't just stand there like a statue," Avalon said, swallowing hard. "What happened to our construction plan in Vietnam? You told me it was urgent that we speak of it. Well, let's speak of it."

Hector did not answer. He just looked at the carbon-tech bracelet that surrounded his wrist and part of his forearm. Numbers and graphs orbited around the cylindrical device, moving or changing according to his will.

"Yes, sir." Hector hesitated for a few seconds. Then he said, "Unfortunately ... unfortunately it seems the local authorities are not inclined to give their consent to our project."

Avalon didn't stop eating, but grunted something at the assistant.

Hector went on. "In their preliminary report, they've raised several issues regarding our proposal. Among other things, the provincial authority cites the specifics of the plan, a lack of funds in the project, the possible negative impact on the environment, inadequate safety standards for the workers, negligible benefits for the local economy and for their workforce, a—"

Avalon closed his eyes and rubbed his temples. He interrupted the list waving a hand full of red sauce.

"Translated, those vomit bags want a more substantial incentive. Is that so?"

Hector shook his head. "Our ... encouragement ... was not even considered, sir. Personally I think they are—"

"I know what they're trying to do," Avalon interrupted, annoyed. "An excuse, like a predator, is easy to recognize."

Avalon bit the inside of his cheek and inhaled deeply. "I don't get it. They must have some reason to keep us out of their territory. The question is: what is it? The reports indicated a strong interest within the local community for our insects. They import more crickets and grasshoppers than Laos and Burma combined, dammit. They need the product. They want it. What game are they playing?"

Hector opened his mouth but closed it almost immediately. The question remained unanswered and the silence lasted for some time. Avalon resumed his meal.

He finished the last fried cricket and drained his glass of red wine, making a disgusting noise with his mouth.

The man snapped his fingers, raised his empty glass and the young server who was waiting silently to his left moved quickly to fill it. When the glass was full, Avalon instructed him to clear the dishes and the empty bowls and to serve the next course.

The man licked his big lips slowly while exploring the vastness of his nostrils with his middle finger.

He looked at the server clear with professional grace the last crumbs, clean the cutlery and offer a new course.

"Nest of scorpions in soy sauce, vinegar and raisins."

Avalon dismissed him by waving a hand, without even looking at him.

Hector was evaluating the data that orbited around his forearm. He seemed nervous and unsure. His back was straight and stiff. His lips merged into a single horizontal line. He closed his eyes, took a deep breath and moved a few steps forward.

"There's more, regarding our plan in Vietnam, sir," he said at last, in a low voice, as if he was afraid of being heard by somebody.

"I'm listening," Avalon said, chewing all the while.

The assistant looked around then went on. "It's a possibility that seems unlikely, but I did not feel comfortable excluding it from the report." Hector pointed to the data emitted by his device. "The true reason behind our problems in Vietnam may not depend on local administration policies, or at least not simply by them. It could … it could have been caused by an external factor."

Avalon swallowed a mouthful, then wiped the trickle of dark sauce from the side of his mouth. "It seems clear to me that they don't want us messing around in their backyard. What external factors are you babbling about?"

Hector didn't answer immediately. For a few seconds, he just watched his boss giving orders to the server with grunts and gestures.

The assistant touched numbers and letters that appeared on top of his device. "The F department has sent a series of data. Individually, they don't seem to have any particular importance, and yet ... I suspect they explain what is really happening in Vietnam, if ... well, if read in a certain way."

"I'm all ears," Avalon said, licking his fingers.

"From the reports, it seems that the Somsak Khon Kaen is importing goods and establishing business relationships with all the edible insect marketplaces in the region, but they have not even remotely considered Vietnam."

"Ha! Proof that those pigs haven't the gift of ubiquity, it seems to me," said Avalon, triumphant. "Damn good news in this ocean of shit."

Hector shook his head. "Sir, the Somsak Khon Kaen has been reported to be active in Malaysia, the Philippines, Indonesia, Burma, Laos, Cambodia and even in southern China -- but not in Vietnam. No activity in that region. I'm not just talking about plans for contracts or contacts with the administration or the local workforce ... import, export, technical assistance, exchange of know-how ... nothing. There's nothing. They've treated the region as a ghost area."

Avalon stopped suddenly, his fork midway between his plate and his open mouth. He let the information sink in. His neck stiffened as his brain elaborated what the assistant had said.

"Let me see," he finally said, putting down his fork and moving his fingers impatiently.

Hector took off his carbon-tech bracelet. After touching it a couple of times, the device changed shape, stretched and flattened by an invisible force. It soon became a simple transparent tablet.

Hector handed it to his boss, who took it briskly and began to study it carefully.

"In my opinion, their moves seem to suggest two possible explanations," Hector said, while Avalon was reading the screen. "Either they don't have the slightest trace of interest in the Vietnamese market, which doesn't seem to make much sense given their past behaviour, or they are trying to—"

"Trying not to get our attention," Avalon finished for him, clenching his jaw. "That they're starting to expand into the East and at the same time they want to prevent us from entering the Vietnamese market."

"I came to the same conclusion, sir."

Avalon continued to evaluate the data, eyes wide and bloodshot. "If that's true, the situation is much worse than we suspected. Not only have they established a presence here, they are now looking to expand into a virgin area while trying to completely exclude us. But how on earth did they ...?"

"Your problem, gentlemen, is that you treat the Somsak as an obstacle rather than as an opportunity."

Both Avalon and Hector looked in the direction from which the voice had come.

The young server had crossed half of the balcony and sat down at the opposite end of the table, without either of them noticing it.

On the ground lay a tie, a jacket, a shirt and a pair of shoes. Now, together with a simple canary-colored shirt and black trousers, he was wearing only a cocksure smile and an impudent expression.

Avalon looked him over from top to bottom.

He appeared to be a completely different person, and yet he was the very same one. The transformation was so drastic and sudden that Avalon thought for a second that he was someone else.

The man kept looking at the smiling boy and at the spot where he had been standing straight and motionless until that moment, as if he couldn't put two and two together.

His eyes were still looking for the server.

The first one to recover from the surprise was Hector, who pointed a finger at the boy.

"What are you doing?" he asked in a low voice, incredulous, with a tone somewhere between amazement and indignation.

"Saemangeum City is a view to be enjoyed while sitting, Mr. Hoberdan."

"What ... what did you say?" hissed Hector, completely taken aback.

The boy shrugged and licked his lips. He leaned forward to pick up a bottle of water. Once he opened the cap, he eagerly began to drink its content.

"I'm calling security," Hector said, his face outraged, fiddling with the tablet that had turned again into a bracelet.

Avalon said nothing. He just looked at the boy carefully, as if he were watching a shape on the horizon of the desert, trying to understand if it was real or a mirage.

It was the first time he had really looked at his server. He seemed young, very young. He was short and thin, with a sharp, tanned face. He had dark hair held up with gel. The almond-shaped eyes were amber and resembled two drops of dew on a face with both Asian and Caucasian traits. A half-blood, thought Avalon. He was probably a cross between a Han and a Westerner.

Avalon did not interrupt the boy while he was drinking his bottle. Instead, he continued to watch him with interest. Clearly, his server seemed to be at ease.

When he finished drinking, Avalon leaned toward him, pointing to the empty bottle with both hands.

"Can I get you another bottle? You seem quite thirsty, son."

"Perhaps later."

"Orange juice, milk, hot chocolate?" continued to inquire Avalon, indicating the door of the balcony.

His server smiled a polite no. "I'm fine now, thanks."

Avalon planted his elbows on the table, crossed his fingers and rested his chin on them, staring at the boy without batting an eyelid. "Are you a nut, a charlatan, or one who has simply decided to get fired with style?"

The boy smirked. "I'm all three things and not one in particular."

"I want to know the reason for this charade."

"It's really simple. I'm here to advise you, Mr. Moon."

"You! Here to advise me? Am I missing something? I thought you were here to clean the crumbs from my table and serve the next course."

"That and make sure that you could become outrageously rich and powerful."

Avalon snorted, clearly annoyed. "This thing is going to end very, very badly for you. I don't like being teased. Kid, do you have the slightest idea who you're talking to?"

"Avalon Yolay Moon," the other replied, indicating the fat man with his pinkie. "Born in Singapore on March 31, 1985. Son of Jin-ho Moon and Anong Kasemsarn. Founder and President of the Sanuk Edible Insects, Inc. Multimillionaire, workaholic, atheist, insectivore and staunch supporter of the movement *six-legged livestock*. You consume only insects or products derived from them. You are a football and basketball lover, single, touchy and extremely stubborn. You have a photographic memory and a questionable sense of humor."

The boy paused and sniffed. "Not particularly fond of personal hygiene," he added, pinching the bridge of his nose. "Favorite color, brown, favorite dish, scorpions grilled with barbecue sauce. You have two great passions: your company and your belly."

Avalon Moon ran a hand over his mouth, his eyes wide. "Who the hell are you?"

"An interesting question that has multiple answers," the boy replied, drumming his fingers on the table. "I'll be frank with you, Mr. Moon. My name is *Nobody*."

Avalon showed his teeth. "Really?" he said, shaking his head slightly. "Well, I guess this simplifies things, doesn't it? Nobody will care if *Nobody*'s body will be found on the bed of a river tonight."

Two women in emerald and gold uniforms appeared in unison at the door of the room. Hector indicated the young server, still sitting peacefully, his legs on the table.

The guards nodded and walked quickly toward him.

"Tell me, Mr. Moon," the boy said, fiddling with the cap of the bottle, with little apparent regard for the two guards who were quickly approaching. "If someone puts what he claimed to be the winning lottery ticket in your hands, would you throw it away before or after making sure that it's not the winning one?"

Avalon raised an eyebrow.

"Wait," he said, gesturing for the guards to step back.

"The Somsak Khon Kaen's new expansion in Vietnam is a matter of fact," said the boy, still fiddling with the cap. "I'm here to tell you how to solve the problem and get an unexpected benefit from it at the same time."

"Let me get this straight," Avalon said, clenching his teeth, "you seriously expect me to listen to a kid who five minutes ago was cleaning my table?"

"Mr. Moon, look at it this way. If I'm a farce, you'd have wasted ten minutes of your time. But if I'm not … well, isn't this what makes the whole thing so damned interesting?"

The two guards looked at Avalon, waiting for instructions. He was unsure of what to do. The kid was definitely a hassle, but his manner sparked Avalon's curiosity. Furthermore, he intended to find out how a child knew so many things about him.

"Wait outside," Avalon said finally, signalling the door to the two women. The guards obeyed, leaving the balcony at once.

Hector started to say something, but Avalon interrupted him. "I want to hear what this noisy little punk has to say, before teaching him better manners."

Hector nodded, although he didn't seem to approve.

"This conversation will continue on two conditions," clarified Avalon with an inflexible tone. "I want to know your name and the real reason for this farce."

The boy snorted, clearly annoyed, as if he had been asked to repeat a frustrating task for the umpteenth time.

"My name is a gift few people receive, Mr. Moon, and you did nothing to deserve it. However, if you really want to associate a series of letters to my face, 'Omnilogos' will do, for the moment."

"Omnilogos," Avalon repeated in a thoughtful voice, as if for the first time he had tasted a tart and unfamiliar fruit. He turned to Hector.

The assistant was already fiddling with his carbon-tech bracelet.

Ten seconds later, he raised his head. "According to DataMorph, it's a cyberio, sir."

Avalon closed his eyelids.

"Should I know what the hell that's supposed to mean?"

Hector continued to read: "It's a term associated in the West with a group of terrorists in the cyberspace, such as The Brothers of Eternity and Anonymous. It's not known whether it is a single individual or a group of individuals."

"Ta-Da!" said the boy, moving his hands in a theatrical way. Then he looked at Hector. "Let me give you a piece of advice for your next research, Mr. Hoberdan. If you want real information, don't use that concentrate of media and governmental propaganda for your sources. Wikipedia is way better."

"You're a terrorist?" Avalon pointed a finger at the Omnilogos, barely holding back a smile. The boy could not have been more than sixteen years old.

"A wise man who never existed once said: If you wanna make enemies, try to change something." The Omnilogos stretched his arms.

"Since I have decided to reveal my speciality in the public domain, terrorist has become my middle name. It is a blessing and a burden that I accept with a smile."

Avalon had nothing to say to that statement. It simply made no sense to him at all.

The boy took advantage of the moment of silence to go on. He held up two fingers. "As for the second question ... well, I think the answer is obvious. I doubt that Mr. Hoberdan here would have gladly set up an appointment with an unknown teenager. Am I right?"

"So you've decided to take the initiative and to organize this show," Avalon said, narrowing his eyes. "And how did you enter my human resources department, anyway?" He then added, with a note of sarcasm in his voice, "*Omnilogos.*"

"Does it really matter?"

A long silence followed. "No," Avalon finally answered, smiling. After a few seconds spent evaluating the boy he turned to Hector. "Who's the head of HR?"

"Jiang Ping, sir," answered the assistant promptly, without even consulting his polymorphic bracelet.

"Right," Avalon said, nodding, "transfer him to the top of the research and development department."

Hector looked at his boss without answering. Eventually he managed to say, "S-sir, there's no research and development department."

Avalon looked at him without blinking.

Hector nodded, understanding. "Yes, sir," he said, touching the bracelet with a quick gesture.

"How old are you, boy?" the man asked, more and more intrigued.

"I'm seventeen."

"Seventeen years old," Avalon echoed, running a hand through his hair. "Well, Omnilogos, congratulations. Looks like your boldness managed to snatch ten of my minutes. Use them well."

The boy wasted no time. When he looked back into Avalon's eyes, his mischievous and cheeky expression gave way to sheer determination. The man was surprised by the sudden change. The Omnilogos seemed to have aged ten years in ten seconds.

He couldn't explain why, but a chill crept up his spine. There was something in that boy that made his hackles rise.

The Omnilogos indicated the insects on the table.

"The reason why I'm here, Mr. Moon, is because I know you. I know I'm in front of a special person, who thinks outside the box and who has a unique ability to concretize dreams and to overcome new, uncharted challenges. You are a man whose choices can shape the world around us."

"Five years ago you decided to invest in what most people believed was nothing but a joke. A joke that wasn't even worth laughing about: a chain of restaurants built around the universe of the edible insects. Your goal was to sell a product considered taboo by half of the world population and to build a business around it. Thanks to your perseverance and your investments, you have created a whole new market and have turned a Thai custom into a widespread practice throughout Southeast Asia. You have created a business worth half a billion dollars that went beyond anyone's expectations. Now, five years after the beginning of that bet, no one is laughing and many eyes have turned with interest to you and to what you're doing here in Asia."

Avalon thought that the boy clearly had something special. The way he spoke, moved and interacted with people was not that of a normal teenager. Confident, enterprising, talkative, even erudite, the Omnilogos was a constant surprise, unpredictable, and at the same time impossible to ignore.

He no longer thought he had a lunatic in front of him. A desire to understand who this person really was grew exponentially.

"I'm surprised, I admit it," Avalon said, raising his hands, as though surrendering to the loquacity of the boy. "I was expecting a pedantic and insolent kid, not a pedantic and insolent kid, knowledgeable in the history of marketing. Now, what do you want me to do with your report about my past performances? Do you think I'm impressed?"

"What you did is no longer important at this point. I'm interested in what you are going to do. That's the very reason I'm here."

The Omnilogos took a clean dish and put one of the fried crickets on it.

"Five years ago, two-thirds of the inhabitants of this planet would have looked at this dish and wrinkled their nose or puked. You, watching the same dish, saw a low-calorie high concentration of amino acids, vitamin B12, riboflavin, vitamin A and protein, incredibly easy to find, keep, process, store and sell. All this by paying a ridiculously low price and obtaining in return ten times the money invested."

"Insects are one of the most underrated and misunderstood products of our time. Misinformation and ignorance cloud them. Insects are incredibly efficient at converting plants into edible protein. Four grasshoppers provide as much calcium as contained in a glass of milk. One hundred grams of locusts contain more iron than beef and less than the equivalent amount of calories and fat. Insects produce less waste and greenhouse gases than traditional livestock. They need a limited amount of land and require less feed. If that wasn't enough, they are much more affordable for the environment, cost less in resources and can generate many jobs."

The Omnilogos took one fried cricket from the plate, looked at it for a moment, then put it in his mouth and chewed with gusto. "Not to mention that they are incredibly tasty."

Avalon didn't say anything; he wanted to see where the boy was going with this speech.

"The creation of your Sanuk has shown the world that insects are a resource no one had really taken advantage of before. And now, as a result of your actions, the edible insects market is about to change radically. Other people have noticed that the time is ripe for investment in this sector, and soon enough your leadership will be threatened. In fact, your leadership is challenged at this very moment, isn't it?"

The Omnilogos pointed at Hector, while he kept looking Avalon straight in his eyes. "In time, you'll lose your leadership and the power of major multinationals will cast you away from the podium. You and your company will be reduced to an ordinary player without influence, forced to scrape the crumbs of what was once your own empire."

Avalon shifted in his chair. He didn't like the boy's words and tone. He didn't like them at all.

"So you're a marketing expert and a fortune teller now?" the fat man said, rubbing his flabby neck. "Your history lesson is interesting, I admit it, but if your advice is to worry about a future that exists only in your head, then this conversation has been a waste of time, *Omnilogos*. What do you want me to do with the predictions of a seventeen-year-old kid? You expect me to believe your words just because you put on this show and somehow managed to sneak in here?"

"No," the Omnilogos replied, leaning further toward Avalon and pointing at him, "what I ask you to do is to stop and think. You are putting too much importance on my age. Forget what I look like. Close your eyes, if you want, but don't be fooled by my appearance. I'm asking you to focus on my message; the *message*, Mr. Moon."

"The message," Avalon repeated, beginning to lose patience. "There is no hidden message, plot or conspiracy against my Sanuk. What you say makes no sense."

"You're not stupid. You listened to Mr. Hoberdan's report and read the newspapers. Like you, everyone knows what's happening."

"Enlighten me," said the man inviting the boy to go on.

"Whether you like it or not, in this very moment the hegemony of a market that you have created from scratch is disintegrating. Think about it! A new player who came out of nowhere has taken root in your territory. That competition took a tenth of your market in six months. More adaptable, aggressive, unpredictable and confident than you ever thought possible, it seems to be always a step ahead of you. This player understands the product, understands the consumer and the market. He knows how to move the pieces on the chessboard and he's a couple of moves away from declaring checkmate."

"You're talking about the Somsak Khon Kaen?" Avalon realized, studying the Omnilogos and beginning to breathe noisily, as if he were running. "I don't understand what—"

"A small U.S. company is threatening your carefully calculated plan, tearing apart your hegemony on the insects market, piece by piece. Foreigners, white muzzles, as you call them, have developed the ability to destroy everything you have worked for."

The Omnilogos crossed his arms. "Now listen to me. The Somsak Khon Kaen is only the beginning. Over the next five years, Southeast Asia will have half a dozen players, faster and more prepared than the Somsak Khon Kaen and ten times the size of your Sanuk. At that point, if you haven't been able to adapt, you'll find yourself completely disarmed. You'll be like a child playing at being a soldier against adults with nuclear weapons."

Avalon's brain laughed at the boy's statements; pretentious, rambling, absolutely without basis. Yet his heart began to beat faster and his hands began to sweat. There was something ominous in the eyes of the Omnilogos and in his words, a feeling of inevitability that echoed in his sentences and entered into Avalon's bones. Another shiver ran down his spine and for some reason, he began to feel cold.

"You keep talking as if you had a damn crystal ball in front of you, but I can clean my ass with your predictions, kid. I don't care what you think you know about my company. You're wrong."

"My statements are based on fact, Mr. Moon. If you have paid attention to what I said, it should be clear that I did my homework."

"So you're aware of information, news, data that we don't have? Evidence unknown to me and my company? Is that what you're trying to tell me?"

"I thought it was clear at this point."

Avalon reflected on what he had just heard. "How did you get to know all this? I mean, your babbling about this incoming war, the entry of new companies in the market. I know nothing of all this crap."

Avalon looked at his assistant for a while.

Hector shook his head.

"Where's the evidence of what you are saying, hmm?" continued Avalon, breathing heavily. "Listen, I can believe the story of the genius, talkative boy who wants to be noticed. I like your style and the way you put up this show, it was fun. However, if you're talking about confidential information, useful to me and to my company, then this is the time to spit it out. Give me a reason to believe your story or get the hell out of here."

"All this is of little importance, Mr. Moon," said the Omnilogos. "Once again, pay attention to the message, trust your instinct. What matters now is your response to this threat and your vision for the future."

"My response?" Avalon couldn't follow the abstract discourse of the Omnilogos, and this irritated him a lot. It seemed like someone had dragged him against his will into the tent of a fortune teller who was reading his hand, telling him his future. He hated that kind of crap.

He started to get up, but the boy kept talking.

"The Somsak Khon Kaen has proven to be seriously dangerous for your Sanuk. They've showed you they can beat you on your own territory. You're not facing a group of farmers that can be scared by some of your men, and you're not against a resourceless Thai businessman who will declare bankruptcy in six months. You're facing an aggressive and motivated foreign company. Their move in Vietnam is just the beginning. If you can't handle the situation fast, it will slip out of your hands. And, believe me, you won't be able to handle it the way you want. The Somsak Khon Kaen is a new breed of enterprise and ingenuity, with an adaptable and unpredictable agenda. If you decide to start this battle, I promise you that it will be long and exhausting, and eventually you'll lose miserably."

"OK. I get it, I get it. You don't want to say how, don't want to say why, but you want to make us believe that you're three steps ahead of everyone else," said Avalon, shaking his head. "You already know everything, right? You may as well put a mole as big as a house on your nose and put up your fortune teller tent. Or ... No, wait! This is the magic moment when you suggest an alternative to avoid my inevitable defeat. This is the reason why you're here, after all, to give me advice, right?"

"My advice is simple," said the Omnilogos, ignoring his tone. "Join forces with the Somsak Khon Kaen. It's the only way to avoid defeat -- or everything for which you've worked will fall apart."

"What ... What did you say?"

"I'm talking about a merger, Mr. Moon. A merger between your Sanuk and the Somsak Khon Kaen is the only way to avoid oblivion."

"A merger you say?" Avalon remained awestruck for a few seconds, intent on thinking through what the Omnilogos had said. Then, as though emerging from a trance, he clapped his hands and giggled like an obese seal. "Ah! This is unbelievable! You're ... Damn, you're a treasure chest of surprises, you little brat. Really! I can't believe half the bullshit you said, but you said it so well I can't even move. Look! I have my ass glued to the chair. I like you. I love you! You are a hoot!"

Avalon wiped his mouth with the back of his hand. "OK, OK, just for fun. Let's ... let's play your little game. What makes you even think that they want ... that the Somsak wants to have anything to do with me?"

"I know it for a fact, Mr. Moon."

"*How?*" barked Avalon, tired of the meaningless conversation.

The Omnilogos had an impassive face, a white mask without any expression.

"I know because I am the Somsak Khon Kaen," he finally said, his lips curling up to form a tiny smile.

∞∞∞∞

A long silence followed the Omnilogos' statement.

His last sentence hung in the air for seconds. No one dared to speak or move.

When Avalon resumed breathing, he burst out into raucous and uncontrollable laughter. He wiped his tears and sniffled a couple of times. He then tried to speak, but was interrupted by another round of laughter that he couldn't control. The tension that had been hovering in the air shortly before was now dead and buried.

"Hector, call the guards," Avalon said, red-faced, waving a hand in the direction of the entrance. "Aye Heeah! We're done with this farce."

Hector nodded and began to touch his bracelet but he was suddenly interrupted by the Omnilogos.

"And miss the look on your assistant's face when the secretariat of the Somsak Khon Kaen calls him? No way!"

Avalon rolled his eyes in disbelief.

"Really?" he said after a couple of seconds, placing his hands on his hips. He looked at the boy as if he were an insignificant but noisy mosquito. "No one less than the secretariat himself will call? And when should this incredible turn of events happen?"

The Omnilogos began tapping a finger on the table. "In seven, six, five, four, three, two, one ..."

Hector's forearm lit with a blue light, and his device began to emit a rhythmic and repetitive ringing.

Avalon turned open-mouthed to his assistant, who returned a blank, expressionless look. He seemed as shocked as his boss was.

When Hector touched the device, the sound stopped.

Avalon looked at the Omnilogos, who looked back at him without blinking.

"It's ... it's the secretariat of the Somsak Khon Kaen, sir."

"Go ahead," Avalon said slowly, holding the boy's gaze. The atmosphere had again abruptly changed. The air was charged by a strange sort of energy mixed with expectations, a bomb ready to explode at the slightest whisper.

"What do they say?"

"Their message simply says: 'It's true'. It doesn't say anything else."

"You will be contacted again," the Omnilogos said. "You must realize you face a choice that will determine the fate not only of the Sanuk and the Somsak, but of all those companies that will decide to enter this newborn market. With our combined forces, we can create an unstoppable union that no other company would be able to counter. We can reach other markets, expand and grow. We could become the monopolist in this sector. And when the big names finally notice the cash cow and the giant multinationals consider entering the stage, we'll be a long-established force, a powerhouse to be reckoned with."

Avalon's brain struggled to process the information he was receiving. Within ten minutes, his heart had stopped half a dozen times.

He wiped his forehead with the sleeve of his jacket, without taking his eyes off the Omnilogos.

"Two plot twists in less than ten minutes," the fat man said, sweaty and breathing heavily. "Forget the tent and the crystal ball. You should consider a career at Broadway. You'd make a fortune."

Avalon took a deep breath and ordered Hector to give him the polymorphic tablet.

When he finished reading the message and confirmed who the sender was, he turned again toward the Omnilogos.

"Do you have other rabbits in your hat? I'd like to know if today is the day the God of insects has decided I'll die of a heart attack."

The Omnilogos opened his arms and showed his empty hands, as if he wanted to reassure him that he wasn't dangerous. "I just have a couple more. But it's nothing lethal. For now, I ask you only to consider a healthy, familiar and profitable business proposition."

"You're talking about a merger?"

"I'm talking about a total fusion, to tell you the truth," the Omnilogos pointed out. "Your Sanuk will de facto absorb the Somsak Khon Kaen. The details have been transferred to your assistant."

Avalon looked at Hector, who responded with a quick motion of assent. The boy wasn't lying.

The fat man scratched his neck. It was still hard to believe that the kid was really who he claimed to be.

"This business proposal seems to me nothing but a gift," Avalon said, reading the data on the tablet and trying to disguise his excited voice. "Unless, as well as a wizard and a soothsayer, you're also Santa Claus' son, 'gift' in this world is a word that doesn't exist."

The Omnilogos laughed. For the very first time, the spontaneous and childlike sound reminded Avalon that he was talking to a mere teenager. The fact disquieted him much more than he cared to admit to himself. Another shiver ran down his spine, but he did his best not to show his discomfort.

"You'll take full control of your rival, its resources, its technology, its contacts and its staff. Everything that is the Somsak will be yours," the Omnilogos said, pushing his hands deep in his pockets. "I wish, however, that the key people who have made the Somsak Khon Kaen a success become members of your board of directors, especially the researchers and the specialists in public relations, the two elements of which your Sanuk has great need."

Avalon nodded. "I expected conditions," he said, looking at the boy with narrowed eyes. "This is another gift. I am sorry to point this out, kid, but you're still going to be one miracle short of sainthood."

The Omnilogos smiled. "The agreement will be arranged if you'll satisfy two non-negotiable conditions."

"Now we're talking," Avalon said smiling, clapping his hands. Finally the boy spoke a language he could understand.

"Come on! Hit me!" The fat man spread his arms and closed his eyes theatrically.

"You'll make sure to expand the market of edible insects in Saemangeum City. I want this place to become one of the hubs of your business empire."

Avalon's smile faded. He looked around, surprised and confused. "What? You mean, here? In this city?"

"Exactly."

Avalon laughed a nervous and uncomfortable laugh. "What are you talking about, kid? This city is an empty shell. It has a population of hard hats, architects and engineers. Who should I sell my bugs to, hmm? The fish?"

"Close your eyes, Mr. Moon. Imagine how this city will be ten years from now, when it will be populated by millions of people."

"I'm sorry," Avalon said, tapping his head. "I have a poor imagination."

The Omnilogos looked around, admiring the profile of some distant, unfinished skyscrapers.

"It's true, after all. Saemangeum City is a gift that few people understand."

Avalon ignored the last sentence. "OK. Let me see … let's see if I understood what you're asking me to do. You want to sell insects to the Koreans. Is this what you want? This would be your first condition?"

"No, I don't want to sell to the Koreans. I want you to enter into Saemangeum's market with your product. When the very first home is built, the first grocery store, the first school, I want you to be there, waiting with your product in hand and a toothy grin on your face while selling it."

"Sorry to burst your bubble, kid, but I see you're quite weak in geography. Let me connect the dots for you. Saemangeum City *is* part of Korea, got it? Why on earth do you speak as if they were two separate things? It makes no sense."

"Trust me, the two things may seem part of the same symphony now, but I assure you that this will not be the case for long."

"A poet." Avalon sighed, raising his arms above his head in frustration.

The Omnilogos ignored him. "Think of Saemangeum City as a separate market, an independent city. It would make more sense if you'd use a bit of imagination, but I'm not asking you to do any of this. I'm simply offering you a possibility."

The boy raised a finger, anticipating Avalon's comment. "This is not a discussion, Mr. Moon. This is a condition. Take it or leave it."

"I swear, kid, I don't get your stubbornness," Avalon insisted. "Today, tomorrow, a year from now, it makes no difference. Even if this damn city were a separate State with a population of ten million inhabitants on the verge of starvation, no one would buy my insects. Consider the geography of the place, dammit. Think of the culture and the traditions. I would have the same probability of selling crickets and ants to Saemangeumians as of selling the same stuff to the French or the Italians. These bastards will never eat insects. They have been trained to think they are the shit of the earth."

The Omnilogos smiled. "Well, you would be surprised to find out what an Italian will eat with just the right amount of tomato sauce on it."

"What?"

The Omnilogos shook his head. "Never mind. I have no way to explain it with words. I just know it. Listen. We are witnessing the creation of the most advanced city that humanity has ever built. A city that doesn't rise from the backbone of a previous city, but a real virgin, urban settlement that has been built in a brand new province reclaimed from nature. This city is a blank sheet we can write on to our own liking, and the people who are smart enough to figure this out will work to shape it as they wish, for better or for worse."

"Of one thing you can be sure. This city won't be what people expect it'll be. It will be a completely different breed; a fascinating and unpredictable gift: international, vertical, advanced, rich and completely self-sustainable. It will be a beautiful and precious jewel that will have no equal in the world. I want the market of edible insects to play an important part in all this, Mr. Moon."

Avalon shrugged and rubbed his hands. "Even if it were heaven fallen on earth, Saemangeum City is still beyond my jurisdiction. Where would I find the resources to even dare to do what you're asking? I don't even have the permits or the contacts to operate in this part of the world, dammit. It makes no sense. Do you realize you're suggesting a titanic investment based on a vision that could never come true? A heavy use of means and resources on something as real and tangible as the air I'm breathing in now."

The Omnilogos stretched an arm and pointed his finger toward the horizon. "Don't they call it capitalism for that reason, Mr. Moon?"

Avalon was not convinced. "The customer will have no interest in my product." He shifted nervously in his chair then added, "If you really know what you are talking about, you should understand it well."

"They'll be interested if you make it so. If you make brave choices that men like you are called to make, choices that can undo simple individuals, or create legends."

Avalon was about to reply again, but in the end he did not. He understood that the Omnilogos was more than determined on that point. He decided on a strategic retreat for the time being.

He grunted and settled back to let his chair bear his weight. The chair creaked dangerously.

He rubbed his chin, waiting for the guy to say something else. He waited in vain.

"I need to shit," the fat man announced farting. He scratched his armpit, but he didn't move from the chair. He also began to feel a discomfort at the base of his right eye. It was the familiar announcement of an unwelcome headache. "And a sparkle of lifesaver dust," he added, touching his nose.

The Omnilogos looked at him with curiosity.

Avalon thrust his hand into his pants pocket and came out with a small vial. He opened it and poured the contents into the palm of his hand. It was a very fine yellow powder.

Avalon covered his nostril with a finger and closed the distance between the powder and his nose. There was a guttural sound, like a strange regurgitation.

Avalon tapped a foot on the ground and sneezed five times in a row. His eyes watered, but he didn't seem to worry about the effects of the sneezing.

The fat man touched his forehead and the lower part of his neck. He then smiled, revealing a row of yellow and crooked teeth that overlapped one another.

The headache was gone.

"After this request of yours, I'm afraid to hear the second one," Avalon said, wiping the yellowish snot with the palm of his hand and licking off what remained on his upper lip. "What is it, exactly? Huh? You want me to solve world hunger with hugs and smiles or simply reduce the ozone depletion with my farts?"

"I need you to put me in touch with Zhongnanhai."

Avalon dropped the small container, which shattered on the floor. He gasped for a few seconds, his lungs unable to suck air, his skin turning to ice. He looked at Hector hesitantly, as if he was in urgent need of a translator. The request caught him completely off guard. Once more, his heart skipped a beat as he repeated the Omnilogos' request in his head.

His face turned from yellow to pale green.

"*What?*" he finally managed to spit out, looking at the Omnilogos with bloodshot eyes.

"You heard it, Mr. Moon. I need to talk with your friend in the Chinese Politburo. Mr. Li, that is."

Avalon's first impulse was to lie, to say that he didn't know what the boy was talking about, but he thought better of it almost immediately. *I know you,* the Omnilogos had said before. Only now did Avalon realize the profound truth of those words. Perhaps, he found himself thinking, the Omnilogos was *really* the Omnilogos.

The thought made him shudder.

Avalon didn't deny knowing what the boy was referring to. His expression of surprise had already revealed everything there was to reveal.

He decided to play another card. "In less than fifteen minutes I found out that a teenager whom I've never seen in my whole life knows more about me than my mother. I don't know what to make of it. That story about the cyber terrorist seems a lot more convincing now."

"You're a person with a lot of resources, but at the same time you pay little attention to detail, Mr. Moon," the Omnilogos said. "You're an open book that leaves many pages on display. Your company is a spitting image of its creator, and some people have learned to exploit this weakness. For this reason, it's easy for me to know what you do and when you do it, your strategies and your contacts. Your problem is that you've never thought of being at war, so you've never bothered to learn how to aim and shoot. It's the problem of the biggest fish in the lake, isn't it? At a certain point, it becomes fat and lazy."

"You mean that besides your ass, there's also a real mole in my organization?" Avalon smiled, but he felt his nostrils flare involuntarily and a spasm of anger shot through him.

"No, Mr. Moon, I'm saying that other than mine, there are a dozen asses that occupy one or more places in some of your departments. All on your payroll, but they answer to someone else."

Avalon closed his hand into a fist. "And this explains why you're here."

"I'm here because I'm a damn good server," the boy answered, smiling thinly.

Avalon shook his head. "Infiltration, deception, lies, probably extortion, those are the best conditions to start a merger between companies, aren't they? Now that I think about it, what good would a merger do for our companies? We're already like the two buttocks of the same, damn ass, right? I can't even begin to figure out where the Sanuk begins and the Somsak ends."

"Are you mad?"

"Mad? I'm furious, you bastard! I'd break your neck with my bare hands if you weren't so damn intriguing. You remind me of myself ten years ago."

"I'm sure we'll become best friends, Mr. Moon. Can I call you Avalon?"

"No."

"That's fair enough. Well, do you agree to satisfy the two requests?"

"What? Are you serious? You don't really expect me to answer this question now, do you? I've just found out that my Sanuk is a sieve of information. I have yet to decide whether to admire you or strangle you."

"Understandable. You've got twenty-four hours." The Omnilogos rose from his chair.

"Hey! Where the hell are you going?"

"It is time for goodbyes, Mr. Moon. There's someone waiting for me outside. Gentlemen, this conversation is over."

Avalon looked at Hector.

"The lobby doesn't report any car waiting outside, sir," said the assistant, studying his bracelet.

"Who said anything about a car?" the Omnilogos replied, picking up his clothes.

"Wait a minute." Avalon rose from his chair. It was a difficult feat. "Can you at least explain yourself, goddammit? Assuming that I actually have a contact within the politburo, what of it? What use is that for a boy like you?"

"I need to deliver a gift," the Omnilogos replied, heading for the door.

Avalon frowned. Did he hear that right?

"A gift? What gift?" he asked, confused. "You need to deliver a gift for whom?"

The Omnilogos opened the door. Before leaving the room, he looked behind him and said, "A gift to mankind."

The Sophist and the Scientist

GLADIA

2025

GLADIA EGEA KNEW she had lost even before she finished her last sentence.

She realized she was sweating. The woman was nervous, and if she could notice it, then the audience could, too.

She could feel her heart beating wildly. She licked her dry lips as she took the glove off her hand and set it on the pulpit. Gladia felt the inquisitive eyes of the crowd observe, evaluate and judge her.

The audience's applause was short. It sounded muffled.

It was a mistake, Gladia thought while abandoning the stage in silence. She simply wasn't cut out for this kind of thing. She wasn't an animal bred to compete in an arena.

Her armor was just a white coat and her sword nothing more than a mixture of graphics and abstract numbers.

Her throat felt swollen. She swallowed hard.

Unfortunately, she was the only one who took up the challenge, the only person crazy enough to jump of her own free will into a tank of sharks and hope to get out alive.

She wished she hadn't. The stakes were too high and she had proven not to be up to the challenge.

When she was finally seated, she took a glass of water and eagerly drank the contents.

"Thank you, thank you, Dr. Egea for your insight," the man sitting to her left with a hand raised to invite the public to silence was saying. "Now, our second speaker is Spine Woodside, speaking contrary to the motion of the day: *Space exploration is a necessary catalyst to the development of our civilization.* Spine Woodside is quite a versatile man: explorer, journalist, and philanthropist. He is best known for founding LAND, which its members call the League for Human Development on Earth."

A three-dimensional reproduction of the symbol of the organization appeared, suspended above the huge room full of people: a man and a woman kneeling on either side of the earth that contained the symbols of the four elements.

"Right, Mr. Woodside," the commentator said, indicating the pulpit. "Let us hear what you have to say. You have ten minutes."

Spine Woodside rose from his chair and greeted the audience with a raised arm. He was cheered by the majority, who applauded and called out his name. Once on stage, he put on the glove that Gladia had left shortly before and focused his attention on the audience. The hall was built on three levels and resembled a huge theater. It contained at least three thousand people.

Woodside, however, knew that the eyes that were studying his every movement were far more numerous. The cameras, greedy for his image, were broadcasting his reproduction to millions of homes around the world.

A unique opportunity, he thought excitedly.

The Landist calmly sipped his water bottle. He made sure that the glove was turned on and cleared his throat.

"My friends, I must confess that after listening to Gladia's speech, I feel lost." Spine Woodside was pointing a finger toward Dr. Egea. "The good woman came here, in front of us all, armed with evidence, statistics, numbers, facts and surveys, displayed with passion and eloquence before our eyes. I admit it, Gladia. You've convinced me."

Woodside pulled his wallet out of his pocket and he put it on the pulpit, so that everybody could easily see it. Eyes and cameras moved accordingly. "I don't need carpets," he continued, raising his voice, "my house is full of them, but, my dear, if you should happen to sell some when we're done, this is my credit card."

The audience burst into laughter. Woodside smiled and rubbed his chin.

He let a few moments pass, allowing the laughter to slowly die. He raised his arms and said, "Unfortunately, my friends, I have no numbers or data to show you. I have nothing to sell. I stand before you with a simple story. The story of Deng, a farmer I met in China some time ago."

Woodside took a sip from the bottle. The audience hung on his words.

"After talking with him about family and politics, I also wanted to know the opinion that this gentleman, a representative of more than three hundred million peasants who live in the Asian nation, had on the recent space station put into orbit by his government. This news, I'm sure you all know, has literally deluged the media all over the world for quite a while. So I asked Deng: What do you think of your accomplishment in outer space? The farmer looked at me for a few seconds before he asked: What the heck is outer space?"

An indistinct noise of people speaking among each other burst from the audience. Spine Woodside moved his gloved hand and at the center of the hall the three-dimensional image appeared of an object shaped like a walnut orbiting the earth.

Woodside pointed at the object he had just summoned.

"This thing, the function of which is not clear to anyone, has cost the Chinese government the equivalent of thirty billion dollars and one Chinese out of five isn't even aware of its existence."

The audience was silent and attentive, eyes and cameras focused on the ruby-colored space station floating over their heads.

"But back to Deng and my story," continued Woodside. "A week ago I returned to the village. I wanted to invite him and his family to be part of a documentary that I and some volunteers were shooting. Well, to my deep regret, I discovered that Deng and half his fellow villagers were gone. They were dead. That's right. Local authorities have informed me that a recent chemical spill from an industrial plant has contaminated the drinking water supply in the whole region. As a result, a total of one hundred and forty people have died from poisoning. Deng and his family were among the list."

Woodside paused. The silence stretched, unchallenged.

"I'm sure nobody in this room knows the least of what I'm talking about. And why should you anyway? The news is bad publicity. An inconvenient truth not meant for your ears. It's certainly not the latest fancy technological pride worth thirty billion dollars and sent into orbit in full regalia. Surely it isn't as fascinating as the wonderful fireworks show that deserves your attention."

Gladia Egea shifted nervously in her chair.

Woodside lifted his chin and puffed his chest out. "In front of you all, I wish to represent those one hundred and forty ghosts and bring them as evidence against today's motion."

"At this point you may wonder what the link is between this motion and a farmer in the Southwest of China. It's really very simple. You see, a routine check of the old industrial plant would have identified the damage, alerted the authorities and saved the village. This control would have cost the government the equivalent of one thousand five hundred dollars. Fifteen hundred dollars that the bureaucrats in Beijing didn't spend because the intervention was considered impractical, unnecessary and, I quote from the official response received by the spokesperson of the factory: 'uneconomic'."

Woodside was interrupted by the growing murmur of the audience.

He waited until the murmurs died down before continuing.

"Our history as a civilization is the result of a series of choices. I believe that what happened to Deng, his family and the rest of the village, is evidence of a bad choice. Deng was a father and a husband, a tireless worker, an incurable optimist and a friend. And now he's dead. And the blame is on us."

Woodside pointed to the audience. "But don't you even think for a second that my story is an isolated case that occurred in a remote place and was the result of a unique circumstance. Today on our planet, thousands of choices like this are made and the vast majority of people don't even realize it. Today, the favorite sport of nations is the launch of expensive pieces of metal through the atmosphere with the sole purpose of being able to shout out from the rooftops, 'Me too, me too', regardless of the real needs of the people living on this planet. Please, take a look …"

Spine Woodside presented a series of three-dimensional images showing examples in support of his position. As they were projected one by one, the Landist commented on them briefly with passion and sagacity.

There was the reproduction of a sparkling probe launched by NASA into the depths of the Solar System, opposed to a young beggar at the entrance of a college pleading, 'Please, pay for my instruction'.

Then came a huge telescope that exhibited the ESA logo opposite the photo of a homeless man in front of the European Parliament showing the inscription: 'Unemployed for twelve years'. It was followed by a short movie showing an army of Indian scientists surrounded by star maps, busy solving complicated calculations while in a little street outside the building stood a group of naked children, malnourished and sick, sleeping abandoned and alone on a pile of garbage.

Woodside had staged the images to be disruptive. It was nothing less than an emotional bomb that was easy to empathize with.

The last image faded away while the Landist slipped off the glove and with icy eyes glared at the speechless audience.

"Every minute governments, private companies and individuals spend millions of dollars on the so-called 'space enterprise' without any real benefit to humanity. Resources that could be used to save lives are used at this very moment for sending high-tech robots to rake sand and ice millions of miles away or to take colorful pictures of space objects that ceased to exist millions of years ago. Nobody can deny this truth! For decades humanity has been wasting money, materials, facilities, ideas and people on a hobby that has never brought and will never bring a real benefit to our civilization. Today's motion, its very existence, signifies the desire to change -- to improve, to admit a mistake and to move on. Today, before the whole world, you can help me make a difference, to take a stand, by voting a resounding, unequivocal 'no' to this nonsense that is plaguing us all."

Spine Woodside stepped down from the podium surrounded by a shower of applause and an almost unanimous standing ovation. The Landist sipped from his water bottle as he walked back to sit a few feet away from Gladia.

"Thank you, thank you," the moderator interrupted, inviting everyone to sit down. "We have heard our two contenders. Now it's your turn, dear friends from the audience. You have a few minutes to think about questions to ask our two speakers. Meanwhile I'll remind you how you voted before the debate began. I want to underline again that the motion of the day is: *Space exploration is a necessary catalyst to the development of our civilization.* Before the debate started, 1,200,109 people were in favor of the motion. Against the motion, were 1,300,005 people. It's important to point out that 700,502 people were undecided at the time of the vote. Dr. Egea, Mr. Woodside, it seems obvious that you'll have to convert this mass of abstentions to your point of view in order to win the debate."

The commentator cleared his throat. "I remind you that shortly we will ask our viewers at home and in the auditorium to vote a second time. We will then compare the results and determine a winner. All right, let's hear some questions."

He looked at the audience and pointed to a man with both hands raised.

"You! Yes, you, jumping on the chair. You seem to have an urgent need to ask this question. You can briefly introduce yourself if you believe it's relevant. Please, go on."

From the audience a tall middle-aged man with curved and sloping shoulders stood.

"My name is John Bernardi, I work at the Jet Propulsion Laboratory in Pasadena. I wanted to ask Spine Woodside if he realizes the nonsense that he's been preaching to us all. You talk of waste of resources, unnecessary research, of a superfluous hobby when referring to the achievements we have made as a civilization in space. I'm sure you don't have the slightest idea of the progress that we have inherited through the Apollo missions, from the Hubble telescope, from the program of the Space Shuttle, the ISS, the—"

"Mr. Bernardi, we are losing you," the commentator interrupted, raising a hand. "Is there a question somewhere in your statement?"

The man nodded eagerly. "From what we've heard so far, people like you think that Queen Isabella made a mistake financing Columbus' expedition." There was a brief pause then the man continued to speak, visibly angry. "You wanted a question? Here's the question: why don't you go home and study some history?"

A portion of the audience applauded the intervention while the commentator nodded toward Woodside, who grinned.

"I'd like to thank our friend from the JPL for his question," the Landist said, showing a bright smile. "Now, together let's dwell on the admirable accomplishments that his space club buddies have really achieved."

"If I'm not mistaken, you've mentioned the Apollo program, the Hubble Telescope, the Space Shuttle and the International Space Station. Well, let's analyze them closely. At its time, the Apollo program cost around 24 billion dollars, roughly 130 billion dollars today, adjusted for inflation. This was the largest commitment of resources ever made by a nation in peacetime. At its peak, the Apollo program employed around 400,000 people and required the support of 20,000 industrial firms and universities. I admit it." Woodside raised his hands, as if he was surrendering to someone. "I'd be a fool not to recognize that with all this we got nearly 840 pounds of rock and lunar dust and we were finally able to solve the stones shortage devastating our planet."

The audience laughed heartily.

Woodside crossed his arms and continued to speak.

"The Hubble telescope has been nothing more than the most expensive camera built in the history of mankind -- and its usefulness is as obvious as its blurred photos. More than ten billion dollars were spent to know that Pluto has a fourth and a fifth satellite and that there are planets around stars other than our own. I'm sure that this has revolutionized the lives of the billion and a half people who live on less than three dollars a day." Whistles and shouts of approval were added to the laughter. The audience started to shout and cheer.

"But let's move on, my friends! Let's talk about the Space Shuttle. What a great deal! This wonderful thing put a giant broken camera in space so that they could justify the cost to repair it. It also made the growth of some crystals in zero gravity possible and has allowed a group of scientists, trained for years at your expense, to take pictures of each other while pirouetting like tech-monkeys in zero gravity. And oh, yes, we can't fail to mention that this program cost the lives of fourteen people. I'm sure the families of the victims who are listening today will be happy to know that the corpses of their boys and girls have cost the U.S. government more than two hundred and ten billion dollars, adjusted for inflation."

Woodside was interrupted by a burst of applause. Gladia whispered something in the ear of the moderator.

"Dear friends, maybe it's just me," Woodside said, raising his voice to be heard over the applause, "but I cannot call this an intelligent use of your tax dollars."

The audience laughed, someone whistled and others stood up and applauded.

"OK, OK, people," interrupted the moderator, "let's move on to the next question."

"But I haven't finished yet, Your Honor." Woodside groaned, looking with a half-smile at the audience, who laughed again.

"I'm sure you'll have other opportunities to continue," said the other. "Now, do we have a question for Dr. Egea? Yes, please, the lady in the fourth row with the chador. Yes, your question."

"Hello. I study solar physics and astronomy at the University of Tehran. I wanted to ask Doctor Egea: What do you think of the amount of funds that the U.S. government has decided to grant NASA in this fiscal year? And what do you think about the role of private companies such as the Virgin Galactic and your SOL in what some people call the space industry of the next generation?"

Gladia settled back in her chair. "Before I answer the questions I wanted to point out to Mr. Woodside, and obviously our audience is educated enough to realize it, that the list he provided is not nearly as funny as a bad joke."

"Really?" Woodside asked, simulating surprise. "I don't know about you, my dear, but I heard a lot of people laughing."

"The question, Dr. Egea," the commentator reminded her.

Gladia shook her head as she looked at Woodside, undecided whether to answer the question, punch his smiling face or do both at the same time.

"Fine," she finally said, trying to avoid looking at her opponent. "It is my opinion that the budget granted NASA today is just another bad joke ..."

"Sure," Woodside stage-whispered with the clear intention to be heard by the public, his voice dripping with sarcasm. "They definitely need more money to produce pens that write in space."

The crowd let out another collective laugh.

"As far as I'm concerned," Gladia continued overriding the audience's laughter, "I stand behind what I've always said about NASA and other governmental agencies around the world. Their role has been important in the past but now it's over. The future of space exploration belongs to the private sector and to people like me who decided to invest heavily in this sector. The SOL, for example, uses much of its budget in space research and sidereal technology. As you all know, the project 'Free Space' was the ultimate result of years of research and the joint effort of thousands of experts. The technology of degradable materials developed—"

Woodside interrupted the woman by clapping politely and nodding. "It seems to me that our audience is scarcely aware of the debt that mankind owes your company, Gladia." The Landist moved his arms up and down, as if he wanted to incite the spectators in a football match. "I beg all present to thank Dr. Egea with a round of applause for once again sponsoring that magnificent vacuum cleaner that has removed the space paint above our heads."

Much of the public followed Woodside's invitation, politely applauding and thanking Gladia.

The woman chewed the inside of her cheek and gave Woodside an angry look.

"OK. Quiet, people. I said quiet," the commentator resumed shushing the public and calling for silence. "More questions. Yes, you on the first balcony. You have a question for Mr. Woodside? All right, shoot."

"Mr. Woodside, from what you've told us, it seems clear that you're not a big Science Fiction fan. I mean, have you ever caught your daughter watching Star Trek, or reading Asimov's books? What would you do in that case?"

Spine Woodside rolled his eyes and stood up. "Are you kidding me? Star Trek is one of my favorite series! I love it! As for Asimov, I gave my daughter the Foundation trilogy as a birthday present."

The audience, obviously confused, looked around, muttering.

"Excuse me," the moderator interrupted, "but doesn't this seem a bit odd to you? Doesn't it seem like a contradiction? I mean, these two sagas tell us about a humanity that lives and travels in space with spaceships. In short, the exact opposite of what you're preaching."

Spine Woodside sat down again. He shielded his face with a toothy smile and turned to the audience.

"There is no contradiction at all. Let me ask you a question. If one day I wake up and decide that unicorns and hobbits are a good idea, do you think that spending the rest of my life to make one might be of some use for mankind? The answer is obvious and people know that these creatures are and will always remain myths; they can't possibly be created because they're just the outcome of imagination. *Imagination*, ladies and gentlemen."

Woodside emphasized the word underlining each syllable. He paused, as if to give the audience time to absorb what he had said. Then he went on, "There's nothing wrong with the imagination. The problem with our society is that someone one day got up and decided to convince the world that Science Fiction was a window to the future -- something real rather than a fantasy that must be taken for what it is."

Woodside turned and looked at Gladia, before continuing.

"Warp speed, time machines and photon torpedoes are marvellous inventions of the mind. The problem is that we've been trained to think that they're also possible. This mental operation is wrong and has a basic flaw. My LAND group and I are not opposing imagination, we are opposing people like *you*," he pointed to Gladia, "who are wasting men and resources to create hobbits and unicorns."

"Your problem is that you have the imagination of a toaster and no confidence in the ability of mankind," answered Gladia, staring back at the Landist and receiving a strong round of applause.

"And the problem with people like you is believing that robbing honest people will make some psychotic scientist's dreams come true," Woodside shot back, returning to focus on the audience.

"Think about it! If I move a piece of wood and I say it's a magic wand capable of transforming a pear into an artichoke, everyone laughs. But if I am a guy dressed up in a white coat with a serious enough face announcing that in five years mankind will terraform Mars, I'm going to end up in the newspapers. Why? Because nobody taught us that there isn't any difference. Both are the fruit of our imagination. Nothing more, nothing less."

"All right, all right," the commentator cut the Landist off, and at the same time, blocked the counter-response of Gladia with a raised hand. "Our next question is for Dr. Egea. Please, silence. Yes, you ma'am. What is your question?"

A pregnant woman got up from her chair. "Dr. Egea, you have spoken about the need of the average family to begin to conceive space exploration as a component of everyday life, as a domestic component, something that fits into our typical day. I believe what you say makes no sense. The funds from private and public entities in space exploration are in my opinion a waste of money. Think about it. Let's say you have a family of five members and you must feed the children, pay for their education, provide medical care, and so on. If your finances are limited, as are the finances of all families, it would be a waste of money to buy a jet and fly as a hobby. Don't you agree?"

"I don't understand the analogy," Gladia said sourly, dismissing the question.

Woodside laughed heartily while a series of boos echoed through the room.

"Who's next? You in the first row. Yes, you with the green jacket, what is your question, please?" said the moderator.

"Mr. Woodside, your movement has grown quite a lot in recent years. This is undeniable. Yet there are millions of people who don't think like your Landists, people prepared to say that the beginning of space exploration has been the advent of a new era for mankind, a unique opportunity, a new brilliant dream of audacity and hope. How can you deny the sincere passion born from the spirit of enterprise of some of our best minds?"

Woodside shook his head and smiled a contemptuous smile. "My friend, believe me, it hurts me to teleport you away from Disneyland, but I think an adult must give you some facts. You see, your wonderful space adventure was born from a squabble between two superpowers that were competing to see which of them could launch more dogs and monkeys into orbit."

That said, Woodside looked at the rest of the room and asked, frowning theatrically, "Good Lord, is there someone else among you who believes in Santa Claus?"

The audience laughed again as the moderator pointed to another spectator who turned to Gladia.

"Dr. Egea, over the past seventy years, the use of vehicles such as cars, trains, ships and airplanes has intensified formidably, and every year their efficiency increases and their cost decreases, allowing them to become more and more accessible by more people. One example: seventy years ago only a handful of people could afford the luxury of a plane ticket. Today, more than three billion people board an aircraft every year. In contrast, during the same period, less than a thousand people have gone into space and the way in which we overcome the atmosphere's gravitational pull of earth is more or less the same, an expensive method used by the rocket that carried the Apollo 11 to the moon. What would it take, in your opinion, to make sure that space becomes more accessible to the common consumer?"

"Competitiveness, in one word," Gladia said, lifting a finger. "This is the element that has always been missing and that has never allowed us to leap forward. Today it costs about ten thousand U.S. dollars to bring a pound of anything into orbit and you can't possibly travel in space if you don't overcome earth's gravitational field. In order to do this we must reach a speed of seventeen thousand five hundred miles per hour, and as you have rightly pointed out, the only way we now do so is by using brute force -- that is, an explosive chemical reaction using considerable amounts of fuel. We need to reduce the costs to leave earth's orbit and I believe that the only way to do that is by promoting a healthy and robust competition among public and private entities involved in the space industry."

"All right, people. Question time is over," ruled the moderator spreading his arms. "It's time to vote again. I remind the public voting from home that you only need to access the Cloud and give your input. The motion of the day is: *Space exploration is a necessary catalyst to the development of our civilization.*"

Gladia shifted uncomfortably in her chair. She sipped a bit of water and waited in silence. Her heart was racing and her hands were shaking. She hid them in her pockets.

Minutes passed that felt like an eternity.

The woman realized her hands were balled into white-knuckled fists as she spied Woodside chatting amiably with a girl in the front row. The girl and the people around were laughing.

Finally the moderator started speaking again and Woodside sat down.

"Dear friends in the auditorium and at home, voting is closed! Let me remind everyone that before this debate started that you voted the motion this way: 1,200,109 in favor. 1,300,005 against the motion while 700,502 were undecided. Now for the final results. The number of people in favor of the motion: *Space exploration is a necessary catalyst to the development of our civilization* has shifted from 1,200,109 to ... 502,223. Silence, please! Against the motion we are now at 2,322,938. The undecided have dropped to 375,455. Looks like Mr. Woodside got quite a victory here. Congratulations to Spine Woodside. Thank you, people. Until the next time ..."

Spine Woodside quickly got up from his chair and heartily strode forward toward Gladia, holding out his hand.

"That was certainly a stimulating debate. We should do this more often."

The woman dodged the outstretched hand. "You can do your gloating somewhere else, Woodside," Gladia said through clenched teeth. "You think you won a race? You've proven nothing today. Nothing! Your fanaticism appeals only to frustrated, dissatisfied and ignorant losers. There is a world of people with brains out there, do you realize that? Your movement is nothing more than a meaningless smoke screen for willful ignorance."

"I'm not sure people feel the same, especially in recent times," said Woodside. "More and more are getting tired of your expensive hobby." He stared at her, his eyes sweeping her body from head to foot. "Just look at yourself, darling, that's all it takes to see that things are changing."

Gladia shook her head. She didn't understand. "Wha ... what's that supposed to mean?"

Woodside approached Gladia and whispered in a low voice, "You yourself no longer believe in what you say." He creased his lips into a smile. Then, unexpectedly, he closed his eyes for a split second and sniffed the air. "The smell of doubt and resignation is all around you. It's a very distinct, unmistakable fragrance."

"You're crazy."

Woodside ignored the last sentence. He then took something from his pocket and handed it to Gladia.

"LAND's doors are always open for people of your intelligence; people who are willing to make a difference. You only need to clear your mind. When you are able to distinguish a unicorn from a horse, call me."

The Landist's hand was holding a business card. Gladia looked at him for a moment, then took it and tore it in front of his eyes.

"Always," Woodside repeated, smiling a wicked smile.

Gladia said no more. She whirled quickly, gathered her things and left the room without looking back.

∞∞∞

Once out of the elevator, Gladia walked into a half-deserted corridor and within a few moments she found herself outside the building.

The limo parked nearby opened a rear door when she touched its smooth surface.

Once inside the car, a mechanical female voice greeted her. "Welcome back, Dr. Egea."

"CP, today's schedule," Gladia was visibly exhausted, closing her eyes. She was thankful that the cockpit was completely dark.

"13:45, business lunch with Mr. Gaspar O'Neil to discuss ..."

"Clear it," said Gladia softly, rubbing her temples.

"16:30, opening speech at the semi-annual fundraising ..."

"Clea— No, wait ..." Gladia grasped her neck with both hands. "Tell Orbit that the program has changed. I will make the closing speech. Tell him that I had ... tell him I had a setback."

"Acknowledged. Transmitting the message... Message transmitted. Continuing today's schedule. 21:00, beginning of the special event organized by the Terawatt Corporation at the Vancouver Convention Centre."

"Jesus." Gladia sighed. "Are you sure it was today?"

"Affirmative. The event is still scheduled for today, March 27, 2025, 21:00 pm PST."

"I need a drink."

Gladia opened the fridge to her right, looking for a bottle, but her hand caught nothing. She frowned and leaned over to check the inside of the refrigerator, only to discover that it was completely empty.

"I was wondering why on earth there was a Chianti Superiore inside that thing," said a male voice from somewhere in the cockpit.

Gladia spun and flattened against the door.

"CP, lights!" she screamed.

"I'm sorry, I cannot comply," the mechanical voice said.

"I mean," continued the figure shrouded by darkness, "you'd never drink a warm beer, right?"

"Who's in here?"

"A big fan of yours."

Gladia tried to open the door. "CP! Open the door, dammit!"

"I'm sorry," the voice repeated, without any nuances, "I cannot comply."

"Relax! CP, lights," the intruder ordered.

The cockpit was suddenly brightened by a quartz colored light and Gladia finally had the chance to see the stranger. He was a young man with amber eyes, almost yellowish-gold, and a crew cut. The woman recognized western mixed with eastern traits: pronounced jaw, high cheekbones, and a pointed chin. He wore a simple pair of jeans and a rumpled shirt. He also wore a strange pendant, a cross between an eight and a snake coiled around itself. It occurred to her that it might have been the symbol of infinity.

"Who the hell are you? What are you doing in my car?"

"Calm down, calm down. You've nothing to fear from me."

"Said the hostage-taker in my car." Gladia recoiled, flattening against her seat.

"Listen. Please, calm down. I don't want to hurt you, OK? I'm a simple person with a business proposition for you. That's it."

"A business proposition," Gladia repeated, bewildered. "Couldn't you take a damn appointment?"

"And risk ending up like poor O'Neil? No thanks, this thing needs your full attention."

"You bastard. Let me go! Now!"

"I'm sorry, but your CP-car seems to believe we are surrounded by lethal doses of organophosphate. We're trapped." The stranger grinned while slowly sipping his Chianti.

Gladia didn't think twice. She threw herself against the door and tried to break through. She received nothing but pain.

Her mysterious kidnapper watched her in silence, without doing anything to stop her.

"Shit!" Gladia groaned in the end, rubbing her sore shoulder. "Well, now what? Should I consider myself a hostage?"

"No, you should consider yourself lucky. If you were a hostage, there would be weapons, screaming ladies, shady types, that sort of thing. Here, on the other hand, it's just the two of us in the comfort of your private limo. I only ask to have a little chit-chat with you."

"I would prefer the comfort of a public restaurant. If you really want to talk, we can do it there."

"No, Dr. Egea. It doesn't work that way."

Silence filled the car.

"It seems you leave me no choice," the woman resigned, leaning back. She looked again at the stranger. His eyes were bright and intelligent. They were the eyes of a cat. He was young, probably around twenty. She considered his clothes for a moment. He had no weapons and wasn't threatening her with one. He didn't seem dangerous at all.

Gladia didn't feel an immediate risk to her safety. She rested her head on the seat and looked upward. "This day is getting worse by the minute." Gladia snorted. Suddenly, she realized that she felt weak and tired.

"You're referring to today's debate? You're damn right." The stranger nodded, pointing an admonishing finger at her. "You could have done way better." He pointed to the building where she had debated with Woodside. Then he went on, "I suppose that's not entirely your fault, after all. All this confirms my old hypothesis: in a public debate, the sophist will beat the scientist hands down."

Gladia stiffened her back like a touchy cat and felt a sudden burst of energy. "What did you say?"

"Come on, Doctor. Woodside humiliated you. You realize that?"

Gladia felt her nostrils flare involuntarily and a spasm of anger shot through her.

"Excuse me? You seize me in my own car and lecture me at the same time? Is everything included in this hostage package?"

The stranger raised his hands. "Look, I'm just saying that as your fan, I was expecting a better performance. That's all."

"So you're my fan, hmm? Well, I am very sorry to let you down! Now what the hell do you want from me?"

"All right," he said, rubbing his hands. The young man seemed excited. "It's been quite a while that I've been following you ... I mean, that I've been following your work and the way you manage your business, Doctor. What you did with the SOL in the past four years has been remarkable. Enough, in fact, to attract the attention of a guy like me looking for a partner for the development of an idea."

"OK." Gladia took deep breaths. "Let's pretend I'm not a prisoner in my own car and I'm not talking to my kidnapper. What exactly do you want from me?"

"Well, listening to you today, I actually think we want the same thing. That is, a fast, safe, and inexpensive way to sell the stars on the market."

Gladia shrugged. "What do you mean sell the stars on the market? I don't even know what you're talking about."

"You said it yourself, Doctor: 'We need to reduce the costs necessary to leave earth's orbit and I believe that the only way to do that is by promoting a healthy and robust competition among public and private entities involved in the space industry'. Remember?"

Gladia raised her eyebrows. He had repeated her exact words.

"Well, yes, I ... I said that, but—"

"Today I'm making that exact proposition," the young man interrupted her, spreading his arms. "A way to do what no one has been able to do before: to make outer space the province of the common person."

Before Gladia could answer, the boy handed her an object shaped like a small pyramid. It had a sapphire color and a strange shine about it.

When the woman turned it on by touching the tip of the pyramid, it began to soar in the air. From each of its sides three-dimensional moving reproductions appeared. Gladia carefully studied the object. She had never seen a trigoy like it. The images were incredibly sharp and stable, while the controls were simple and intuitive. She watched the projections for half a minute, breathing quickly.

"I've never seen this model," she admitted, touching the trigoy with her fingers. "Who's the manufacturer?"

The boy raised both his hands. "My sparkling hands," he replied simply.

"*You* made this?"

"Me. But the resolution of the images on my trigoy are really not the point here. The reason I'm in front of you, Doctor, is the content. Please, go ahead. Let me know what you think about it."

Gladia did as she was asked. She studied the images and the data that flowed back and forth following her gestures.

After five minutes of silence, she forgot she was a prisoner in her car. She emerged from the reading as if she had left an important financial transaction open.

"Is this really what I think? I mean … building this … thing. It's not a joke?"

"No, it's not," he answered while rubbing his chin. "Although I know a pretty good one that involves …"

Gladia was not listening to him. "I've never seen anything like it," she went on, her eyes reflecting the shining projections. "I mean, the idea is … brilliant. Tell me, who do you work for? Who gave you this data?"

"Nobody," replied the young man, "and I work for myself."

"Alone?"

"I like to think of being a lone ranger, but the truth is that I work with other people. Special people, like you, Doctor. You see, if I want to make sure to turn this mixture of equations and images into something concrete, I have to go to the next level -- and that's why I need your help."

"Why do you need my help?"

"I need the resources of your SOL to move the project forward. I need your technicians, engineers, laboratories and your matrix, among other things."

Gladia looked at the stranger, but she didn't respond.

The woman went back to studying the data projected by the trigoy with deep interest. She realized that her heart was pumping faster and faster.

"So, what do you say? Are you in?" the young man asked excitedly.

"What do you mean?"

"Oh, come on. I'm talking about the project, Doctor. The project you're looking at. Do you want to be part of it?"

Gladia shook her head. "Of course not," she replied, almost laughing, but continued to read the information. "I don't even know who the hell you are! Furthermore, do you really believe that I can make a decision like this on my own? You must be crazy. I answer to investors, shareholders, interest groups, not to mention the matri—"

"Bullshit," the stranger said hotly, cutting her off. His ears became suddenly as red as tomatoes. "I'm not stupid. I know how these things work, Doctor. You always have the first and last word, which is exactly what I need. I'm asking what you think, Gladia Egea. What do you think of those specs? Is this feasible, in your opinion?"

"Feasible? You mean this Science Fiction idea here?" She pointed to the projections that revolved around her. "I can't even start guessing how much it could cost a thing like th—"

"Forget about money," the young man interrupted her. "Imagine you have a lot of it. Is the idea feasible?"

Gladia looked again at the projections, then to her kidnapper.

"What do you want me to say? In theory, an antimatter propulsion engine is feasible."

"Well, that might please Star Trek fans," the young man said impatiently. "But what do you say of this, hmm?" He pointed with both hands to the pyramid.

A few seconds of silence passed.

"It has potential," Gladia finally said, deliberately slowly.

The boy sighed with relief. "It's a start."

"A start?" Gladia laughed. Despite the situation she found herself in, she couldn't help but find his comment quite ridiculous.

"Am I missing something here? Do you really think that my opinion makes any difference?"

"Your opinion is the only one that has any importance to me, Doctor. It makes a world of difference."

"OK. You've got my opinion. Now what do we do?"

"Now we start to build," the boy answered, as if it were the most obvious thing in the world.

"Wha—?" Gladia looked at him with wide eyes. "Listen, I don't know who the hell you are and I don't give a damn. I admit that this thing here"—she pointed to the trigoy—"is the best trigo-projector I've ever seen. I'm also ready to admit that the data that's inside it is good stuff for Sci-Fi junkies. What else do you want from me?"

"You yourself just told me that it's potentially feasible. That's more than enough for me."

"It's not enough, dammit!" snapped Gladia, exacerbated by the insistence of the weird guy. "God! Who do you think you are? Did you really believe that by forcing me to look at an equation and some images you would have got a countersigned contract? You must be insane! Every day, I get dozens of proposals, but if I had to finance each of them, my SOL would have failed long ago."

"It's a question of money, then?"

Gladia couldn't hold back a wry smile. "Isn't it always?" Then she leaned toward the stranger. "Look, it doesn't matter what I think about your project, assuming it's really yours. If you want to submit this data to my experts, I have no problem. But it'll take time, compliance with a protocol and you'll have to answer a lot of questions before you even hope to—"

"I hate questions, they waste a lot of time," he said, his eyes fixed on the glass of wine. "Plus, there is no need for your experts to do the math to determine whether the calculations are accurate or not. They *are* accurate. I understand, however, where you are coming from. After all, I didn't give you any reason to trust me. OK, let's say that you receive an anonymous donation to preliminarily evaluate my data and determine whether this project is possible or not. What would you say in that case?"

Gladia bent the corner of her mouth, showing a contemptuous smile.

"I'd say that it would have to be a damn generous donation. Nothing you can afford, anyway." She glanced at his worn jeans.

"CP," called the boy, patting a seat, "please, update Dr. Egea on her current financial situation. Specify the activities related to her bank account in Andorra considering only the last half hour."

"The bank account has received eight money transfers of unknown origin in the last twenty-eight minutes," said the mechanical voice.

"Really?" The boy asked, feigning astonishment. "Well, well." He folded his arms across his chest, as if thinking of something. "It seems your day just got a bit brighter, eh?"

Before Gladia could say anything he preceded her by lifting a finger. "CP, specify the total amount transferred."

"The total amount transferred is 3,291,980 USD."

Gladia's eyes widened. Did she hear that right?

"Mmm. 3,291,980 is a curious amount," the young man remarked thoughtfully, rubbing his chin. "Really curious. Maybe this figure contains some secret information, a coded message. Let's see. If we turn this number into a date, it turns out to be 3, 29 and 1980. Wow! Guess who was born on the 29 March of 1980? That's right, it's you. Isn't it wonderful? Happy Birthday!"

"Seriously," Gladia said, looking into his eyes, "who are you?"

"Another person bound to titles and names." He looked disappointed. "All right, if you really need a label to attach to my face, you can call me, Omnilogos. You'll have to earn my real name."

"Omnilogos?" Gladia murmured. Her brain felt slow and clumsy, but the word sounded familiar. It took her a few seconds to connect the word to her thoughts.

Finally she burst out, "You mean, *that* Omnilogos?"

"Today there are so many, too many, I admit it," he said, touching his chest, as though confessing a sin. "I was the first but I have no power over the others who have taken my name. Crackers, hackers, rebel teenagers, dreamers, psychopaths, dissatisfied middle-aged criminals, artists and virtual clowns -- many have taken my name or joined my cause for similar or discordant reasons. However, no one has my style."

The Omnilogos smiled and looked up, as if recalling an old memory. When he looked again at Gladia, his expression changed radically; a transformation almost impossible to conceive. The young man seemed to have aged ten years in an instant.

"I am a collector of hopes and peregrine truths, a shepherd of thoughts, ideas, projects and dreams too important not to be realized. I'm an abstract concept that has no body, no smell, no boundaries, no shape and no color. I am *the* Omnilogos."

Gladia had yet to recover from the avalanche of surprises. If what this guy said was true, she was sitting in front of a sort of living legend. The Omnilogos was a figure that everyone talked about but about whom no one really knew anything. Was he part of a terrorist organization? Or was she dealing with a single person? Perhaps he was none of these things, or all at the same time. Whoever she, he or it was, people blamed this abstract concept for crimes and at the same time praised it for outstanding discoveries such as the cure for osteosarcoma that it was said he or she had downloaded to some of the major research institutions of the planet.

When the Nobel Assembly at the Karolinska Institutet made public that they would award the Nobel Prize for medicine to anyone who proved to have created and spread that data, many waited for the Omnilogos to somehow show up in Stockholm to receive the prize. But a lot of people were disappointed that day.

Gladia was looking out of the window. She roused from her thoughts when she noticed that the boy was staring at her.

"The Omnilogos, then," she said, clearing her throat and moving uneasily in her seat. "Fine. Let's ... let's say you've sparked my interest. Aside from the fact that if you really are who you claim to be, then I'd be talking to a terrorist wanted in three continents, let's assume that I like this project of yours and that I decide to support it, putting aside all the legality and the bureaucracy. That's what you want, right? But why have you chosen SOL? Why me?"

"I've chosen you because you're the final piece of a puzzle started many years ago, Doctor. I've always wanted to do this thing my own way, without any compromise and without any constraints that would have limited my choices. Look, I could have given these schematics to the Pentagon or the Chinese PLA and I would have saved myself a lot of hard work, but my creation would have been crippled, corrupted, limited. I need visionaries, believers in the cause of space, just like you, Doctor. Only then will I be sure that what comes out of those abstract projections is really what I wanted, what I will be proud of."

Gladia turned once again to study the trigoy and its data.

The truth was that she didn't know what to say. Every second that passed, her curiosity and her uneasiness grew hand in hand. She had to take time and find out more about that matter.

"According to this data, your project seems to involve other companies and corporations, in addition to mine. Here, I see the Paragon Corporation, Gaia, the I & I ... and this Archetype Unlimited."

"Exactly."

"The CEO of Gaia, Mark Strutzenberg, is a friend of mine," she said, shaking her head. "If your idea is to rope in that old Kraut then I wish you good luck. You'll soon have your hands full of shit, I promise you."

"Mark can be a real son of a bitch, that's true, but he knows a good deal when he sees one."

"You mean you know him?"

"I mean we play chess when we don't tell dirty jokes. We have collaborated on several projects before. He has already said he will do his part."

Gladia pursed her lips, then stared at the Omnilogos intently.

"Did the old fart keep pulling on his La Flor Dominicana as if he had a noose around his neck?"

"La Flor Dominicana?" the Omnilogos repeated, smiling thinly. "Mark would smoke dirt before even touching a Double Claro. His hands don't linger on anything that's not a Maduro or an Oscuro. But you know this better than I do, right?"

Gladia nodded. The Omnilogos knew Mark.

"Well, congratulations. Now that's news. But you haven't convinced me yet. What about the I & I? I don't think it's really a company that you can rely upon too much these days. I've heard they're sailing through stormy water after the Joshua scandal."

"This is why they won't say no."

"I don't understand."

"I own the majority of their stock equity and I have several contacts at the upper levels of their management. Let's just say that in the past I made sure some unflattering information about the company filtered out when the right people were listening."

"You mean it'll be easier to blackmail them?"

"Blackmail them? No, of course we wouldn't do that. But I'm sure they'll have an open mind when they hear their biggest shareholder is promising to save them from doom."

"It really seems you've done your homework." Gladia moved the information in front of her as she spoke. "And what is this Archetype Unlimited? I've never heard of it."

"That is because it doesn't exist yet."

"What do you mean it doesn't exist yet?"

"That is exactly what I said."

She heard a finality in his tone that told her the subject was closed.

"All right, forget it. What about Paragon? I don't think they have anything to do with what you're looking for. They definitely don't produce artefacts related to the aerospace industry. How could they? They're specialized in pharmaceutical products."

"They'll produce what I say."

"Oh, really? And why is that?"

"They will do it because I am the Paragon Corporation."

Gladia was doing everything she could to appear in control of the situation. But the last ten minutes were just too much to digest. She realized that she was finding herself in the middle of a plan that had been hatched long before, whose dimensions were difficult to fathom.

If this guy was really what he claimed to be and if he really had access to these kinds of resources, then the project he was proposing was not a farce. It was a real possibility. And this, she suddenly realized, frightened her.

Many, many questions still remained unanswered.

Gladia turned off the device and the little pyramid rested gently in the palm of her hand. She handed it over to the Omnilogos without speaking.

There was silence for a while. Both of them stared at each other, without blinking.

"How much will it cost?" Gladia finally asked. She realized she was shaking.

"You want an estimate on what will likely be the single most expensive object in the history of mankind?"

"I want the truth."

"The truth is that I haven't the faintest idea."

"So this is a gamble. If I decide to embark on this thing it would probably mean the largest commitment of funds to one project that the SOL has ever made. Am I wrong?"

The Omnilogos nodded. "True, there are risks for you, for me, for your SOL and for all the people involved. Dr. Egea, you know better than I do that risks are an essential part of any bet worthy of the name. Listen to me. Use your imagination. I want you to focus on the bigger picture and not to think about what your company has to lose. I want you to think of what mankind has to gain. Think about what you have to gain. If you succeed in this endeavour, your name will be on people's mouths more often than good ol' Coca Cola."

The woman stared at the Omnilogos without saying a word, as still as a stone.

She thought of the lost debate and of the public's reaction. She thought of the bitter taste in her mouth and felt a growing sense of frustration that was eating away at her gut. She thought of the strange encounter and the guy who claimed to be the Omnilogos himself and she thought of his idea, his promises, his speech and his vision. Then she thought of Spine Woodside, his impeccable hairstyle, his handsome face, his square jaw and his stupid toothy grin.

"Becoming more famous than a soda," Gladia finally said, unable to suppress a smile.

She took an empty glass from a nearby shelf and handed it to the young man, pointing to the bottle of Chianti.

"It's always been my dream."

SPINE

2028

SPINE WOODSIDE TOOK the trigoy from his pocket.

From the other side of the oval table, three people looked at him; two men and a woman. Woodside waited for a few seconds, carefully evaluating them one by one.

In the dim light of the room, the woman was the closest thing to a giant praying mantis. Her eyes, large and bulbous, were closer to the tiny ears than to her short and pointed nose. She was wearing a pair of rectangular glasses with thick lenses which amplified the ice-blue of her eyes. She had thin and protruding lips, sealed and curled in a strange smile. It looked as if she was about to kiss or spit on someone else's face. Her head was a nearly perfect triangle that began with a long, sharp chin and ended with a forehead covered by a helmet of shaped hair.

The short man to her left was decidedly less noticeable. With a flat face, a broad forehead, and small watery eyes, he resembled a stray dog. His neck was bent and his shoulders hunched, as if he wanted to hide from someone. The man rubbed his hands together while his eyes darted from one side of the room to the other.

The last of the three seemed at ease with his feet on the table and his fingers knitted behind his head. The dark beard, short and symmetrical, easily got lost on his black skin. The black hair and skin were paired well with his black suit. If it had not been for the white, opaque matter of his eye and his silver tie, the man would have disappeared in the darkened room.

Woodside turned his gaze to the object in his hand, on which everybody's attention was focused. The Landist lit it with a gesture, letting it slip away from his fingers.

The trigoy spun on itself for a split second, then hovered in the air. It stopped about six feet from the floor.

The three-dimensional reproduction that appeared in front of them was both familiar and unwelcome at the same time.

A short person with dark hair and a sharp face was performing a deep bow.

"Good evening everyone. My name is Wei Wang."

Woodside motioned near the trigoy to raise the volume and magnify Wei's image.

"My name will tell you nothing," Wei continued, touching his chest. "I am only a stranger who knocks on your door to advertise a product. I like to consider myself as the last link in a chain forged long ago by the needs that nourish mankind. A chain made of ideas that has moved and continues to move our civilization beyond the boundaries of explored knowledge. Like all of the curious, brilliant and arrogant people who have preceded me, it is my belief that I can offer you all something you need but that nobody else has ever been able to give you."

Woodside fast-forwarded the projection for a few seconds. Wei appeared again, but in a completely different pose.

"The next step is to give flesh to the idea," Wei was saying, gesturing with his hands. "The inventor is working with a company that believes in his or her vision and that invests time and resources to develop, refine and test it. In ninety-nine per cent of the cases, the idea proves too volatile, fragile, and tenuous. What is the result? The idea is overwhelmed by reality's hardship and sinks into oblivion. But in the one per cent left, we find a world of possibilities hidden in uncharted territory, a challenge to be met."

Wei moved sinuously like a snake, as if he was trying to dodge an invisible bullet. Then he clasped his hands, throwing his arms up toward the ceiling of the room. Before their eyes the reproduction of a very old car magically appeared.

"In that one per cent rests the Model T, produced by Henry Ford in the early twentieth century, the first car cheap enough for the common middle-class American. It forever revolutionized the car industry, thanks to the introduction of the assembly line."

Wei paused, then moved his hands as he did earlier and from no-where produced a white symbol. It was a bitten apple.

"Steve Jobs, for those of you looking for a more recent example," Wei continued, pointing to the symbol. "His Macintosh in 1984 and the I-Phone in 2007 revolutionized the personal computer, telephone and music industry, among other things."

Wei turned around, like an Olympic diver preparing for a two-and-a-half somersault. He folded his arms and formed an X. The symbol of the bitten apple and the car disappeared into thin air and the focus of the viewers returned to him.

"Two men with two companies changed the lives of hundreds of millions of people. I, like them, had an idea and I have dedicated my life to making it real. But this idea is a bit different from all the others. First, it's different in its proportions. The two ideas of the past were each brought to life by a single company. On the other hand, I needed five multinationals just to make my own creation feasible."

Woodside moved his hand again and sent the projection forward. This time, Wei was pointing to something.

"Now imagine yourself finding two thousand dollars in a white envelope. I don't know about you, but I'd look around, pick up the envelope and go on my own way with a smile on my face. After the fluke, I would start thinking about how to use the money. Today, there are several ways to spend two thousand dollars." Wei moved his fingers, creating forms and imaginary figures. A series of images followed one another as he spoke.

"I can offer my buddies a dinner, I can buy groceries for three months, I can buy a non-stop plane ticket from Vancouver to New York or maybe a stay in a luxury residence for my girlfriend and I. Two thousand dollars will not change my life, but it'll surely make my day."

Wei put his hands behind his back. "Now imagine a world where with this amount of money I can also buy a ticket to see our planet … from the orbit of earth itself. No, it's not a movie ticket, it's a ticket to get on one of these."

Woodside enlarged the object that Wei was showing. The Landist narrowed his eyes to see more clearly, as if he was trying to memorize every detail.

"Welcome aboard!" Wei joined thumb and index finger of both hands to form a virtual picture frame. An oval object with several grooves on the surface instantly appeared in the frame. It looked like a gigantic dragon egg.

"What you're seeing is a magnified image of Polaris, ready to begin its ascension. Polaris is … well, it's hard to explain. I can't make any comparison because it is the first of its kind. Let's just say that it would be fair to call it an orbital car, or rather, an orbital wagon. What is its destination? It travels to an observatory several thousand miles above the earth's surface. What is its purpose? To open up to you the outstanding spectacle that is our planet."

Woodside fast-forwarded the projection once again. Polaris had disappeared. Wei was now sitting on a chair. A wide smile graced his face.

"Yes, I know. 'Science Fiction' is certainly not the trend of the moment." Wei stood up and began to walk. "We live in a world where some people want to deny us the right to reach for the stars. I am talking about the so-called Landists and their followers."

"Well, I have a new concept for all of them: to *dare*. Here, in front of all the people of earth, I declare that I am a Hyperist, a person who aspires to the stars. I am a Hyperist and I'm damn proud of it. I am a person who raises his head and sees new possibilities for our species, obstacles to overcome, battles to win. I know that when I look up, I see my long forgotten home. And I dare to think that one day I will reach it again. Stardust to stardust."

Wei clasped his hands and a sparkling powder that seemed made up of myriad multi-colored diamonds appeared in the room. The cloud of light slowly gathered in a few points until it started forming concrete shapes. They were letters. The sparkling powder so assembled forged the words: 'Stardust to Stardust'. It was a slogan and a declaration of war.

Woodside felt his heart beat faster, threatening to burst from his chest. He clenched his jaw and fast-forwarded the projection one more time.

Polaris, the orbital wagon mentioned by Wei, was again the center of focus. This time, however, it was not alone. It seemed somehow linked to a very long cable on which the wagon was moving at an ever increasing speed.

Wei was pointing to Polaris.

"After all," he was saying, "I'm talking about launching a satellite into a geostationary orbit and attaching it to a station in the Pacific

Ocean with a 22,000 mile long cable. This cable, ladies and gentlemen, will be just a few inches thick. On it will travel vehicles driven by inexhaustible energy capable of transporting people and material into earth's orbit. All of this at the cost of a plane ticket."

Wei paused for a moment and then said, "Most of you will be puzzled at this point, while others will probably be laughing. I understand you very well."

The Hyperist scratched his forehead. "It's odd for me, too, but not for the reason you're thinking." Wei joined his hands behind his back. "You see, some time ago, the writer Sir Arthur C. Clarke -- the author of *2001: A Space Odyssey* -- said that 'the space elevator will be built about fifty years after everyone stops laughing'. Well, my team and I stopped laughing a while ago, and we look forward to making Science Fiction your greatest adventure once again."

Woodside turned off the device and the three-dimensional image disappeared.

A long silence followed the last sentence.

The mantis woman adjusted her glasses, moistening her lips with the tip of her tongue. The short man shifted uncomfortably in his chair, looking around, as if he was desperate to find a window he could throw himself out of. The black man was an island of calm in a stormy sea. He toyed with his tie while keeping his feet on the table.

"Yesterday afternoon, any mammal linked to the Ether could see this fantastic commercial spot." Woodside spoke slowly, emphasizing each word carefully. "Now, I want to know who the hell is this Wei Wang, and what the fuck is he talking about. Arvin?"

The short man jumped to his feet, as if the chair had been kicked out from under him. The small and flickering eyes were fixed on the data in front of him.

"Wei Wang," squeaked Arvin, avoiding Woodside's blood-shot eyes, "born in Richmond, B.C., Canada, on January 1st, 2005. He moved three years later with his family to Orlando, Florida. His father, William, was a rope technician. His mother, Erika, was a housewife. Both died in a car accident when Wang was a child. After a short period in a children's home, he was adopted by a couple of professors in Pasadena, where the boy remained until the age of thirteen." Arvin cleared his throat. There was silence in the room.

"I'm listening," said Woodside, inviting the other to go on.

"That's ... erm ... all, sir," Arvin murmured, staring with scrupulous attention at his shoes. "I don't … we have no other information at the moment."

"That's all?" Woodside repeated, grasping the edge of the table with both hands. An intricate web of veins emerged on his neck. "This is what you've been able to find out in twelve hours on the most clicked person on the planet?"

Arvin looked at the mantis woman and the black man. His eyes seemed to beg for help. No one lifted a finger.

"S-sir," mumbled Arvin, short on words. His eyes were moving so fast that they seemed about to burst out of his head. "I—"

"You're fired!" Woodside bellowed.

"Sir, that's … this Wang is a damn puzzle!" Arvin tried to defend himself. "There's no bank account registered in his name, no medical report concerning him. He doesn't … he doesn't even appear in the database of any school. I did … I did what I could with the time given to me. I've got a group of people busy searching for any useful data related to Wang on the Ether and in loco. I have men in Richmond, Orlando and Pasadena as we speak."

"So you're running a cross-search of cyber and physical reports, huh?" Spine Woodside evaluated, carefully eyeing the sweaty man. "I like it, you're hired again."

Arvin collapsed into his chair, exhausted. He wiped the sweat from his forehead with a trembling hand.

"Tenoderia." Woodside turned to the woman. "Tell me that this is the biggest, shameless hype of this century. That thing"—he pointed to the spot where Polaris had appeared shortly before—"is clearly impossible, right?"

Tenoderia ran her slender fingers through her hair. She had incredibly long and well-groomed nails that ended with just a hint of scarlet red nail polish.

"I'm afraid not," she replied, staring at the trigoy. "Thirty minutes after the speech, the five companies named by the subject released a joint statement confirming to the press what he said. A few hours ago the named companies also issued generic schematics of some of the technologies introduced in the presentation."

For the second time Tenoderia let her tongue dart around her lips. Her bulbous eyes glowed with a strange light. She smiled in a perverse way, as if she were about to reveal a chilling secret to a friend.

"The subject, this … Wei Wang, he's not lying. I had little time to read the data, but the technologies he mentioned, the magnetic solar engine, the design of the device and the super-intelligent material the cable is made of are all theoretically possible, according to the information they gave us."

"You mean this guy is really building a thing like that somewhere in the Pacific Ocean?"

"No, I mean that anyone who has issued this information has solid scientific basis that supports him and a technology ten years ahead of anything I've seen in the fields of robotics, biochemistry, megastructures, nano engineering and renewable energy. The only direct evidence of Polaris, the orbital carrier described by the subject, is that provided in the presentation."

"For Christ's sake." Woodside ran a hand over his forehead. He found it cold and sweaty. "I was hoping for a good ol' 'you fell for it'."

The Landist turned toward the black man, imperturbable as ever.

"Komla! Jesus ... Would you like, I don't know ... a deckchair or would you prefer a damn mattress?"

Komla pulled his feet down and off the table but he didn't abandon his sly smile.

"Thaaaanks," Woodside said, shaking his head. "Now, have you got anything interesting for me?"

"This thing is on everyone's lips, Spine," Komla said, in a deep voice. "The birds tweet it, the dogs bark at it—"

"Yeah, yeah," Woodside cut him off, raising a hand and closing his eyes in exasperation. "And the cats meow at it. Good God, Komla! Spare us your penny humor, will you? I want to know what the buzz is on the *outside* of the zoo."

Komla leaned forward, placing both hands on the table. "Whoever designed this campaign is a genius. A genius, I tell you. The timing of the news, the way it's been released, the channels used and the information provided, all of this form a masterpiece of public relations like I've never seen in my whole life. If what Wang said in the presentation is true, the mere fact that such a thing has remained secret for nearly three years is incredible. If only the echo of a sigh would have leaked out, we would have known it. However, until a few hours ago, no one knew anything about this at all."

After a long pause, Komla went on, "I have a theory that explains how they managed to keep this thing a secret until yesterday. Spine, I think that most of the people involved in the project didn't even know what they were working on."

"What the hell are you talking about?"

"I'm saying that whoever has overseen this project has made sure that no information leaked out. It's … it's like making a movie by breaking down the script into separate parts. Every single actor is required to act in his or her scene, ensuring that he or she knows nothing about the general plot of the story. In the end, the director puts together the shots and gets his movie without the characters knowing anything about the script. As Tenoderia said before, this space elevator is the sum of different components, but developed in areas related to each other. Consider this new super-material Wang describes in the presentation. It can potentially be used in any field, but he decided to use it as the backbone of his invention."

Woodside scratched his neck as he brooded on what he'd heard. His gaze fell on the trigoy.

The Landist stretched out his arm, turned the pyramid shaped object on and began to scan the projection once again. He stopped at the time when Wei was using his fingers to evoke images, videos and sounds. He looked like a snake charmer, he thought, amazed.

Woodside put a fingernail between his teeth and began to chew nervously. He saw the presentation two, three, four times then stopped the trigoy while Wei conjured the slogan, 'Stardust to stardust'.

"Damn it!" Woodside exploded, indicating the projection to the others. "I can't see any trigo-projector around him."

"Mmm. I don't think he's using one," Komla said, toying with his goatee.

That answer brought a bitter twist to Woodside's mouth. "No? And how in hell can he play with those … things? How can he evoke images out of thin air, hmm? Is he a fucking magician?"

"Could be," Arvin ventured, looking hypnotized by the way Wei moved his arms.

Woodside grunted and turned to Tenoderia, a hint of hope in his eyes.

The woman shook her head. "He's not using a trigoy, that's obvious. He's not even using a source, or any other type of projector that we know."

"Then *what* is he using?"

Tenoderia shrugged.

Woodside returned to gnawing at his nail and rewound the projection. He listened to the moment when Wei declared himself a Hyperist, then stopped the video again.

"This story of the Hyperist ... does anyone know what he's talking about? What's a Hyperist, anyway?"

"A person who aspires to the stars," Arvin answered promptly, quoting Wei.

Woodside threw him a withering look. Arvin's eyes were downcast.

Komla indicated the projection. "Shortly after his speech, some provinces of the Ether merged into a region called HYPER. The merger came about a bit too fast not to look like something organized. It could be linked to the concept of Hyperist inaugurated by Wang."

"HYPER?" repeated Woodside.

"Yes." Komla nodded. "It includes blogs, websites, social networks and other units and utilities of cyberspace. Apparently they all had one thing in common ... well, being opposed to the Landists."

"How big is this HYPER?"

"The last time I saw it this morning, it counted about 27,000 subscriptions, 110,000 users—"

Komla was interrupted by Woodside. "Forget it. How many are there now?"

Tenoderia touched her glasses with a flick of the hand that spoke of old habit. Her eyes moved quickly up and down, right and left.

When she finished reading, she took off her glasses, rubbed her eyes and said nothing for a few seconds.

"Well?" Woodside asked, drumming his fingers on the table.

The woman put her glasses back on and straightened her back. "Right now three regions of the Ether have merged under the effigy HYPER. The number of users and subscriptions is growing rapidly and—"

"How many are there?"

Tenoderia cleared her throat. "995,000 subscriptions, seven million users, sixty-four million accesses..."

Woodside stopped her with a raised arm. "I got it, I got it ..." he faded off into a whisper.

The Landist clasped his hands over his mouth and nose. He stood still and silent for half a minute. Nobody else spoke.

All of a sudden, Woodside clapped his hands and shook his head to clear it.

"All right, folks, one thing at a time. Let's go back ... let's go back to that thing ... that space elevator, or whatever it's called. I mean, what are we exactly talking about here? Is it even possible to build it? How does it work? Why have I never heard of it before?"

Tenoderia crossed her legs and straightened her shirt. "The basic principle of a space elevator is quite simple to imagine. If you tie a string to a tennis ball and twirl the string above your head it will remain taut and straight as long as the twirling motion is perpetuated. The earth is spinning faster than your hand could ever manage, about 1000 miles per hour. If you anchor an incredibly resistant ribbon or cable to the earth's surface at the equator, and then attach the other end to a large enough mass -- for example, a space station or a small asteroid -- to keep it taut, you end up with a railroad track right into space. Once constructed and set up, wagons can ride it up and down via some sort of powered rails, or the ribbon itself could be the rail, with the wagon crawling up the cable with clamp-on wheels, thus easily delivering cargo into orbit without the use of expensive rockets."

"Wagons such as Polaris?" asked Komla.

"Exactly." The woman nodded. "With that type of carrier available, we could considerably reduce the cost of travel between earth and space. The space elevator idea is theoretically simple to implement but with an important complication. The structural stress that the cable would have to bear would be immense. No existing material has the properties required to meet this need. At least ... well, at least not until yesterday afternoon ..."

"When that clown came up with his 'fictionite' idea," Woodside finished for her while repeatedly tapping his fingers on the table. "What do we know of this material that would make his spatial devilry possible?"

"Not much," the woman admitted. "As I said, information is still being processed. This super-material should work like an extremely sophisticated artificial intelligence, capable of adapting to external physical and atmospheric conditions with the sole purpose of keeping itself both lightweight and incredibly resistant. Technically, the cable is made of special carbon nanotubes held together by a cybernetic system that is responsible for maintaining its stability, and if necessary of modifying its physical properties. This 'fictionite', as you called it, not only has the tensile strength needed to support the weight of this huge 'bridge', but is also capable of resisting abrasion, adverse weather conditions and cosmic and solar radiation without losing its basic properties, lightness and strength. The cable also has a system of automatic maintenance. This means that if something were to ultimately damage or alter the chemical properties of the nanotubes, a specific program, similar to an anti-virus, would launch a diagnosis identifying the problem and solving it. Theoretically, this cable is almost indestructible."

Woodside shook his head. He wasn't convinced. "I don't give a rat's ass how technologically advanced this damn thing of yours is or how many elephants this sparkling awesome ribbon can support. We're not in Wonderland, dammit! At a certain point, everything breaks! Gentlemen, we are talking about an object longer than the circumference of the planet! You got that? What would happen if this enormous object were to break and fall on our heads?"

"I can't say I have a satisfactory answer to that," Tenoderia replied cautiously. "It would largely depend on the exact physical properties of the material used to build the cable -- information we are not currently aware of. It would also depend on the location of the space elevator, the exact point where this supposed break would happen, and a multitude of other factors. It could be an isolated incident with few or no casualties or a global catastrophe."

"For Christ's sake! Are you listening to yourself? I'm getting goose bumps! Do you realize the gravity of the situation? If this Wei Wang is really capable of doing this, we are facing the most dangerous psychotic megalomaniac of the century. This asshole is risking the safety of human life for the simple pleasure of a little advertising. It's absurd! We need to start throwing everything we've got at him before this thing gets out of hand."

"Spine, listen to me, please," Komla said, raising a hand, "SOL's and Gaia's shares rose by nine per cent in the last five hours. Ordinary people from all over the world are following the invitation launched by Wang, buying in bulk the 'book the stars' package advertised in yesterday's presentation. Other companies at this very moment are investigating the data regarding the technologies in the orbital elevator, to evaluate the opportunity to collaborate on the project or start one of their own. If this product has the potential that we have seen and is already at an advanced stage of development, we are talking about the news of the century."

Woodside stared at him.

"Come on, don't look at me like that," Komla said, shaking his head. "You know I'm right. People are now excited rather than scared, it's important that you understand that. They want to know everything they can about the scoop of the moment, and they want to speculate and to dream. They want to be part of it all. Imagine snatching a huge candy bar from the hands of a hungry child, telling him that it does damage to his teeth. Shouting out to the public that this thing is dangerous may not be the right move to make at this time. If you want to go against this thing, you'd better be well prepared. Let's wait till the child gets a bad stomach ache."

"Jesus, Joseph and Mary, Komla, I pray to God that your plan is better than your comparisons. Go ahead, what's your idea?"

"Sooner or later, the excitement will fade and the common person will start asking what one usually asks when there is so much at stake, especially in a huge project like this: 'What if something goes wrong?' Well, we'll be ready to answer that question, pointing out the flaws and dangers of the space elevator, flooding the media and the information channels with our version of the story. There are also other factors to consider before unleashing an offensive. This project has natural enemies. I guarantee you they just need an excuse to throw everything they've got at Wang and his friends."

"I'm not following you."

"Think about it," Komla said. "How do you think that Kinoper, BT or Extros Mobil will react to all of this when they realize that along with tourism and space exploration, the main purpose of Polaris is to promote the use of renewable energy? If Wang is right about the potential of his invention, in less than a decade the CEOs of companies like these will have to get a real job."

"God is my witness, it seems like—"

Spine Woodside was interrupted by Tenoderia, who suddenly raised her hand.

"We're getting new output from the Ether," she said, looking carefully at her glasses, as if she was reading a book.

All waited without speaking.

After a few moments Tenoderia looked at Woodside with an unreadable expression.

"The CCTV has just made it known that a satellite of no specific characteristics will be launched in a week from the Xichang Space Launch Center in China. The launch was requested by the I & I and has just been approved by the government."

"The I & I. Wasn't that one of the five companies named by Wang?" Arvin asked with a trembling voice.

"It's already started," Komla murmured in disbelief. "Wang is doing it for real."

"It's all happening too fast!" Woodside jumped up from his chair and began pacing. "We have to keep up, be focused on what to do and on how to do it."

The Landist massaged his temples and closed his eyes. When he opened them again, his gaze suggested urgency and determination.

"OK, listen up." He pointed to Arvin. "Time is of the essence. You've got twenty-four hours to get your hands on something useful. I don't care how you do it, but I want to know everything about this Wang. Everything! When you bring me his pants, I hope for you they're full of shit! Is that clear?"

"Cle ... Y-yes, sir."

It was Tenoderia's turn.

"Analyze Wang's data," Woodside ordered. "Analyze it well. Find me reasons why this space elevator should never be built. If you don't find any, do more analyzing. There's something important that we're not getting in all this, I can feel it, and this thing just can't be the miraculous invention that wordsmith is advertising."

"Very well," said Tenoderia, nodding.

"Komla, work your magic. Act on people's doubts and hesitations. Mobilize any contact you have and as soon as you get useful info from Tenoderia, give it to anyone who can put it to good use."

Komla gave him a thumbs up. "You got it, boss."

"As for me," Woodside went on, "if there's a reason why LAND exists, it is to prevent this kind of madness from happening. This *Hyperist* has no idea of the ocean of shit he's going to drown in."

CANTARA

2029

GLADIA EGEA POINTED out the images projected by the trigoy to the man gnawing at his cigar.

"Woodside and his lackeys couldn't have possibly chosen a better time to spread their message on the Ether." Gladia touched the back of her neck. "There are people who already speak of burning the headquarters of the Gaia, the SOL and the I & I to the ground to prevent the launch."

Mark Strutzenberg breathed noisily. After a while, a jet of smoke came from his nostrils, for a few seconds obscuring his broad face. The man absently scratched his platinum-colored beard. "Well, can't say the landfuckers don't have a sense of humor, eh?" he murmured, staring at the pictures. The tip of his cigar exploded for a second of bright orange light while the man inhaled nicotine and exhaled the smoke from his mouth. He bit his lower lip. "Spine has finally decided to come out of his hole and use his nuclear weapons," he concluded dryly.

The co-founder of the SOL gave Mark an annoyed look, not particularly happy with the metaphor he used to describe the situation.

"This leaves us very little room to maneuver. We're running out of time." Gladia huffed, scratching her forehead while still staring at the trigoy's data. "The Planetary Court's decision is scheduled for next Friday."

Mark Strutzenberg grunted at that statement. Gaia's CEO stared at the flux of information in front of him with much more than simple attention: the vertical line that furrowed his brow spoke of nervousness, confusion and plain irritation.

"Well, this doesn't help a bit, that's for sure," he said. "The members of the Court contrary to the launch were waiting for something like this to throw buckets of shit against Polaris. They could point to this to screw up all our efforts." A pause, then the man added, "As if we didn't have enough to think about already." Mark turned to face Gladia. "Have you received Shimao's report?" he asked, looking intently with an expression that didn't leave much room for interpretation.

Gladia nodded gravely and stared back. "Of course I have. Bad news never comes alone." Silence followed. Gladia closed her eyes for a few seconds. When she opened them again, the muscles of her face showed stress and fatigue. She swallowed hard and licked her dry lips. "Shimao, Trudeau and Nazarov are doing what they can with the time and resources they've got," she said, trying not to sound resigned. "I'm confident they'll be able to solve Infinity's structural problems but we can't ask them for miracles. Woodside's allegations will turn them into the favorite topic of the etheric grape vine and we can't do much to prevent that."

There was silence again, punctuated by a few heartbeats. Then Mark said, hesitantly, "What does our young man ..." Abruptly he cut himself off. His mouth was still open, but it seemed he lacked the spit to continue talking. He straightened his back and cleared his throat, then resumed, lowering his tone to the point that Gladia had difficulty hearing. "What does he think of Spine's move?"

The woman held her breath. She put both hands on her hips and looked away from Mark. "Wei doesn't know anything about what's happening and I made sure that it stays that way."

Mark jerked his head toward Gladia so suddenly that his cigar almost darted from his mouth.

"*What?*" cried the man — his eyes were two huge, bloodshot bulbs threatening to explode out of his skull.

Gladia calmly replied to her colleague's surprise. "Wei has enough on his hands right now," she said, shifting her weight from one foot to the other. "He doesn't have time to spare in order to personally take care of this. Don't look at me like that, old man. You know I'm right. Also, I've already thought through how to deal with Woodside. We don't need Wei to babysit us. We can deal with this ourselves."

For a long time, Mark looked at the projections surrounding the trigoy. Then he went back to study Gladia's expression. "I pray to God that you know what you're doing, woman." He waved a hand, inviting her to keep talking. "What's the plan?"

"We have to catch up. *Quickly*," settled Gladia, drumming her fingers on her hips, "and in order to do so, we need to resort to exceptional measures."

"*How* exceptional?" Mark asked, two deep greenish shadows besieging his eyes. A piece of ash broke away from his cigar and fell to the ground. Neither of them noticed it.

"Enough to involve someone who can turn the situation around and give us some space," Gladia said. "This is a battle that has moved faster than we ever thought possible from the talk shows to the public opinion. We didn't see this coming. Up until the last moment Woodside has made us believe he was a fool, hungry for applause, just to give us *this* gift at the last minute. He took us completely by surprise, we can't deny it." Gladia pointed to the pictures with a slow movement of her head. "We underestimated that sophist and the charlatans around him and now we are paying the consequences. We need someone who can rescue us quickly from this situation and who at the same time can put enough pressure on the Planetary Court to save Polaris and Infinity."

Mark looked at the doctor with an expression that betrayed skepticism. "And let's hear it. Who would you have in mind in order to make this miracle happen?"

Gladia waited an outrageously long time. Finally she said, "Does the name *Cantara* ring a bell?"

Mark's jaw twitched. "Cantara Handal? The Black Widow of the Ether?" The man spat out the name as if the words were made of acid. He stepped back without even realizing it. "You're kidding me, *right?* That woman would dismember her daughter for a few dozen subscriptions to her region!"

"She *would* have dismembered her daughter," remarked Gladia. All of a sudden, she seemed ten years older. "That's the problem. It seems that Cantara has abandoned her Ether-related business, confining herself to some kind of ... isolation from the media, so to speak."

"Confined," Mark repeated, clearly surprised. "You mean ... you mean she retired? At her age?"

"As far as I know, you can't retire from a job like hers. But Cantara has apparently suspended her involvement on the Ether, delegating her business to someone else. Now it seems that all she does is give private lessons to a bunch of teenagers. We don't know much more."

"She went from world famous etherion to babysitter? This story reeks of dirty underwear," Mark said, grunting. "Anyway, who talked you into involving her in this mess?"

Gladia licked her dry lips again. "I spoke with Gregor and the Board of Propaganda, at the public relations department. According to the smart folks, bringing Cantara to our side could mean a huge difference for us. We are losing this media war, Mark. Think about it! It makes sense to get one of the most influential etherions on the planet to stand on our side. I'm planning to talk to her tomorrow."

"The public relations folks have suggested this? Are they insane? I don't see how the solution to our problems could be that ... that ... *woman*."

"Despite her withdrawal, Cantara continues to have a strong presence on the Ether and a very particular impact on the slice of public opinion that has remained neutral until now," Gladia said, her eyes blank while fixing on the far side of the room. "There is an ocean of people who listen to what she says and trust her judgment. Not to mention the special relationships she has with many of the most influential etherions. That woman is a real treasure trove of resources."

Mark did not seem convinced. "Even if that's the case, why should you be the one to talk to her?"

"Public relations discovered that Cantara shows respect for enterprising female figures with an attitude: '*women with balls*', according to what Gregor says." Gladia made a half bow, as if she were introducing herself to an audience.

Mark's face suddenly relaxed in a wicked smile. "Modesty aside, of course," he said, pointing to his colleague with his cigar.

"Of course," Gladia answered, smiling back. "However, Gregor stressed that Cantara seems to especially respect my position and that she knows my personal history very well. In short, it seems that I intrigue her. This makes me the Hyperist with more possibilities of getting her on our side."

Mark continued to maintain his frown. He looked once more to the trigo-projector and pointed to the images. "You mean, she could be *our* atomic bomb?"

"Something like that."

Mark slowly breathed in and crossed his arms. He seemed to wait for Gladia to say something else, but she remained silent.

"Right. So, what are you up to?" he finally asked. "How are you going to convince her to come out of her hole and help us?"

Gladia looked at the man. She raised her eyebrows and a smile flashed across her face. "I have studied her psychophysical profile very carefully. It seems that Cantara demonstrates a propensity to be involved in something bigger than herself, in projects where one person can make a difference. This ... behaviour of hers, is very special, something that I can work on, something I can bend to our advantage."

"I don't get it," Mark said, shaking his head. "How could that be helpful to us?"

"I'm going to make her an offer she can't refuse," Gladia said, winking at the puzzled man.

Mark frowned again. "Does this *offer* include a gun and the threat of brains scattered over a contract?"

"No." Gladia shook her head, barely holding back a grin. "Let's just say I will offer her the opportunity to watch a show that will give her a lot to think about."

Mark waited once more for Gladia to continue. He waited in vain. "Well?" he asked with increasing impatience, twisting his beard. "Are you going to make me die of curiosity?"

"You seem agitated, old Kraut." Gladia pointed to his cigar. "Breathe. I suggest that you turn on another one of your bazookas and relax. We wouldn't want your blood pressure skyrocketing, would we? Trust me, you have nothing to worry about."

Mark shook his head and flashed a grin. He took two steps forward and pointed to the woman with a finger. "This is your way of keeping me out of the party? Nice try, but I'm going to do my part. If Spine has decided to bombard us, I could buy you a few extra days throwing everything at him that I've got."

"No, Mark, I want you to stay put. Listen to me. The last thing we need now is to throw fuel on the fire. Furthermore, this is my prerogative. I am the coordinator of the Polaris project and I'm going to do this thing my way."

Mark didn't answer, but one corner of his mouth twitched. He seemed undecided on what to do.

"I have a bad feeling about this whole thing," Mark admitted in the end, shaking his head. The man pressed the burning end of his cigar in the ashtray and put an end to the stream of smoke that had flooded the room with its exotic aroma.

"Mark, you've got a bad feeling on any matter at any time," Gladia said as she turned the trigoy off and caught the object with a quick wave of her hand.

"Statistically speaking, this proves me right fifty per cent of the time," Mark pointed out, a sly smile on his broad face.

Gladia pocketed the device and started toward the door. "Well, my old friend," she said before leaving the room, "let's pray that this time you're dead wrong."

∞∞∞∞

Cantara Handal looked at the seven students in a semicircle around her and crossed her arms. "Well?" she asked, her eyes lingering on each of them. "Does anyone have any ideas?"

The students looked at one another for a few seconds. Then, seven arms shot up almost at the same time.

Cantara smiled. She looked to her right. "Angelica," she said, nodding toward the girl and inviting her to speak.

Angelica was tall and lean, with almond-shaped eyes partially hidden by the glare of light reflected by her glasses. She looked at the trigo-projection in front of them.

"I don't think ... I believe ..." Angelica paused for a second, thinking hard on her next words. She breathed in and cleared her throat, then continued, "I think that the four units we're examining have no mutual affinity and that they'll probably never reach the merging process. There's more. Judging by the preliminary analysis, they'll probably disappear in the coming weeks. I also think that we should spend no more time studying them. It seems to me a waste of resources that could be better used in other directions."

"You said one correct thing and two wrong," ruled Cantara, clasping her hands behind her back and evaluating the young girl. The other students followed her with their eyes as she approached the trigo-projection which was showing charts, numbers and images. The woman pointed to the data with a nod.

"Forget everything you think you know about their past performances. Concentrate instead on their Baussial curve. Judging by their etheric reciprocity, the four units have much more in common than may seem from the simple preliminary analysis. Now, remind me: what is it that I always say about the merging process?"

Angelica immediately responded to that question. "In the merging process, the first impression is always the wrong one."

Cantara nodded and waved a hand. A new three-dimensional graph appeared in front of them.

"Exactly. Also, you're wrong in saying that the units will disappear in the short to medium term," the woman continued, moving an index finger and highlighting some parts of the graph. "Their activity hasn't grown much in the past few days, true, but this doesn't necessarily mean that the units are about to shrink or disappear. If you take into account the column of interactivity, you can clearly see that the number of subscriptions has now stabilized to over five hundred per day. See here and here? They are no longer trying to expand; they are trying to solidify and to hold their ground. In a nutshell, they're striving to balance each other, even if it means for now that they must sacrifice their size and the number of subscriptions. It's a clever move. Whoever the architects are of these units, it is clear that they're looking at the broad picture. Their aim is to eliminate inconsistencies and find a common ground on which to develop in order to aspire to the rank of province."

Cantara turned slowly, her back now facing the class, and headed toward the desk. Once in front of the table, she picked up a steaming cup and gingerly drank the contents. The unmistakable fragrance of green tea relaxed her senses. For a few seconds, there was no other sound but the woman's slow sipping.

Meanwhile, behind her, some students were nodding as they revisited the graph explained by Cantara. A couple of them moved their hands quickly to add impressions, images and sounds to their devices.

Cantara put her cup down and swallowed. She raised her head, straightened her back and looked in front of her.

The circular shaped mirror on the wall of the room caught her attention. The woman spent a few moments to assess her reflection.

Cantara Handal was a tall, slim woman, with thin arms and long legs. Her slender and sinuous body made her seem a rare cross between a model and an ice skating dancer.

She ran a hand over her face, caressing her honey-colored skin. The features of her face were as sharp as the blade of a knife and almost accurately pinpointed the boundaries of her high and pronounced jaw. Her beautiful eyes were a triumph of green streaked with silver grey. Her whole face was crowned with a heavy mask of makeup, the color of the night that stretched toward the temples and almost reached the ears, giving her the look of an Egyptian queen.

There were many who might argue that Cantara was one of the most attractive public figures on the planet and that she could have been even more beautiful if it had not been for her completely shaved head and her completely hairless face. No one knew why Cantara had banished hair from her life. It was one of the mysteries that added to the many others that surrounded her, such as the meaning of the pendant, shaped like an hourglass, that she always wore as though it were a wedding ring.

Her sensual but dangerous appearance, her known predilection for dark and green colors along with her reputation as a ruthless etherion had earned her the nickname the 'Black Widow of the Ether'.

Cantara touched her lips, two inviting and soft portions of skin dressed up by a bronze colored lipstick. Then, for no apparent reason, she began to bite the edge of her lips. When she felt the taste of blood in her mouth, she ran a thumb over the wound and in silence contemplated the crimson red exhibited on her finger. Finally, she took a handkerchief from her pocket and covered her wound.

Cantara breathed in through her nose and out her mouth. She looked away from the mirror and turned around again, facing the class.

When she looked back to Angelica, a satisfied smile lit up her face.

"However," she said, "You're right in saying that devoting attention to this imminent merger is a waste of resources. Whatever will arise out of it, it's still too early to make predictions about its usefulness for our region. Better to wait for future developments while keeping our eyes open."

Angelica nodded, a thoughtful expression on her face.

Cantara clapped her hands a couple of times, then spread her arms, as if to welcome the whole class. "Very well. Now, let's analyze last week's subject." The woman extended an arm toward the trigoprojector and the object was attracted by her open hand. Cantara pocketed the trigoy and looked back at one of her students. "Sebastian, remind the class of our subject."

Sebastian, a boy with short-cropped hair and an expression that suggested a seriousness not appropriate for his age, stood up. "Yes, Madame," the boy said, lifting his chin and inflating his chest. "You requested that we consider the following phrase: *Now and then: From the conservative Internet to the everlasting Ether.*

"Phenomenal," Cantara said, clasping both hands behind her head as she rested her back on the desk. "Sebastian, let's start with your work. Illustrate for the class your analysis. Start with your sources, then continue with the synopsis and close with your own conclusions. You have five minutes from now."

Cantara turned her thumb up and a countdown appeared.

Sebastian looked at the numbers in red hanging over their heads. He cleared his throat and took his trigoy from his pocket. When he tossed it into the air, the little pyramid-shaped object positioned itself at the exact center of the room. Pictures and letters began to swirl around the trigo-projector.

"For my research," Sebastian began, putting his hands in his pockets and nodding to the data, "I consulted a number of sources and interviewed half a dozen people involved in the media and specialized in Ether-related sectors. In my thesis, I consider the evolution from the Internet to the modern Ether as a gradual transition from one type of worldwide computer network to a virtual community of people connected directly to each other via one or several regions of the cyberspace. In my analysis ..."

"Your eyes, Sebastian: Look your audience in the *eyes.*" Cantara pointed to the other students with a green enamelled nail.

Sebastian paused for a second, then shifted his gaze to the rest of the students who were watching him carefully. Sebastian's cheeks took on a tinge of red, but the boy did not let the nagging feeling disrupt his performance. When he spoke again, his voice was as calculated and steady as the CEO of a multinational, intent on explaining the latest quarterly report.

Cantara continued sipping the content of her cup as she nodded occasionally at what Sebastian was saying. When the countdown signaled just over one minute left, Cantara raised her hand and squeezed it into a fist.

"OK, Sebastian. Could you express your final thoughts?"

Sebastian glanced at the remaining time. He cleared his throat then looked back at the rest of the class. "In my opinion, the transformation undergone over time from this global system of interconnection between devices has reached a stage where the control has shifted from a physical device to the organic consciousness of individuals who today are directly connected to the Ether. This type of evolution from the technology to the organic will open the possibility to process and to share in the future virtual world not only images, colors and smells, but also feelings and emotions. The Ether may soon become the catalyst for a whole new way to define the very meaning of virtual and real interrelation and, in time, to merge the two concepts."

Sebastian sat down. The room remained quiet for a few seconds.

Cantara took a couple of steps toward the students. She stopped a few inches from Sebastian.

"I can't give you more than a Delta in posture and exposition," she said, looking steadily at the student without blinking. "Sebastian, you need to learn to look into the eyes of your audience or of your interlocutor and to stop hiding your hands in your pockets. Just clasp them behind your back if you can't hold back the tremor. This gives you a better posture and elegance. In a public debate, these qualities of presentation could make the difference between victory and defeat."

Cantara read embarrassment and frustration on the boy's face, but not resignation. In that moment, a small hurricane was probably raging inside Sebastian's brain, she thought. She left her words hanging in the air and then continued, her face slightly more relaxed. "You deserve however, a Gamma for the approach you have chosen to analyze the essence of the subject. You did a great job in reviewing the sources and your conclusion is plausible, given the premise of your argument. But sometimes you have to risk something to give more originality to your work. You must understand that standing on the shoulders of giants is not always a good idea. Learn to trust your instincts and remember that you're telling a story: a *story*, Sebastian. You can better sell your point of view if you show the audience a calculated range of emotions, rather than a simple list of data and statistics."

Cantara walked away from the boy. "All right, Asha," she said, turning to the girl next to Angelica. "Show us what you've put together. You have five minutes from now."

It was with well concealed pride that Cantara listened for the next twenty-five minutes to intelligent, witty and never predictable expositions, one after the other.

Her pupils had made progress by leaps and bounds, she thought, but the kind of life they had chosen was not simple at all. In order to be an etherion -- a shepherd of the public opinion -- sacrifice and unparalleled mental effort would be required of them. It was a constant challenge to expand their own awareness and skill, in a competition with other aspiring etherions contending for professional standing and public acceptance as opinion leaders. Only a handful of them would ultimately be successful and an insignificant percentage of this fraction would make a real difference. In a world like theirs, failure and success might be two equally dangerous sides of the same coin.

"Let's think about this point for a while," Cantara finally said, indicating with her emerald nailed, talon-like hand, the last student who had just finished speaking. "Lucius's hypothesis is quite interesting, isn't it? To consider what once was known as the 'network' no longer as a simple virtual hangout where you can connect and exchange information, but as a chessboard on which countless pieces are arranged and controlled by different players who collide against each other. The contenders in this match are therefore committed to doing everything to checkmate their opponents. Now let's try to push this concept beyond its boundaries. Can some of you tell me what the important implication of Lucius's exposition is, if taken to the extreme? Hmm? What would happen if the Ether really became a huge battlefield?"

The hand of James Ark, the boy at the far left of the semicircle of students, was the only one to rise.

Cantara turned toward the skinny, short boy dressed all in black, with the usual dark glasses hiding his eyes.

"James," Cantara called, inviting the student to speak.

While keeping her eyes on the boy, the woman licked her lips with a slow, obscene gesture reminiscent of the movement of a feverish and excited arachnid preparing to suck the belly of a prey.

The boy lowered his arm. "It means that the Ether can be conquered," he said.

Silence followed those words. For an instant, the woman could swear she saw a wry smile flashing on the boy's face, but the next instant she was sure she'd only imagined it.

Cantara looked away from the pupil. She nodded toward the class, visibly pleased. "It means that the Ether can be conquered," she repeated, pointing to James. "It means that the Ether could become a battleground in which those who manage to conquer and stabilize more regions under a single hegemony have an unprecedented control over ..."

A beep coming from her arm interrupted her. Cantara took some time to understand what it was. Then she touched her wrist and said in a clearly irritated tone, "What is it, Ebony? I asked not to be disturbed."

"Madame, your appointment with Dr. Egea is scheduled in fifteen minutes."

Cantara's eyes widened. Without realizing it, she had completely lost track of time.

The etherion sighed and clapped her hands a couple of times.

"Right. Well, time's up. You can go," she said looking at her students. "James, we haven't had time to hear your exposition. Leave your file in my In-Stat. I'll have a look at it tomorrow."

James nodded and transferred his file in the input station with two quick movements of his hand. The input station glowed with a scarlet light to emphasize the presence of a new file not yet read.

The students quickly gathered their things and left the room. Cantara waited until the door was closed.

"Control," she said when she was alone, addressing the ceiling. "Return to the office configuration."

When the last word was spoken, the room came alive.

The chairs and the seven input stations arranged in a semicircle in the center of the room were absorbed by the floor while the large desk was disassembled and reshaped in a more compact and elegant version. Two armchairs and two tables emerged where the input stations had been and a minibar appeared where a few seconds before there had been nothing but empty space.

The room completed the new configuration just in time before a voice from everywhere and nowhere announced Gladia Egea, cofounder of the SOL, second vertex of the Hexahedron and the coordinator of the Polaris project. Shortly, there was a knock on the outer door and an older woman stepped in.

Cantara stepped toward her guest and shook her hand, then

pointed to one of the armchairs.

"Gladia Egea, it is an honor," the Madame said, smiling. "Would you like some tea or coffee?"

"Hot water with lemon wedges, thanks," Gladia said with a polite smile as she sat down.

Cantara walked to the small minibar. She returned a few seconds later with two steaming cups and a glass filled with lemon wedges.

When both were seated, Cantara looked unflinchingly at the other woman, evaluating her very carefully. She took a sip from her drink then placed her cup on the nearby table. "I am confused," Cantara began, exhibiting a forced smile, "I heard that Wei Wang personally harasses the people that he needs. It's been all day that I've been expecting him to jump out of my wardrobe or a drawer. But no, I deserve only the visit of his second in command." She pointed to Gladia with one of her bright fingernails, while adding a sugar cube to her cup. She then concluded, "Well? Should I consider myself offended?"

There was not really any trace of irritation in her voice, only a slight tinge of sarcasm.

"Madame Handal …" Gladia began.

"Cantara, please," she said. "Let's leave the formalities at the door."

Gladia nodded, then resumed. "Cantara, I will be very frank. The first Hyperist knows nothing of this visit, and even less of …" She paused, as if to find the most appropriate word, then continued, "… of the *information* disclosed by Woodside and his followers. I have personally seen to it that he remain unaware of all this."

Cantara stared at her guest. "*Unaware?* How is this even possible? The news has been out for more than twenty-four hours. My table knows of what we're talking about! Is Wang still on our planet or has he found a way to ascend prematurely to the stars?"

Gladia smiled a thin smile. "The first Hyperist is currently engaged in a matter that requires all of his attention. I decided not to distract him with the rumors that are raging on the Ether."

"Rumors," Cantara repeated, as if the phrase had been very poorly worded. "That's a huge understatement to describe Woodside's counter-offensive. My dear doctor, these *rumors* are the reason why Polaris will never rise. I would rather call it the uppercut that puts an end to the boxing match. Not that I'm personally interested in the matter," she pointed out, spreading her arms.

"That having been said," she continued while absently touching the rim of her cup with her thumb, "it seems clear that anyone who has a pair of ears knows that the Landists are eating you guys alive. I don't see how an *intelligent* person like you can ignore such a fact."

"That ... Woodside's allegations have raised some interest among the public and in some of the members of the Planetary Court is undeniable, but I would wait before jumping to conclusions." Gladia tilted her head a few inches. It was her turn to smile. "You know what they say in this kind of situation: 'listen to everything, believe nothing'. I don't see how a person as *cautious* as you are can ignore a saying like that."

The last sentence lingered in the air for a few seconds.

"Touché!" Cantara finally exclaimed, nodding toward her guest and placing her hands under her chin theatrically.

"And that's exactly why I'm here," Gladia continued, indicating the other woman.

"You get straight to the point!" Cantara said, crossing her legs and looking at Gladia with a toothy grin. Never taking her eyes off her guest, she put her lips on her cup and sipped the contents. She took a moment to breath in the fragrance from the cup, then continued, "The kind of woman I prefer."

Cantara swallowed and then set the cup aside. "Allow me to be as frank as you were," she said, leaning toward her guest and clasping her hands, "I'm sure you have heard rumors of my early retirement. I am enjoying this time away from the annoying background noises of everyday life, trying to instill common sense into young minds that are not yet completely corrupted by modern society. I have no intention of entering into the game again, let alone into *this* kind of game. I'm sorry," she concluded, sounding anything but. Her smile was a long curve that went from ear to ear. "You seem to have come all this way for a cup of hot water and a few slices of lemon."

Gladia moved slightly in her chair. "May I ask you why? I mean, I'm curious. There are advantages and disadvantages in the ..."

"Because I'm too good at recognizing a lost cause," Cantara interrupted her unceremoniously, picking the cup up again and drinking the contents.

"Mad ... Cantara." Gladia paused. She breathed in, then took a piece of lemon and squeezed it over her cup. She decided to change strategy. She sipped her hot water then said, "I'm sure someone in your position will understand that this matter is far from being the end of the Polaris project."

"I don't understand what you're talking about," Cantara said, waving a hand over her head, as if spreading incense in the room. "Woodside has provided the Planetary Court a damn good reason to put an end to Polaris. That the projections and calculations of his experts are reliable or not ... well, it doesn't really matter, does it? Now that most of the public opinion *believes* they are, nothing really counts. Your well-publicized campaign for the construction of Infinity is over. Its days are numbered."

Gladia started to say something, but Cantara raised a hand, interrupting her. "As if that were not enough, my dear, the Ether is packed with not so encouraging rumors about the construction of the Infinity control center itself. Rumors concerning complications in the design of your space elevator, about the growing difficulties to mass produce the intelligent hyper-filament that must support your prodigious creation, and of other technical difficulties that not even your best brains seem to be able to understand. Half of your mythical Hexahedron is busy trying to solve structural problems that you guys hadn't even foreseen at the beginning of Infinity's construction."

"For a retired woman," Gladia said, "it seems to me that you're fairly up to date on the ... What did you call them? Oh, yes! *Annoying background noises.*" There was a bitter twist on Gladia's mouth.

Cantara shrugged. "Nonsense," she replied, smacking her lips after sipping some tea, "let's just say that I consider myself a woman who keeps her ear to the ground and who loves elaborating on conjectures." The Madame kept her smile as wide as possible. "And my conjectures tell me that other problems and complications will arise in the near future and that the departure of Polaris will be an increasingly complex and unpleasant business to handle for you Hyperists. Now tell me, my dear, did you manage to keep the genius boy unaware of *this* too?"

Gladia stared at Cantara without blinking. "The first Hyperist is well aware of our progress and is more than confident that his team will be able to solve any complications."

The Madame let out a giggle that Gladia found particularly annoying. When Cantara had finished laughing, she settled back in her armchair as she watched the co-founder of the SOL with a condescending look. "Sure," she said, as she took a napkin and passed it over her lips, "this can be the encouraging chorus that you guys repeat to each other, but the people that keep both feet on the ground don't seem to feel the same way, and I'm not referring only to Landists. My dear Gladia, there are things that simply can't be done, regardless of will, power or money."

"I don't understand what you mean," Gladia said. "Anything can be done if there's enough will."

"Oh, come on, Doctor! Let's try at least to behave like adults." Cantara crossed her arms. "I admit it, what you want to do may seem incredibly simple: to drop something toward Earth from a satellite hovering just above the equator. A child could grasp the concept. And yet, and I'm sure you'll agree with me, we both know that in an experiment like this, *simple* is a very complicated word. Don't you agree?"

Gladia smiled thinly, and remained silent.

"Think about it," continued Cantara. "If you try to take a shortcut, you waste more energy. If you try to slow down, you speed up. If you aim for one direction, you go in the opposite. No one before has ever tried to drive a probe attached to a forty thousand kilometer long cable: and for a good reason."

Gladia didn't hide her surprise. "I didn't know you were an expert in aerodynamics."

"I'm not, but my consultant in orbital transportation is paid handsomely to be in my place, and he tells me that your Polaris project has several fundamental flaws, many of which can't be overcome, not with our current technologies, at least. Maybe in fifty years your space elevator *could* be feasible, but nowadays it is a little less ridiculous than the idea of flying pigs."

"The space elevator is an idea that has no flaw, mathematically and technically speaking." Gladia straightened her back and puffed out her chest. "In theory, there is nothing to prevent it from happening."

Cantara laughed again, this time a sparkling and genuine laugh. She attentively studied the nails of her hands. "In theory," she repeated, still smiling. She sipped her tea, then continued, "My nail polish costs five times the equivalent that you find at Walmart and in *theory* it should last for a month, should be completely odorless, always remain shiny and not contain any trace of chemicals. In *practice*, the color begins to fade after a week and there is something in this formula that causes me a slight itching. As if that were not enough, sometimes I could swear I smell a distinct odor of tar while applying it. What do you think all this means, my dear?"

"It means that you need a new nail polish," Gladia replied dryly, not sure where the other woman was driving at.

Cantara nodded. "Sure. *That* and also that you should never trust what a label says, or what's written in a psychophysical profile." She pointed to Gladia with her cup. "In *theory*, I should be before a woman who has her head firmly on her shoulders, gifted with a critical and analytical mind. And yet, I find myself staring at a person who drinks the words of a twenty-four year old megalomaniac with an ego incredibly more developed than his brain."

Gladia rested both hands on her knees.

Cantara resumed drinking her tea. There was silence for half a minute.

The Madame set her cup on the table. Again she wiped her lips with the napkin. "Technically, my dear, this is when you fall on your knees and start begging me to help you and your Hyperists to rescue your crazy lot from the ocean of shit where Woodside is drowning you," Cantara said, showing a row of white teeth.

Gladia knew well that this was a lost battle. But it was something she had known long before setting foot in that room. After all, she said to herself, she was not there to convince Cantara to join their cause. She was there simply to invite her to a show.

"No," Gladia finally answered, crossing her arms over her chest. "I think this is when I invite you to witness a story that will make you believe in miracles."

Cantara shook her head. It was her turn to be surprised by the answer of her guest.

"My dear Gladia," she said, slightly moving her shoulders. "Of all the things I thought you were, I didn't expect 'believer' was part of the list." A pause, then she asked, sarcastically, "Let's see. Does this story begin about two thousand years ago, in a remote province of the Roman Empire?"

Gladia smiled. "No," she answered, looking to the other woman, "it is a story that began a few years ago and that is still in progress. And I'm offering you the chance to be part of it and to shape the world around you as you've never done before."

"I beg your pardon?" Cantara said, clearly confused. "I'm not following."

Gladia pointed to the Madame and smiled. "How would you like to make a difference?"

∞∞∞∞

Cantara almost couldn't believe that she was actually there.

Curiosity and a sense of adventure might have been two of the main reasons why Gladia had convinced her to board SOL's jet, but she thought there was something more than that.

However, little did it matter now that she was sitting there, in a room shrouded by pitch black darkness that reminded her so much of a huge movie theater. The woman was almost expecting that someone would approach and offer her a bag of popcorn and a can of Coca Cola.

The only difference between this place and the replica of a cinema was the peculiar, spherical shape of the room and the countless bluish lights that covered the walls and the ceiling like a giant, phosphorescent plant. There was also a solitary raised platform in the middle of the vast space that had no apparent reason for being there. Cantara had no idea what the purpose of the place was and Gladia hadn't revealed much.

Almost without realizing it, she found herself watching, for the hundredth time, the veins of bluish light that snaked to the sides of the room, the only source of light in a space otherwise shrouded in the deepest darkness. The place, the Madame soon realized, instilled in her a sense of anticipation and wonder, as if she were in a huge cathedral where a secret religious function was about to start.

A shiver ran down her spine. She swallowed hard, forcing herself to think critically and to look for answers to her questions.

"So *this* would be the place where miracles happen?" Cantara asked, breaking a silence that had lasted several minutes.

Gladia, sitting to her left, was staring at the distant platform. "No," the doctor answered, keeping her voice down, as if to respect the sacred silence of the place. "This is the place where miracles are *created*."

Cantara skeptically studied the other woman, but did not reply to that statement.

The Madame recalled the events that had led her to this strange place. The fact that she found herself in a restricted area didn't surprise her so much. HYPER headquarters was a Spartan structure, simple and very unwelcoming. The only sections she managed to see while passing from one checkpoint to the next had revealed a small army of security drones, dozens of armed men and very few smiles. She suspected that Gladia Egea had to call on quite a few favors to give her the privilege of sitting in this very chair.

After all, the Madame thought, if she had agreed to come all that way to end up here, it was only because Gladia had somehow convinced her that the event she was about to witness would be something really quite special. No, not merely special, she thought. It would be something very unique and exceptional.

She really hoped that the trip had been worth the trouble.

Just as she was about to ask another question, the already dim light of the room went out and total darkness enveloped the surrounding environment. Cantara lost sight of the platform at the center of the enormous spherical space, the only point of reference in a temple of silence.

It was as if something had suddenly sucked away all the energy in the room.

The Madame looked around and her eyes caught sight of a figure moving in the darkness, near the platform.

A subdued light began to glow somewhere above their heads and Cantara was finally able to see the figure that had appeared out of nowhere. When she recognized him, her eyes widened. She put a hand over her mouth in amazement.

Before them, a few dozen yards away, was Wei Wang, visionary mind, first Hyperist and creator of the orbital carrier Polaris. And he was stark naked.

Cantara blinked half a dozen times. She rubbed her eyes vigorously but Wei Wang continued to stay where he was. His pale skin, barely illuminated by the dim light of the room, made him look like a ghostly presence.

Cantara whirled toward Gladia, but the doctor did not seem at all surprised by the sudden appearance. The Madame forgot what she wanted to ask, and looked again at the first Hyperist. The light was getting progressively more intense. Now she could see Wei's body.

Her first impression, she realized, was disappointment. Wei Wang was short -- much shorter than he appeared in the media. Yet Cantara was surprised to find out how much his body, albeit minute, was defined and incredibly dry, not very different from that of a Greek statue. The muscles precisely delimited the anatomical boundaries of his body.

From that distance it wasn't easy to see every detail, such as the expression of his face, but other than that, the boy's identity was unmistakable. Cantara could not believe that she was a stone's throw away from possibly the most famous and controversial person of the moment.

Her thoughts were suddenly interrupted when the first Hyperist began to speak.

"EVE," Wei called out, addressing the ceiling. "Open the file: *Spacefaring Civilization.*"

A solitary note reverberated in the enormous room.

"Close your eyes," Gladia said suddenly.

Cantara didn't understand what the other woman meant. "Wha …?"

She never finished the question. Without any warning, a cobalt blue light mixed with yellow gold exploded in the huge room and Cantara was forced to protect her face with her arm to avoid being blinded.

When her eyes adjusted to the brightness, she saw that a multitude of lights and colors had replaced the darkness. A gigantic shape loomed in the center of the room.

It was a circle … *no*, Cantara thought after a few seconds of silent amazement, it was a sphere … a huge blue sphere interspersed with portions of white, green and brown; portions with a very familiar shape.

Cantara found that she was staring at Europe a few moments before the Old Continent rotated out of her sight, revealing the American continent, followed by the Pacific Ocean, Asia and Europe once more. What she was seeing was an incredibly faithful reproduction of the planet Earth that revolved peacefully before her eyes.

Cantara glanced around, looking for the source of that titanic multidimensional projection, but could not see any trigo-projector in the area near them. Her mind was spinning. It was impossible to conceive that an image so impressive had appeared out of nowhere in the space of a split second.

The reproduction of the Earth was so detailed, so realistic, that Cantara felt like an astronaut staring at her own planet from several hundred kilometers above the ground. This made her think. She was neither in a cinema nor in a cathedral, but in the room that was the closest thing to a huge planetarium that she'd ever set foot in.

The Madame noticed she was holding her breath. She rested both hands on her chair and swallowed hard as her eyes adjusted to the incredible reproduction of the planet. She shook her head to clear it and licked her dry lips as she tried to compose herself.

Cantara's eyes slowly moved from the giant sphere, which rotated above their heads, to the infinitely smaller and insignificant Wei Wang, who was apparently stretching arms and legs, like an Olympic swimmer preparing for a competition.

She wondered if the boy knew that in that very moment someone was spying on him. She and Gladia, she realized, were wrapped in an area of darkness that seemed immune to the light coming from the reproduction of the Earth.

From his attitude, Cantara judged that Wei Wang thought he was alone.

The Madame turned back to Gladia who was smiling, her eyes shining with a light that had nothing to do with the glow coming from the crystal clear reproduction of the planet.

"Remember to breathe," Gladia whispered, clearly amused by the expression of the woman sitting next to her.

Cantara was about to open her mouth to answer, but she was forced to stop when Wei started speaking again.

"EVE," the first Hyperist called while flexing his knees. "Let's load the most recent data. Give me the overview of the situation."

A mechanical voice with a feminine tone replied to Wei's request. "In the file you've selected," the ubiquitous voice said, "we are at the end of the year 2041. In this scenario, there are no significant threats to the Master Project and the dangerous variable has been eliminated or prevented successfully by your past actions."

"All right then, let's begin!" Wei said, clapping his hands repeatedly. "Let's leap into the future. Determine when the next major threat to the Master Project will occur."

Cantara didn't understand what was going on. She looked at Gladia once more, but the only answer she got was a pointed finger that invited her to keep watching.

169

The Madame snorted and turned to focus on Wei.

"Processing terminated," the voice was saying.

The reproduction of planet Earth vanished for an instant but re-appeared less than a second later. Cantara didn't notice any difference between the previous planet and the one that rotated now before her eyes -- except perhaps for some small forms that now seemed to be orbiting above Oceania. The woman leaned forward in her chair and squinted, trying to put her eyes into focus but with no success. The forms were too small and too far apart to be distinguished from the background.

"This is the beginning of the year 2047," EVE, the mechanical voice, announced. "The emerging space economy is revealing some chronic problems that are due primarily to an inability to increase the volume of orbital traffic while maintaining reasonable protection standards in the transportation of goods and people. Polaris is no longer able to adequately meet the growing demand of transport. Private companies providing orbital shuttles must comply with strict safeguard requirements that prevent them from substantially increasing the tonnage of their vehicles or testing new propulsion systems. Three incidents occurred in five years, in which thirteen victims are reported. Laws and regulations that prohibit the expansion of human transport in orbit will be approved. The transport of goods will be affected by similar regulations. As a result, the GXP of the space economy will enter a recession for the first time in history. The projections show that the GXP will also decrease in the coming years, threatening the expansion of so-called astral tourism, orbital trade, the astral industry and in general, the entire space economy."

Wei nodded, clearly deep in thought, while assimilating EVE's report. After a few seconds of silence, the first Hyperist began to move his body in a slow and sinuous way, reminding Cantara of the movements of a dancer who follows the rhythm of an alien music. Wei's movements were smooth and precise, without any hint of hesitation, as if he had performed the same routine countless times. The 'dance' seemed to generate a series of characteristic blue data—graphics, numbers, images and such, all of the same blue color—that began appearing seemingly out of thin air. The data started to orbit around Wei's head. He spent a couple of minutes studying them while mumbling to himself.

Eventually, the boy sighed and made the data disappear with a quick jerk of his index finger. He turned to look to the ceiling with a thoughtful expression.

"The most important cause of the GXP contraction seems to be a new series of strict orbital transportation regulations. My understanding is that they were created by the new Planetary Court following the three accidents you were talking about."

"That is correct," EVE replied.

Wei seemed to think about EVE's response for a while. Then he formed an X, crossing his arms -- and the movement of the Earth instantly froze. Cantara watched with eyes full of wonder for what seemed to be for Wei, a common gesture -- but one that made him look rather like a deity in her eyes. Once again, the Madame spent a few seconds searching for the source of the multi-dimensional reproduction of the planet but without any luck. It was as though Wei controlled that show of lights and shapes with the power of his thought -- which was clearly impossible, she reminded herself. There had to be a plausible answer. She continued to scan the room, looking for a detail that could explain the mystery.

Meanwhile, the young man was enlarging the area over Oceania where Cantara believed she had seen tiny forms. As the visual scale expanded, Cantara realized that the forms were actually structures of different sizes that orbited many hundreds of miles above Earth. They appeared to be just a bunch of silver grey shapes, with no apparent meaning.

"EVE," Wei suddenly said, "which was the company with the highest spatial turnover reported in 2046?"

"Titan Asteros Corporation," the voice replied immediately.

"What is the most significant source of its income?"

"Titan Asteros Corporation obtains forty-five per cent of its revenue from the construction of orbital astrals, twenty-five per cent from astral tourism, seven per cent from the production of ..."

"OK, I got it," interrupted Wei. "Who are its major clients?"

"Are you referring to its customers or its contractors?"

"Both," Wei explained. "I'm referring to anyone whose work depends on the performance of a service or for the construction of an astral."

"Titan Asteros Corporation provides services mainly to private agencies and private citizens. Do you want a detailed list?"

"No." Wei shook his head. He seemed disappointed. He made a

half-twirl with his body and raised both arms in unison. The silver colored shapes disappeared instantly, replaced by another area of Earth's orbit apparently free of any forms.

The Hyperist produced other data, these too shaded in a characteristic blue color. After having studied them for a few seconds, he asked, "EVE, which space companies do the US, the EUROCON and China use most?"

"Are you referring to military or civilian companies?"

"Both."

"In this case, these three political entities are served mostly by a union of corporations called Astrocorp. This union comprises eleven companies specialized in different sectors of the space economy and of astral technology."

"Provide a list of the services they offer."

EVE replied instantly. "Astral tourism, orbital transportation, manufacture of military and civilian equipment, refinement of ..."

"I understand." Wei crossed his arms and repeatedly tapped his foot on the floor. He seemed lost in his thoughts for several minutes. After a while, he began to read a new string of data that he had evoked. He assimilated them quickly and then asked, while he was still reading, "EVE, how many of the disputes that the Planetary Court is expected to settle this year are classified as important?"

"Three thousand and eighty-eight," EVE answered.

"Well," Wei said, suddenly stopping the tapping of his foot on the floor. He straightened his back and shoulders, then continued. "Maybe we can put a bit more pressure on their shoulders."

Wei became busy evoking data and moving his hands and fingers relentlessly.

Cantara noticed soon enough that the omnipresent voice, EVE, not only provided information, but also described the events that apparently occurred following the decisions that Wei made from time to time. To Cantara, that show reminded her of an extremely complex real-time strategy game that changed and adapted depending on Wei's choices.

The Madame began to understand that what she was seeing was an incredibly realistic simulation of a possible future. EVE created the scenario which, if completed in an appropriate manner, allowed advancement to the next level. Wei had to figure out what the problem was and use the information and resources he had to solve it, thus fulfilling the mission objective.

Cantara witnessed the latest decision of Wei completed with an elegant dancing movement of his body.

EVE's evaluation of Wei's choices was swift. The voice said, "Wei, my analysis indicates that four of the eleven companies that constitute Astrocorp have established a block of all orbital activities. The block looks like a form of protest against the regulations of the Planetary Court concerning orbital transportation."

"You can call it a *strike*, EVE. And I'm not done yet." Wei moved his arms again and described an imaginary square with his hands.

"EVE, activate a three day time ellipse."

EVE carried out the order and Cantara saw the reproduction of planet Earth becoming opaque for a split second before returning exactly as it was before.

At that point EVE said, "Time ellipse confirmed," then it commented the result of Wei's actions. "Three days after the decision of the four companies, Blue Galacta, Asteroid Dominion, Farpoint Alfa, Sinospace, JAXA Earth, Terracorp and Equinox also have suspended or drastically limited their presence on or below orbit. Astrocorp as a whole seems to have blocked any form of space activity. It appears that your … strike is contagious."

"How are the US, the EUROCON and China handling this strike?" Wei quickly asked.

Cantara couldn't be sure from where she sat, but she would have bet that the first Hyperist was grinning.

"The three political entities have asked Astrocorp to justify this unexpected strike. The cessation of all Astrocorp orbital activities could result in a substantial loss of income for three political entities. A legal dispute seems about to begin between the two parties."

Wei nodded. "Yeah, I'm sure they didn't take it very well. The big players are sharpening their knives but they have no idea that their prey is much bigger than they expect. EVE, the eleven corporations forming Astrocorp should respond with a joint statement to the pressures of the three political entities. Shouldn't they?"

"Correct," EVE confirmed. "Astrocorp publicly declared its inability to complete its work and remain faithful to its contracts due to the current rules governing the orbital transportation."

"Sweet." Wei put the blue data tables aside—those which he had used up to that point—and began completely different research with a new kind of data characterized by a bright white color. Wei spent some time evaluating the new information.

If this simulation really worked like a real-time strategy game, Cantara imagined that those different colors were referring to different types of resources that Wei could use to fulfill his goal. Hers was just a speculation, but the show seemed after all quite simple to understand. The Madame continued to watch events unfold, finding herself much more interested than she wanted to admit in a simulation so similar to a chess game, but at the same time reminding herself where she was and why she was there. She couldn't risk being ruled by the impressions of the moment. The advice she gave to her students, after all, was a general rule. *The first impression is always the wrong one.*

Wei spoke again as he nervously rubbed his neck with both hands.

"EVE, what does the slice of public opinion not politically involved think of the space economy?"

"Your question is beyond the scope of this scenario," EVE said, as if the question made no sense at all.

Wei cleared his throat then rephrased the question. "According to the Ether and to traditional media, what seems to be the opinion that the planetary population, not declared Hyperist or Landist, hold toward the space economy? What do the *neutralists* think?"

"The subject is too recent to generate consistent data," EVE said. "However, from the information available on the Ether, it seems that most of the public classified as 'neutralist' consider the space economy as an interesting new element with potential. A recent survey determined that seventy-five per cent of respondents that define themselves neutralists, would take an astral holiday if he or she had the money to afford it."

Wei nodded, then began again to move his body, relentlessly making forms, charts and numbers appear before his eyes while shaping new events.

EVE evaluated Wei's decisions and the use of his resources. "You seem to have started on the Ether a campaign of protest against the regulations regarding orbital transportation."

"That I did," Wei said, while making one decision after another. It seemed to Cantara that the greater the amount of information EVE provided to Wei, the faster the boy's processing speed needed to be in order to match the scenario. Consequently, even the movements of his body had to keep pace with the increasing speed of the simulation. Soon, the naked body of the Hyperist began to shimmer with a sheen of sweat, partly reflecting the light of the room. The Madame understood in that moment why Wei had chosen to be completely naked. The boy preferred total freedom in order not to limit his movements or affect his performance. The clothes were disregarded as a form of obstruction.

As time went by and with the increasing difficulty of the scenario, Cantara began to notice that Wei was showing the first symptoms of fatigue. The first Hyperist was clearly affected, mentally and physically, by the increasing pace of the simulation. His breathing became more rapid and irregular and he seemed to spend more time assimilating and evaluating the volume of data that orbited around his body. At that time dozens of numbers, graphs and reports exhibited half a dozen different colors demanded his attention.

Wei wiped away the sweat beading his forehead with one arm, then puffed. "OK, that's it." He swallowed a few times then continued speaking. "I want a two week time ellipse."

"Confirmed," EVE said. The planet became opaque for the second time, almost out of focus before resuming its configuration. "We are now two weeks into the future."

Wei held his breath. "How many of the disputes are now classified important by the Planetary Court?"

"Five thousand two hundred sixty-six and growing," EVE answered. "Most of them are caused by Astrocorp's strike, by the protests coming from the EUROCON, the US and China and by a growing movement in public opinion favorable to the relaxation of the orbital transportation regulations."

The first Hyperist now seemed excited. While feverishly moving hands and arms, Cantara thought she could hear him giggle.

"Give me another week-long time ellipse, EVE. Report!"

EVE carried out the order and continued with its report. "Wei, the Planetary Court is undergoing multiple pressures from the world of business, media and politics to relax the constraints on the orbital transportation. EUROCON, the United States, China and eighty-six other political entities are voting in order to remove different decision-making powers from the Planetary Court regarding the space economy. Strong pressure from public opinion is also favoring a heated debate, in traditional media and on the Ether, concerning the need to establish new safeguards, without limiting the orbital transportation of goods and people."

"Give me another time ellipse. I need five more days," Wei ordered, breathing heavily while studying his data. Then he impatiently repeated, "Report."

EVE answered promptly. "It is expected that the Planetary Court will make a new decision regarding the orbital transportation shortly." A pause, then EVE continued. "The vote has just ended. Seventy-five per cent of the members are now in favor of the new regulations. Moreover, the day after the vote, the Planetary Court undergoes a substantial downsizing of its powers in orbital and space related business."

Wei sighed loudly, clearly satisfied, then asked, "Can you generate at this point of the scenario, a report on the performance of the space economy two quarters into the future of the approval of the new regulations?"

"Affirmative," EVE responded. "The GXP of the space economy will grow slowly but steadily over the next two quarters. Polaris will be modified to carry double the tonnage in the past. The modernization of the space elevator will be completed by 2052. In addition, thanks to the relaxation of the rules on orbital transport, new companies will spring up. In the future, the supply of services will be able to appropriately meet the demand."

Wei took a bottle of water that Cantara had not seen until that moment and finished half of the content in a few gulps, then wiped his mouth with the back of his hand. After a while, he asked, both hands resting on his hips while inhaling large gulps of oxygen, "EVE, illustrate the consequences of the victory of Astrocorp over the Planetary."

"Astrocorp, which emerges victorious from the clash against the Planetary Court, will see its membership grow considerably. Twenty-nine corporations and companies involved in the astral industry, in astral tourism and in astral commerce will become part of the union. In 2049, Astrocorp will officially change its name to Stellar Guild. Titan Asteros Corporation will join the Guild in the following year. Wei, this scenario no longer presents significant threats to the Master Project and the dangerous variables have been eliminated or successfully prevented by your past actions."

Wei raised his fist to the air, a clear sign of victory.

"EVE, save the file *Spacefaring Civilization*," said the boy, exulting.

"Confirmed. The file has been saved."

Cantara could barely digest what she had seen. Confusion, disbelief, suspicion, wonder and amazement were fermenting inside her, battling to gain the upper hand. She turned to study Gladia's expression and was surprised to find the woman sitting on the edge of her chair, as she absently nibbled her thumb. Gladia whispered something inaudible, eyes fixed on Wei who stood at the center of the huge room.

"What did you say?" Cantara asked, watching the woman.

"He never, ever managed to get past this scenario before," Gladia whispered, speaking more to herself than to anyone in particular. Cantara could read excitement and anticipation on her face.

"I don't understand. What do you mean?"

"I mean that he was never able to reach this point: *Never* before. Now he's in a completely uncharted territory."

Cantara returned to focus her attention toward the first Hyperist who was wiping his sweaty face with a towel. She saw him again drinking, gulping eagerly. When he finished, his voice still saturated with excitement, Wei said, "Right, EVE. Let's do it again. Let's leap into the future. Determine when the next major threat to the Master Project will occur."

Again the planet disappeared and abruptly reappeared in the blink of an eye.

Cantara carefully studied the new multi-dimensional projection. This time she could see a greater number of geometric shapes spread like wildfire in some parts of Earth's orbit. Their presence still did not seem significant, but it was definitely increased compared to the previous simulation.

"Processing terminated," EVE informed Wei. "We are now at the end of the year 2058. In this scenario, there are multiple threats to the Master Project."

Wei was rubbing his arms, apparently trying to soothe his sore muscles. He breathed in and out for a few seconds, then said, "EVE, describe the three major threats in order of severity."

EVE immediately replied, "First threat: a growing tension between the US and China due to a territorial dispute in South-East Asia which is deteriorating rapidly. It is expected to degenerate into a full-scale armed conflict in the short term. All diplomatic relations between the two powers ceased a month ago. Both nations are conducting repeated military exercises on the borders of their respective spheres of influence. Some attempts made by the Planetary Court and other supranational entities to mediate the growing tension don't seem to have any effect."

A brief pause, then EVE continued. "Second threat: the construction of a second space elevator christened 'Sirius' began about a year ago. Its completion would dramatically increase orbital traffic, allowing the construction of triple the number of astrals in half the time currently required. This second structure is the result of a joint effort between several nations participating in the Commercial Covenant. The construction of Sirius has already requested the equivalent of one-seventh of the world GDP and is proving to be more complex than expected. Some nations are abandoning their involvement in the project because of rising costs. In addition, a protest movement originated from public opinion begins to question the usefulness of this infrastructure and the huge resources needed for its completion."

Cantara saw Wei warming up, again moving his arms and shoulders. This time, it seemed that the boy was preparing for a real boxing match. Her thoughts were interrupted by EVE, which resumed the list.

"Third threat: a new group of Landist extremists known as the 'Children of the Sun' has grown rapidly in recent years, perpetrating several successful terrorist attacks at some of the major corporations involved in the space economy. The construction of Sirius seems to have increased the influence of this movement. In a recent statement, the Asian section of the 'Children of the Sun' says they are preparing an attack against Sirius itself, should its construction continue."

Wei opened his arms and legs and planted his feet on the ground, as if he were preparing to stop an avalanche with his bare hands. Abruptly, dozens of data of different colors exploded around him. The first Hyperist began as quickly as possible to become familiar with the historical situation in which he found himself. This time, the young man seemed to Cantara incredibly tense, almost nervous. It was clear to the Madame that the difficulty of the scenario had grown exponentially.

It soon became obvious that Wei was unable to assimilate the enormous volume of information as quickly as he did in the previous scenario.

"EVE," Wei said at the end, shaking his head reluctantly, "I need more time to figure out a proper line of action."

The automated voice did not seem inclined to satisfy his request. "Wei, remember that you have exhausted your supply of temporal stasis two scenarios ago. The situation in this scenario must proceed according to the rules established by the program."

Wei cursed loud enough to be heard by Cantara and evoked possibly double the amount of data that he began to study while muttering something Cantara could not catch.

"Wei," EVE interrupted him, breaking a silence that had lasted less than a minute, "the tension between China and the United States has worsened as a result of military exercises conducted by the Chinese fleet in the Gulf of Alaska."

"Shit!" Wei blurted out, quickly making the data he was working on disappear. Finally he began to move his body. Cantara, however, could not help but notice that something had changed in his movements with respect to the 'dance' of the previous scenario. His actions were fluid and harmonious, but he had undeniably lost the dexterity that had characterized his movements only a few minutes before.

"Wei," EVE called, while the first Hyperist was busy describing a series of concentric circles with both arms, "your attempt to involve Canada in the negotiations for a ceasefire between the two powers seems to have partially affected the scenario. The US government has agreed to meet the Chinese if they cease to deploy their fleet on US waters. The politburo agreed. Official delegations of both powers are expected to meet in three days in Vancouver."

Wei allowed himself to relax for a moment. He summoned the data back and tried to study them in silence but he was interrupted again by an update of the situation.

"Wei, the terrorist group known as the 'Children of the Sun' has successfully completed an attack on an astral refinery owed by Equinox. Result: nine victims, damages totalling fifty-nine million bancors. The news is broadcasted everywhere. Two other attacks are announced against other companies forming part of the Stellar Guild."

With a nearly superhuman effort, Wei summoned around him a cloud of information of a dozen different colors. With increasing speed, the Hyperist read the information and made one decision after another in order to counter the most urgent threats.

Yet, this time it seemed there was simply too much to consider, too much to handle. Cantara saw him shaking his head more than once while trying to keep up with the increasing complexity of the scenario.

"Wei," EVE interrupted him again, "your action enabled the destruction of the Asian section of the terrorist movement, but the 'Children of the Sun' operate in separate and independent cells. Your actions do not seem to have destabilized the operational capacity of the movement as a whole. EUROCON, African, American and Arabic sections of the 'Children of the Sun' just announced actions against multiple installations related to the astral industry."

There was a pause no longer than a minute then, while Wei was frantically assimilating data and moving his body to shape new events, EVE concluded, "Wei, the terrorist group has successfully carried out an attack on the Half-Way station of Polaris. Seven passengers were stranded twenty-five thousand kilometers from the ground. The Infinity control center seems also to have been contaminated in some sections by a gas of unknown origin. Infinity is being evacuated at this moment. Meanwhile, the group has declared that it also intends to carry out an attack against Sirius."

Wei was clearly at the limit of his strength. As he faced the unravelling of the events with increasingly slow and imprecise actions, the first Hyperist cried almost imploringly, "EVE! I'm using my etherions to give birth to a movement in the public opinion to put pressure on the CC to temporarily stop the construction of Sirius. Are there any consequences?"

"Wei," EVE said with what seemed to Cantara an unyielding tone, "the use of your etheric resources will not affect the construction of Sirius. In addition, the Secretary of the Commercial Covenant has publicly stated, and I quote: '*We will not bow to terrorist threats of any kind. The work on the construction of Sirius will continue as planned*'. The statement was just released on the Ether. The terrorist group has responded by intensifying its attacks on the headquarters of the Stellar Guild and of the CC."

There was a brief pause, before EVE continued relentlessly, "Four attacks carried out successfully. One hundred and thirteen deaths, about two hundred injured. Damages for a total of four hundred and nine million bancors resulting in ..."

"Damn it!" Wei shouted, clearly frustrated, while the mechanical voice continued inexorably its report. "EVE," the first Hyperist said, interrupting the list, "I want to use an emergency resolution of the Planetary Court to suspend the construction of Sirius and ..."

"Wei," it was EVE's turn to interrupt him, "the Planetary Court doesn't have any power over this matter. Your maneuver in 2047 has drastically reduced its involvement in space economy related affairs. Your actions do not appear to affect the intensifying chaotic situation. The degeneration of the system is reaching a critical point. The status of equilibrium is shifting away."

"Shit, shit, *shit!*" Wei shouted angrily, now completely besieged by data, images, graphics and numbers. No matter how fast he assimilated information or made decisions, it seemed that for every situation that he solved there were three others popping out of nowhere.

"Wei, the negotiations between China and the United States have failed. An accident between the fifth US fleet and the aircraft carrier Deng Xiaoping has just provoked a localized conflict between the two powers two hundred miles from the Gulf of Alaska."

"No," Wei said through clenched teeth, frantically moving hands and arms, sweat covering every inch of his body. "Not now!"

EVE continued, insistent and relentless as a jackhammer. "The conflict between the US and China has escalated into war." This statement followed a few minutes of silence that seemed to last for hours. Then EVE continued to update Wei on the evolving situation.

"After several clashes between the two fleets off the American coast, Mexico and Canada declared their neutrality. The Planetary Court and other peacekeeping forces do not seem to be able to stop the conflict. The estimated loss of life as a result of the hostilities is now rising to six thousand and six units and the number is growing rapidly. The damage to the economies ..."

Wei did not pay attention to the rest of the report and tried a desperate countermeasure to turn the tables. EVE evaluated his action then ruled, "The Planetary Court and other major peacekeeping forces cannot stop the conflict even with the heavy sanctions approved by the majority of the Nations of the world. The President of the United States authorizes the use of nuclear weapons."

A minute of silence followed. Cantara felt Gladia hold her breath. The woman seemed completely absorbed by the events.

EVE spoke again, "The first atomic bomb has been dropped for demonstration purposes about five hundred miles from Shanghai, in the East China Sea."

A dome spawning a shining white light suddenly appeared in the area named by EVE. Cantara and Gladia gasped in unison, completely taken aback. Again Cantara was surprised by the quality and detail of the projection. The simulation had quite clearly ceased for her to be such. Now, for some unknown reason, her brain seemed to classify the images she was seeing as a window on the future, something no less real than the room she was in.

EVE's voice roused her again from her thoughts. "The Chinese Politburo retaliated against the US two days after the attack, dropping three nuclear devices in the Sonora Desert, in Arizona. To this moment, the conflict has caused fifty thousand three hundred and twenty-two casualties."

The situation seemed to get worse by the second.

Cantara listened to the calm and quiet voice of EVE which, with merciless efficiency, brought news of death and destruction upon them.

"Wei, the world GDP and the GXP of the space economy are collapsing rapidly. It is estimated that both will lose around ten per cent in the next quarter. It is also estimated that fifty-five million people will become unemployed in the same period. Crime and social unrest are increasing, especially in areas affected by the conflict. The 'Children of the Sun' attributed the outbreak of the conflict to the exorbitant costs required to complete the space elevator Sirius. The public is witnessing the collapse of manufacturing and of their standard of living. Martial law has been declared in one hundred and seventeen capitals of the world ..."

"EVE! Goddammit! Stop the construction of the second space elevator! I'm using all that I have left of my ..."

The ubiquitous voice silenced him mercilessly. "Wei, the construction has already been suspended for lack of funds and manpower. The Commercial Covenant has effectively ceased to exist. Other attacks are perpetrated against companies and institutions related to the astral industry. The authorities are unable to isolate the ever growing extremist groups." EVE continued down the list overlaying one piece of information over the other. Cantara could only catch glimpses of information among the flood of news of disasters that followed each other like an unstoppable domino effect.

"... It is estimated that the world GDP will fall another fifteen points in the next quarter ... The standard of living is decreasing exponentially ... Half a million deaths caused by the conflict ... The explosion of an epidemic ... collapse ... loss ... unrest ... poverty ... war ..."

Wei Wang collapsed, exhausted. The young man was gasping for air and coughing convulsively, his hands on the floor, his body shaking uncontrollably, hit by waves of spasms. He appeared to struggle to breathe. His muscles, tense and tested by the enormous effort, no longer seemed able to support his weight.

The first Hyperist tried to say something, but neither Cantara nor Gladia nor EVE were able to hear it. Wei fell first on his knees, then on his back, eyes closed and arms wrapped around his body, in a desperate attempt to stop the spasms.

"What's the matter with him? Why is he shaking like that?" Cantara asked, holding her breath.

Gladia did not answer. She just looked at Wei with an expression that Cantara thought was equal part sadness and helplessness.

Meanwhile Wei lay motionless on the floor. He was no longer trembling, but he was also barely breathing. EVE continued to update him with a matter-of-fact tone.

Then, after what seemed to be an eternity, the first Hyperist raised a solitary hand. To Cantara that gesture resembled a white flag waved in front of an enemy army.

"OK, EVE," Wei eventually murmured, in a voice so low that Cantara struggled to hear, "close ... close the file *Spacefaring Civilization.*"

EVE executed the order and the colossal Earth suddenly vanished.

For the second time the room fell into pitch black darkness.

Everything around was still and silent. Only then did Cantara realize she had both hands wrapped around her knees. She shook her head, trying to regain her composure, but the knuckles of her hands were still white.

After a few minutes, the familiar aquamarine light returned to the room.

Cantara glanced around, relentlessly. Her head was spinning and she was trying to process an incredibly wide range of information while inspecting the room. The planet Earth, the multicolored data and Wei Wang had disappeared, as if swallowed by the darkness.

Even EVE's voice had deserted the hall.

"Where ... where is he? Where is Wang?" the etherion asked, visually searching for the naked body of the Hyperist without finding it.

Gladia shifted in her chair. She looked at Cantara. "The most probable answer is that he went to take a shower. He will sleep for a few hours and then start all over again."

"All over again ..." repeated the Madame, clearly confused, "to start all over again *what*, exactly? What ... what was all of that?" She motioned to the platform on which a few minutes before the Earth's reproduction was revolving.

A tired smile flashed on Gladia's face. "I call it *Wei's bet*."

"Wei's bet?" Cantara repeated, puzzled. She spread her arms and showed her hands, revealing her confusion.

With a quick movement of her head Gladia pointed to where a few minutes before Wei had performed his dance. "Nobody really knows what he's up to -- not even us, the members of the Hexahedron. We only know that for the last few months Wei has confined himself here, doing ... well, probably doing what he does best."

"Really?" Cantara looked at the other woman, her face showing confusion. "And what would that be?"

"Trying to make a difference," Gladia said, as if it were the most obvious thing in the world.

"I don't ..." Cantara didn't finish the sentence. She didn't even know how to continue it, she realized, surprised. Wei's bet seemed to her the best way to define what she had seen. But was it really a bet what she had seen? And even if that was the case, why was the possibly most intelligent and eccentric person on the planet spending his time doing this? And most importantly, why had Gladia Egea wanted to show her the process?

Then a thought struck her like a bolt from the sky; one question that arose spontaneously after watching the simulation and remembering why she was here. Cantara carefully studied Gladia's face and asked, "This simulation ... What happens ... in the simulation, I mean ... What happens if Infinity is not built?" She pointed to the platform in the center of the room. "What happens if Polaris doesn't rise? Wang has never tried this eventuality in one of his scenarios? It seems that all ... *this*, started from the fact that Polaris has been built and that it is operational."

"No," Gladia shook her head resolutely. "He has always assumed the departure of Polaris in each simulation as a matter of fact. This is why he refers to Polaris and to Infinity as two sides of the same coin. It is the first milestone from which everything else begins."

"Maybe he assumed it, but not you, right? Not you." Cantara didn't realize she was on the edge of her seat. Her desire to understand increased her determination. "You have considered that possibility, haven't you? You wanted to see with your own eyes what happens if Polaris doesn't come to be."

Gladia bit her lower lip. "I used this program once, breaking more than one rule. Something I'm not particularly proud of," Gladia admitted.

"Well?" the Madame pressed her. "What happens in that case?"

"Cantara, you have to understand I don't have Wei's skill in using the program. Even more importantly, you don't have to ..."

"*What happens?*" Cantara repeated stubbornly, interrupting her.

Gladia sighed. "In *that* scenario, our civilization continues to develop some technologies that greatly enhance Ether's control over mankind. We close in on ourselves and never develop a space economy of significant size. We become increasingly dependent on the virtual world and on its related services." Gladia paused. She rubbed her hands on her pants and looked away from Cantara. Then she continued, staring at the floor.

"In the year 2069, humans live fifty-nine per cent of their lives on the Ether, surrounded by automatic mechanisms that pump life into their bodies. In 2111 the human race is a complex mechanism of automated and artificial interconnections. We live our whole lives in a world carefully planned to meet our needs. At some point, however, something happens. In the year 2133 a deficiency in the Ether that EVE calls the 'Singularity' begins to attack the delicate mechanism that keeps this complex artificial world together. There are neither engineers nor experts left to fix the problem and the sentinel programs designed by humanity to protect our virtual sleep fail to solve this discrepancy. Eight hundred and twenty nine million lives, all that's left of our species, cease to exist in a heartbeat on March 31st, 2134 at five-thirty in the afternoon, Greenwich time, when the Singularity irreversibly compromises the system."

Gladia's eyes were closed, her hands clasped, an unreadable expression on her face. Eventually, she looked at the Madame again and concluded, "The human race dies out lying in bed."

Cantara swallowed hard. Even though she understood that she had witnessed a simulation, the result of a program's calculations, even though a part of her brain was laughing at those apocalyptic statements, a sense of urgency and inevitability began to invade her body.

Again a shiver ran down her spine.

She rubbed her arms with her hands vigorously. This place was starting to get cold.

She had seen nothing but a game, Cantara harshly reminded herself, repeating that phrase as a mantra while she recalled the hours spent watching Wei Wang shape the future of the human civilization; just a game. But was it really just that?

Was Wei's bet really what Gladia had described it to be? Was it a way to make a difference?

"What did I see?" Cantara suddenly asked, without noticing that the question was in fact addressed to herself.

Gladia crossed her arms. "Over the years, I've learned that trying to define Wei's actions and intentions would be like hitting a bullet with another bullet while you are tied up, upside down on the back of a running horse. What did you see? You have seen a vision of a future that could be, a shadow cast on a wall, a column of smoke in the darkness. You saw a dream. You can call it whatever you like. One description is as worthy as the next. None has any value, and all of them have the meaning that you choose to give them."

"A dream," Cantara repeated skeptically, looking at the empty platform. "This is why you come to me; because you want my help to realize the fantasies of that boy? Because you really think that his dream will become real ... really... all *this?*" She pointed to the room lazily lit by the bluish light.

Gladia looked intently at the other woman then said, "I've known Wei for five years and if there's one thing I realized over this time it is that he has a gift for turning his dreams into reality. I look at you and I look at Wei and I see two sides of the same coin, two people who are satisfied only when they shape the world around them, when they can make a difference. And what I'm proposing now, Cantara, is just that: to make a difference."

"There you go again with that sentence: 'To make a difference'. But I ask you, *how?*" Cantara laughed, in order to exorcise the sense of frustration she was feeling. In fact, although she tried to hide it, she felt dizzy and insignificant after witnessing the spectacle created by Wei and EVA. She continued to speak, her tone less steady than she would have liked. "To make a difference in what way? Helping you guys to build castles in the clouds?"

Gladia held her breath, then. After a tense silence, she laughed uproariously.

Cantara blinked, amazed. Gladia's reaction at her words had taken her completely aback.

The Hyperist clapped her hands over and over again as she bent over on herself, unable to hold back the laughter. She continued to laugh for some time. Cantara kept staring, not understanding what had caused this wave of euphoria.

"Gilbert Keith Chesterton," Gladia finally managed to say, coughing while wiping her eyes with the backs of her hands.

"I beg your pardon?" Cantara said, slightly moving away from the woman, as if expecting another unpredictable reaction.

"Gilbert Keith Chesterton," Gladia repeated, straightening her back while rubbing her jaw. "A British writer Wei would have loved, I guess. You reminded me of something ... something he said: 'There are no rules of architecture for a castle in the clouds.' Yes. Yes, indeed. Don't you find it funny and incredibly enlightening at the same time? What better answer to your question?"

Cantara found Gladia's words totally senseless. Was the Hyperist just making fun of her?

"This is ridiculous," she blurted, rising from her chair and pointing to the other woman. "Are we talking about fairy tales and chimeras, about fairies and mermaids, now? Don't you have any real answers to my questions? Or are you just completely nuts? I mean, do you seriously believe that Wei Wang is planning the future? Here? In this very room? *Now?*"

"No." Gladia shook her head. She smiled. "I don't believe that. What I believe is something else entirely. I believe that Wei Wang is not merely planning the future, but the future of the future."

∞∞∞

Cantara couldn't sleep that night.

No matter from what angle she tried to analyze the whole thing, the Planetary Court was going to vote against the Polaris project. It was inevitable.

Spine Woodside had done an excellent job in the past months, making everyone believe that he had lost the battle against the Hyperists when in fact he was simply preparing his counterattack.

There was no possibility whatsoever that the decision of the Court would favor Polaris' departure.

The days of Wei Wang and his project were numbered.

Cantara sighed, frustrated, as she shifted uncomfortably in her bed. This knowledge had not bothered her twenty four hours before. So why now should the thought of that eventuality make her uneasy, preventing her from sleep? What had changed after witnessing *Wei's bet*? Why did she feel as if she had left unfinished business in that room, an important task that had to be accomplished?

She could not deny it, not to herself. Something had clicked inside her. Yet, no matter how hard she tried, she could not really understand what it was. It was like a premonition that flashed occasionally on the border of her consciousness and lasted for a few heartbeats before disappearing, swallowed up into darkness.

After turning again and again in her bed, Cantara decided she might as well get up and start her day a few hours before schedule. She sat on the bed, put on a crimson-colored robe and headed for the bathroom.

After freshening up, she walked through a dimly lit corridor and opened the door of her office. Once there, she immediately noticed that the input station at the very end of the room was glowing. Cantara approached the object, warily. She frowned and cocked her head, surprised. Then suddenly she remembered her student's homework; James's homework.

It seemed as if a year had passed since her last lecture, not a simple day.

She walked through the room and waved a hand.

When the input station answered her gesture, showing the requested file, Cantara sat in one of the armchairs. *I might as well start from here*, she thought as she began opening the file.

Cantara read the title: *The War of the Ether*. She could not suppress a smile. It was a presumptuous and catchy title, typical of the boy.

She began to evaluate James's work and, as she went on, she found herself fascinated by its content. The homework's execution was not only original, engaging and well written, it was also incredibly accurate. She paused for a few minutes on one of the last sentences. She read it aloud, "Sometimes the final victory cannot be obtained without a calculated number of losses. A strategic retreat can sometimes be the best alternative to avoid total defeat."

That sentence made her think for a few minutes.

She thought hard, staring at the words. It did not sound at all like the deliberations of an aspiring etherion. It was more like the declaration of a general who is preparing for a battle. James' entire approach was incredibly challenging and fascinating. Cantara read the last sentence again. She felt there was something important hidden in that simple sequence of words, some implication that escaped her, like a word on the tip of her tongue that she could not quite remember but she felt she must know.

Then, the awareness hit her like a bucket of icy water out of the sky.

The woman eagerly jumped up from her chair. She looked around, then quickly walked toward the desk and, once there, put her wrist on the communication panel.

Cantara Handal suddenly knew exactly how to make a difference.

∞∞∞∞

The Madame studied the symbol of the Hyperists—a silver colored infinite—over her head. It was several feet above the ground, in the exact center of the room, and revolved slowly but surely, recalling the constant movement of the Earth. There were no wires or support to justify its position, no visible trigo-projector explaining its silvery sheen. The symbol of the HYPER was hanging in the air seemingly without any plausible explanation, defying with impunity both gravity and common sense.

"So? What is your answer?"

Cantara smiled. Gladia's question did not catch her off guard. She had expected it since she entered that room.

"My answer is a clear, unequivocal '*no*', my dear," Cantara said, looking at Gladia sharply. "I'm going to continue to enjoy my retirement."

Gladia started to speak but Cantara cut her off.

"Save your breath, Doctor. My decision is final."

Gladia's face became a mask without expression. She spent a few moments in silence, clearly metabolizing what she had just heard. Then she frowned and said, "And you came all this way to tell me this personally? A simple call would have …"

"Moreover," interrupted Cantara, raising a finger, "the Planetary Court will decide *against* the construction of Infinity. Of this you can be sure."

Gladia shook her head, looking puzzled and outraged at the same time. "I don't understand. Did you simply come to waste my time with …"

"I haven't finished, yet," the Madame continued inexorably, her eyes shining with a fierce light. "In a few months there will be another decision of the Planetary Court concerning the construction of Infinity and the launch of Polaris and, once again, Woodside and his Landists will win."

Gladia approached the woman, raised an arm in the direction of the door, ready to invite her to go out, but Cantara continued speaking. "Still, I promise you that on its third consideration, the Planetary Court will approve the project. The departure will be postponed twice, but not canceled. The third time will be the only one that really matters."

"The *third* time?" Gladia's eyes widened. She seemed unable to follow the other woman. She raised both arms in frustration then continued, "What is this? Is this a joke? What you're saying makes no sense! The Planetary Court has never ruled three times on the same dispute!"

"It will do so, for this case. Believe me. It will set a precedent."

"Do you really think so? And how could you be so damn sure?"

"Rumors," Cantara answered vaguely, carefully studying her long and glazed nails.

"Rumors?" echoed Gladia, without even trying to hide her impatience.

"Well, let's just say … rumors in the right hallways," Cantara pointed out, nodding a few times, as if to give strength to her own words.

"So I should … *we* should trust your 'rumors?' Is that what you're saying?" Gladia asked, shocked. This conversation was beginning to seem like a mockery to her.

"It seems to me that you don't have any other choice at the moment, do you?" Cantara straightened her back and showed her teeth, smiling triumphantly, like a chess player ready to checkmate the adversary.

"Oh really? And let's hear it," snapped Gladia, undecided whether to oust the Madame or to slap her in order to suppress that arrogant smile. "What should we do to make sure that all of this happens? Mhm? That the *third* time Polaris will receive the green light?"

"Nothing," Cantara replied calmly, placing both hands over her crossed legs.

"Right," Gladia said, beginning to walk up and down the room, "let's see if I understand what you're suggesting. Not only are you telling me that you won't help us, you're also asking us to do nothing while Woodside dismembers us piece by piece?"

"That's right, my dear. You'll have to wait. You will need these two setbacks in order to achieve the final victory."

"The final victory …?" Gladia froze in the middle of the room and rolled her eyes. She looked back at Cantara. "What the hell are you talking about, for God's sake?"

"Listen," the Madame said calmly, leaning on the chair. "This Friday the Planetary Court will reject *de jure* the construction of the Infinity complex and the departure of Polaris, but *de facto* the Hyperists will be able to continue their plans. Think of it as a planned setback to prevent total defeat."

Gladia curled the side of her mouth. Despite herself, the muscles of her face relaxed for a moment and the Hyperist allowed herself a smile. She reflected on what she had heard, then studied Cantara curiously. "Now you're talking in plain legalese," she said. "I didn't know you were an expert in planetary lawmaking."

"I'm not," Cantara answered, "but my consultant in law …"

"… is paid handsomely to be in your place," finished Gladia, nodding. "Yes, I should have expected that kind of answer."

There was silence for a few heartbeats, then Gladia spoke again, while walking the entire length of the room. "So the fate of Polaris would depend solely on these *rumors* you're talking about and your word?"

"The *presumption* of my word," Cantara pointed out, raising a finger. "I would deny to anyone that we have had this nice conversation."

"One question nudges at me, then." Gladia studied her guest carefully. "What exactly are you hoping to get from all of this?"

"You mean besides the gratitude of one of the most influential women on the planet?" The Madame blinked at Gladia, flashing a sly smile.

"Yes, in addition to that." The co-founder of the SOL sighed, nodding. "What would you like to get in order to prove your *rumors* are true?"

Cantara licked her lips slowly, very slowly, as if she was preparing to taste some delicious food, then said, "I thought of the … show you invited me to and I have decided that there is something that you have that might come in handy, especially now that I have made a decision about my future."

"And what is it that you need?"

Cantara rubbed her long fingers. She smacked her lips and said, "I want EVE and I want the simulation program used by Wang."

For thirty seconds even the echo of a noise deserted the room. Then Gladia shouted, "What?"

"I have thought about a possible, alternative application of that program," Cantara continued, not paying attention to Gladia's bewildered expression. "You see, adapting that program to my needs, I would turn it into a catalyst capable of making my lessons much more interesting, and my students much more engaged."

Gladia's amazement seemed to melt away. She smiled, shook her head, revealing what seemed to be interest. "You'd do all this for the promise to have a program that increases the performance of your students? Is this—is this really what you want?"

"My students are incredibly gifted, Gladia. Some of them have what it takes to become real engines capable of shaping the future public opinion, to be truly remarkable founders of trends, linchpins, and builders of cultural empires. However, the industry in which we move changes at the speed of light and it's a minefield that has claimed more than one life. I want my boys and girls to have the best chance that I can offer them when they go out there, trying to make a difference in the real world. Wang's program could help me do just that."

"So you would like to use Wei's bet as—as a kind of simulator to forge the best etherions of the world? Is this what you want?"

Cantara crossed her arms and smiled. "What I want is none of your business. Now, pay attention because I will not repeat this again. You have thirty seconds to give me an answer." Then, looking at the

Hyperist with eyes that shone like polished emeralds, she added, "Today is *your* turn to make a difference, Gladia Egea, co-founder of the SOL, second vertex of the Hexahedron and coordinator of the Polaris project."

Cantara stood up and waved a hand. A rush of scarlet light appeared in front of the symbol of infinity.

Gladia speechlessly watched the trigoy launched by the Madame which projected a simple and yet captivating countdown.

Thirty seconds.

Gladia looked at the numbers and then to Cantara. She took a step back, almost without realizing it.

Twenty-nine seconds.

"I want EVE and I want the program used by your genius boy," ordered the Black Widow of the Ether with all the majesty conferred by her features, at the same time dangerous and irresistible. "Give me these two things, Gladia, and I assure you that Polaris will rise. Give me what I want and I promise Wei Wang will continue to build unchallenged, his castles in the clouds."

ERIK

2030

"SONNIE, IS IT time yet?" Erik asked, absently chewing his gum. The boy was lying on the couch, his eyes glued on the images projected by the telegoy.

"The launch is scheduled in one hour, thirty minutes, twenty seconds."

"That long? I'm bored!"

Erik sat up. Annoyed, he stared at the transparent visor of the autotron that was serving him a tuna sandwich and a glass of milk. He was the most recent, expensive prototype his mother was working on. It was expected to go into mass production in two months and as usual, his mother had decided to use her son as a tester.

Sonnie was physically thinner than its predecessors, somehow more basic and meager. It was the first of a completely new generation of Pentanidus.

When his mother assigned the automaton to him, Erik immediately noticed that the sinskin -- the autotron's covering -- had been removed, replaced by a simpler translucent carbonglass. When the child touched Sonnie's smooth, hard surface for the first time, he'd asked why this autotron had no skin.

His mother had replied that the average consumer was a capricious beast. Apparently, people did not want an autotron to be too different from an autotron.

Erik had been thinking a lot about that sentence, never really understanding it.

"Whole-grain bread, tuna and tomatoes with partially skimmed milk," Sonnie said, holding the tray.

"Not hungry."

"Erik, I received precise instructions regarding the fourth meal of the day."

"I said I don't want it!"

"Refusal to comply with a direct instruction is non-acceptable behavior. Mrs. Deringer ordered to call the number 667 883 98854 in case of non-compliance."

"What? Mom told you to call uncle Ramor if I didn't want her smelly ..."

"Done. Standing by and waiting for an answer."

"Hey, hey, *hey!*" Erik moved his hands in front of the autotron's visor. "OK, you won. I'll eat it."

The boy spat out the chewing gum and took the sandwich, shoving it in his mouth.

"I'hm heatin', chan't ya shee?" Erik shouted, the words garbled by food.

Sonnie waited until the child had finished his meal.

"Call aborted," the automaton said finally, taking the empty glass and dish and going back to the kitchen.

Erik wiped his mouth and watched Sonnie go away. He snorted. This time his mother had created a real monster, he thought. With previous models, he had always been able to find a way to do what he wanted. However with this new Pentanidus, things were different. Smarter, faster, more adaptable, Sonnie was a completely new class of autotron designed and built specifically to supervise the offspring of mankind.

His mother was expecting to sell quite a few of them.

Erik looked back at the giant platform in the middle of the ocean that had been displayed on the telegoy for the past three days, without interruption.

The platform was actually a giant mega-structure packed with bridges, walls and towers. To the child, that colossus resembled an imposing silver fortress; an artificial monolith that inspired a kind of awe. The Hyperists decided to name this enormous structure 'Infinity'. No one was surprised by the choice of the name when it was announced. The symbol of the Hyperists, after all, was a silver colored infinity.

Erik focused on the highest tower of the mega-structure, the heart from which the cable of the space elevator aspired to the limitless vastness of space. The tower itself was shaped like a giant infinity.

The telegoy commentator interrupted his thoughts. Flushed with excitement he was saying, "All systems are on standby and waiting for the impending launch. Polaris is ready to ..."

Erik moved his hand and the commentator's face was replaced by another man in a suit with an even more excited look.

"After yesterday's press conference, where Wei Wang answered questions regarding the safety and reliability of Polaris ..." With another gesture, another channel was displayed. "... huge groups of Landists poured into the main squares of dozens of different cities to protest against the upcoming launch, while the headquarters of SOL, Gaia and I & I were assaulted and damaged. Numerous clashes between Landists and Hyperists have left several dozen wounded on the street, some of them in serious ..."

Sonnie returned from the kitchen and examined the spreadsheet left earlier on the table by Erik.

"You have answered ninety-six per cent of the questions correctly. Your performance does not require any action on my part. I'm sending the data to Mrs. Deringer."

The autotron barely left Erik time to look away from the red face of the commentator.

"Your result has been acknowledged by Mrs. Deringer." Then the autotron froze on the spot. Its visor flashed with a green light. "Incoming message," Sonnie announced. Immediately after, the automaton's visor was replaced by his mother's face.

"Honey, I'll be late again today," said the woman with a shrill voice, her long blond hair tousled and two greenish grooves under her eyes.

"Again?" Erik muttered unhappily, "but you said ..."

"I know, pancake, but Professor Kurosawa and I have some stuff to fix. How's Sonnie?"

"It's a nightmare, Mom! Please, turn it off."

The mother nodded. "Excellent," she said, smiling.

"Please, don't sell it," Erik pleaded, joining hands.

"Why shouldn't I sell it?"

"It'll kill thousands of innocent children from boredom."

"No, it won't. This is precisely the point, isn't it? With autotrons like Sonnie, mothers like me can sleep soundly. By the way, are you getting ready for nighty-night?"

"But, Mom," Erik protested, indicating the telegoy. "They're broadcasting live ..."

"Lights go out at nine o'clock, Erik," said his mother, inflexibly. "Not a second later. Sonnie knows it."

Erik cursed under his breath. His mother didn't hear him.

"Now give me a kiss."

The boy grimaced. "Do I have to? It's cold."

The mother turned her head and showed him her cheek.

He snorted and reluctantly kissed the autotron's visor.

"Love you."

The little boy said good-bye to his mother. Sonnie's visor went transparent again.

Erik wiped his lips with the back of his hand. Then he looked back at the images projected by the telegoy.

The channel was showing a variety of cities as they prepared to celebrate the upcoming launch.

Erik was fascinated by the number of people crammed into all those places.

"Wow! Look how many people are packed in there! Sonnie, what place is that?"

The autotron stared at the projection. "Beijing, Tiananmen Square," the automaton replied.

"How many are there? I've never seen so many people in one place."

"The authorities estimate a total of three million two hundred thousand people."

"And this one? What place is this one over here? How many are there?"

"Saemangeum City, U-complex, almost three hundred thousand people."

"And this one?"

"Rio de Janeiro, Copacabana, about one million seven hundred thousand people."

"It looks like they're really having fun, right?"

Sonnie looked at the boy, but didn't answer.

Erik changed the channel and this time a familiar face appeared. The commentator was saying, "After twice successfully stopping the launch and refusing to give up at not even less than an hour from countdown, Spine Woodside is currently busy with his supporters in a violent campaign against Wei Wang and his space elevator."

"Sonnie, how long before Polaris takes off?" asked Erik, watching Spine Woodside surrounded by a sea of people.

"Fifty-three minutes, thirteen seconds."

"Well, that means this time he's screwed," said the boy, smiling. "He's not gonna' make it. He's got no time."

Erik didn't fully realize the difference between a Hyperist and a Landist, but if Wei Wang was a Hyperist, then he was one, too.

The child extracted the last channels from the telegoy he had seen and put them on, one next to the other. In front of him there were now five screens with the live image of the mega-structure surrounded by the ocean, two commentators excitedly talking, the channel that broadcasted for the cities and Spine Woodside busy speaking to his public.

Woodside was egging on his crowd, describing in great detail the danger of the space elevator.

"Sonnie, what is the probability that the cable of the elevator breaks?"

"Detailed information on the composition of the cable has not been made public," the autotron began. "For this reason, I can't give you a satisfactory answer to your question. The cable has a tested tensile strength of around 200 giga-pascal and a multi-purpose AI that maintains the physical properties of the material. The probability that such a cable may be damaged is extremely small."

"How long will it take to get Polaris to its destination?"

"Ideally, keeping the cruise speed constant and considering altitude, temperature and humidity at an ideal rate, Polaris should reach its destination in one day, two hours, eight minutes and ten seconds. Problems with the equipment, the module and adverse weather conditions may, however, require different types of interventions on the speed of the vehicle, thus increasing the total duration of the ascension."

Erik nodded, thoughtfully. "What is it carrying exactly? No one is saying that."

"Wei Wang and the board of directors of the project Space Zero have kept Polaris' cargo secret. Several dozen independent agencies and NGOs, however, have assessed the content, considering it harmless. Each inspector was required to sign a binding contract that forbade them from disclosing the exact nature of the cargo."

The child listened to Woodside. "Hmm, I see. So there can't be any weapons inside it, right?"

"According to several statements made by the inspectors, Polaris is carrying a non-organic object of negligible economic value, negligible weight, and negligible mass, devoid of any technological or electronic component."

"Oh, come on! It's impossible that no one knows anything! I mean, how many people have inspected that cargo?"

"345."

"And no one said absolutely anything? Not even a whisper?"

Sonnie turned its visor toward Erik. "There are rumors. Most of them speak of a metal key. Wei Wang himself announced that it would have been a unique object, structurally compact, with a simple, symbolic value."

"OK, I got it," the boy said waving a hand and making Spine Woodside's image disappear.

Erik kept asking questions for another forty minutes while his curiosity grew, thanks to the images broadcasted by the telegoy.

The boy suddenly stopped speaking and excitedly whirled around when the commentator said, "Only five minutes remaining before Polaris' ascension from Infinity!"

"Did you hear that? It's almost time, Sonnie. Aren't you excited?"

Once again, the autotron did not answer, it just looked at the child fidgeting on the couch.

Polaris, an oval-shaped vehicle, was slowly climbing the majestic tower shaped like an infinity. It was connected to a cable that apparently had no end, like a bridge that was thousands of miles in length that started in the ocean and threw itself into the infinity of the universe.

"Three minutes remaining!" the commentator was saying with growing excitement. "The system is being powered up at this very moment and the cable responds to the signals from the Infinity control center. Polaris is ready to go, waiting for the thrust that will mark the beginning of the first stage called 'the five minutes of terror'."

"Erik," Sonnie said turning toward the boy, "do I start playing the tune you have requested for the event?"

"Geez! I almost forgot," said the boy, clapping his hands. "Well said, Sonnie! Yes, give us some atmosphere. Rock and Roll!"

At exactly one minute from the launch, Sonnie positioned itself at the center of the room and its electronic amplifiers exploded suddenly with rhythmic music, powerful, intense and full of energy.

"Less than fifty seconds to the launch, ladies and gentlemen! The airspace around the structure is clear!"

"*Back in black, I hit the sack, I been too long, I'm glad to be back!*"

"We have a go from the control center. The start of the automatic countdown begins now!"

"*Yes, I'm let loose, from the noose, that's kept me hanging about!*"

"Twenty seconds! Polaris is fully energized! The AI on board has now complete control of the functions of the carrier."

"*I keep looking at the sky 'cause it's gettin' me high!*"

"Fifteen ... twelve ... ten, nine, eight, seven, six, five, four ..."

"*Yes, I'm back in black!*"

"Polaris comes to life! It rises, accelerates ... continues the vertical ascent! No sign of structural failure. We're getting the preliminary data from the control center ... and ... everything is going according to plan! Polaris has almost reached—"

"Look at it go!" Erik cried out, standing up and bouncing on the couch. "Yes! Go, go, *go!* Don't try to push your luck, just get out of my way!"

Sonnie looked at the boy who was following the rhythm of the song, then the images of Polaris, which was moving fast and gradually increasing its speed.

The journalist commenting on Polaris' ascension had a purplish face and bulging eyes. The autotron calculated thirteen percent chance of a heart attack.

Sonnie moved its visor and focused on the images of people celebrating in London, on the Molotov cocktails thrown by demonstrators in Washington and Moscow, on the violent clashes between Hyperists and Landists in dozens of different cities despite the intervention of the police.

The autotron turned back to look at Erik yelling excitedly while waving his arms in the air, dancing on the couch, and following Polaris' unstoppable rise with bright eyes.

It noticed that the boy's heartbeat sped up considerably, that his breathing seemed irregular and that his pupils were dilated compared to a few minutes earlier. These were all disturbing but not life-threatening parameters, the automaton decided in a few nanoseconds, classifying the abnormal physical state as 'euphoric human behavior'. It crossed out the pending decision to call an ambulance but at the same time stopped the music and the television broadcasts.

"Wh—? Sonnie! Why did you do that?" Erik shouted, furious.

"Erik, I have classified your current behavior as moderately dangerous. Also, your bio-values are out of scale. Please bring your physical parameters back within acceptable levels."

"You sonofa ... Turn it back on. Now!"

"I have not registered a significant change in your bio-values. Please stand by."

Erik let out a frustrated shout but in the end he sat down and tried to breathe normally. He threw a look of pure hate at the autotron, but said nothing more. He stood still, quiet, and breathed slowly, eyes closed.

"Fluctuating but acceptable bio-values."

"Good. Now could you turn it back on, please?"

"I'm powering up the telegoy."

The images returned to brighten the room, but there was no longer any more music.

"What about the music?" Erik asked.

"AC/DC, *Back in Black* has been considered by my analysis to be the main cause of your distress. The playing of the song has been interrupted to ensure your safety."

Erik raised his middle finger. Sonnie didn't seem to grasp the meaning of the gesture.

"Let's now go live with the Infinity control center," the commentator was saying with the image of Polaris behind him. "Once the five minutes of terror passed, Wei Wang is now expected in the press room to comment on the performance of the launch and answer questions."

There was a moment of silence, full of expectations.

"The door is opening," the commentator finally said, his forehead glistening with sweat. He was holding his breath. "Yes, there he is! Wei Wang is greeted with applause and a general standing ovation."

Erik's anger slipped away instantly when the reporter announced the arrival of the star of the moment. He made all the other projections disappear and focused only on the image of Wei, followed by five people. The boy immediately recognized Mark Strutzenberg, the

CEO of Gaia, with his usual cigar in his mouth and Gladia Egea, the co-founder of SOL, Wei's right arm in the titanic project of the space elevator. They were immediately followed by Patrick Trudeau, Chief Engineer of I & I, Isaac Nazarov, the founder of Archetype Unlimited and Toshio Shimao, head researcher at the Paragon Corporation.

Erik focused on Wei Wang. The Hyperist looked thinner than the last time he saw him on the telegoy. His face was skeletal and almost blue. He was breathing very slowly and with little conviction, as if he didn't remember how to do it. His eyes were besieged by deep dark shadows, his hair was tousled and the muscles in his neck were tense. He smiled and waved his hand, but he didn't really seem to realize where he was, or what he was doing.

Erik thought of a zombie that was wearing the skin that once had been Wei Wang's. *The Polaris project has destroyed him*, the boy thought worriedly.

The commentator didn't echo his thoughts as he excitedly described the triumphal march of Wei and his colleagues.

Only after a few minutes did Erik notice the glow that surrounded the stage where Wei and the other five sat. He enlarged the image and leaned forward to see better. It was a force field. The boy nodded, approving the precaution.

When the crowd was finally seated, the commentator disappeared, substituted by the image of Wei Wang, who was introduced by a mechanical voice as: visionary mind, the first Hyperist, the creator of the module Polaris and the director of the project Space Zero.

A silence full of excitement permeated the packed room. Erik tightened his grip on the edge of his chair and waited, without moving a muscle.

"To write history is a wonderful experience," Wei began, smiling at his audience. "It gives you a very special perspective on the world around you and helps you understand one very important thing: impossible is only a possibility that has not yet been discovered."

A standing ovation from the public prevented Wei from continuing his speech. Twice he tried to continue the conversation and twice he was interrupted by whistles and applause.

Erik imitated the audience by clapping and cheering wildly. Then he looked at the autotron, staring at him in silence. The boy sat down again and huffed.

It all happened in a matter of seconds.

A sudden explosion erupted from within the room, throwing half of the audience to the ground. Almost immediately it was followed by a wave of multicolored light.

Erik gasped, completely taken aback. He held his breath in astonishment, one trembling hand on his mouth.

He saw the majority of the audience screaming and throwing themselves on the ground, or rushing to the emergency exits in disorder, pushing and stumbling over other people.

The child's eyes widened, unable to process what was happening. The room transformed into a chaos of screams, bodies and sounds without any meaning. Security drones came out from their slots in the walls, dozens of men in black and silver uniforms moved quickly, shouting orders and warnings to each other.

Then time stopped.

Erik saw Wei Wang rise from his chair, slowly, his face devoid of emotion. His eyes were fixed on a specific point in front of him.

It was in that moment of panic and confusion that the boy heard the second explosion.

Erik couldn't see what hit him, but Wei Wang was thrown by an unknown force. The first Hyperist violently struck the wall of the stage. He fell, first on his knees, his hands stiff at his sides, and then to the pavement, slumped back like a lifeless mannequin.

Wei remained motionless.

Erik clamped his hand over his mouth and screamed into his palm.

The child heard the voice of the commentator, but he was so shocked that he didn't understand what the man was saying.

"An explosion, we think, ..." A pause, followed by cries for help and two other explosions tore through the room.

"They're still shooting! Strutzenberg and Shimao ... lying on the ground! They've been hit by something! I can't see ... Almighty God!"

The commentator disappeared from the screen. In his stead, Wei Wang appeared with eyes wide open, lying on the pavement in an unnatural position, with Gladia Egea weeping at his side.

A security man picked her up and carried her away.

Just in time.

Another explosion occurred.

A crowd of people invaded the stage, moving frantically, shouting and shoving other people.

"Oh, no," Erik whispered with a hand still covering his mouth and a shocked expression. "Please, no ..."

The cameras recorded Wei being hurriedly transported out on a stretcher.

Sonnie analyzed the images without commenting on them. "Erik," the autotron called after a few minutes. The boy was shivering in silence, shocked. "The cessation of all activities is scheduled in sixty seconds—"

"What? You're ... you're kidding, right?" the child interrupted looking at the autotron, eyes shining with tears. "Do you even realize what happened? You want me to go to bed now? Forget it!"

Sonnie interrupted the broadcast and dimmed the lights of the room.

"Wha—? Are you crazy? Turn it back on. Immediately! I want to know what happened to Wei!"

In an instant Sonnie elaborated the answer to give the boy.

"Wei Wang died four minutes ago."

Second Chance

ARIUL

7 days later

THE SKY WAS covered with thick, dark clouds the color of dirty water, motionless in the inexorable vastness.

Gladia Egea opened the urn. She looked at it, undecided, as if she didn't remember what she should do with it. She closed it.

The woman clenched her jaw. She felt her heart beat wildly. Slowly, very slowly, she opened the casket a second time.

The wind ruffled her hair. The salty air had a strange smell. It was like being in the middle of a garden made of marine algae and shells, salt and sand.

Gladia looked at the contents. Simple fine and light grey ashes that were all that was left of Wei Wang, Gladia thought.

Reluctantly, the woman threw the ashes into the air.

They disappeared in the blink of an eye, collected by a gust of wind.

Gladia closed the urn and sat down on the sand.

The ocean was calm that day, an immensely wide and still table, like a sheet of glass enclosing an endless world within the world.

Somewhere around there, in a corner of Florida, was the Kennedy Space Center, the outpost from which mankind had sent its messengers, daring to challenge the infinite and the unknown, aspiring to the stars.

Long forgotten past.

Now the place was little more than a tourist attraction.

Wei had told her that that place constituted his first clear memory, the starting point from which he began his history in the world.

Not very far from where she was sitting, Wei and his father had admired the powerful engines of the Atlantis, the last Space Shuttle to leave Earth.

It had been the last light that heralded the end of an era.

Gladia reached into the sand and began to dig. It was pleasant to feel the grains between her fingers and under her nails, almost therapeutic.

A few minutes later, her hand emerged, clutching a mixture of yellow and white sand.

Looking at it, the memory of that strange morning overcame her. She closed her eyes and recalled the smell of bacon and pancakes.

She smiled.

"Damn it," she had said, when the sugar bowl rolled and spilled its contents on the table.

Her hand had been full of white grains, a pearl-colored sand.

"Leave it," Wei had said, while grabbing the small container before it fell off the table.

"Geez, I'm so sleepy I can't even keep my eyes open," she had complained, shaking the last grains of sugar off of her hand.

"Would you like another napkin?" Wei had handed her one.

She had waved it away.

"Rather, tell me what am I doing here in the middle of the night?"

"I need your opinion," Wei had answered.

"Here? In this place?" She had looked around. A server was bringing sausages and scrambled eggs to a customer, a couple of tables away. The room had smelled like maple syrup.

"Wouldn't it have been better … you know, in the lab?"

"The laboratory stinks of work," Wei had replied impatiently. "Now shut up and listen, will you? Close your eyes."

"What?"

"Close your eyes."

"You want me to fall asleep on the spot?"

"Just do it."

She had obeyed, snorting.

"Now imagine," Wei had continued, "you are in front of a door. It's locked but you have the key. However, there is a chain with a padlock that keeps you from opening it. Are you listening?"

"Hmm."

"Good. What do you do if you want to enter the room?"

She had massaged her temples. "Wei, Jesus Christ. You woke me up at four in the morning for another one of your stupid mind games …"

"Stay with me," Wei had said snapping a finger. "Closed door, chain locked. You got it?"

Gladia had yawned through her words. "Yeah … Augh … I got the picture."

"How do you get in?"

"Well, I guess I need to open the damn lock."

"Exactly. Now, let's pretend that a Good Samaritan passing by opens it for you."

"A Good Samaritan?"

"Yes, a Good Samaritan. What happens at that point?"

She had shrugged. "This stupid door opens and—"

"No, no. The door will not open. Don't you remember? The door is still closed. You have to use the key to open it."

"OK," she had said, propping her cheek with her hand and yawning again. "Before I open the door with the damn key"—she'd pointed to a nearby table—"do I at least win a pancake?"

"Think about what we're doing," Wei had continued, his eyes alight with excitement. "Don't you understand? Polaris is the Good Samaritan who opens the lock, but it must be humanity that decides to open the door. Entering the room is not a consequence of the action of the Good Samaritan, but of your action. It's a consequence of your willingness to find out what's inside the room."

Wei had rummaged in his pockets and come out with a padlock; an open padlock.

He had placed it on the table.

"What's this?" she had asked, frowning.

"Polaris' cargo," Wei had replied, as if it were the most obvious thing in the world.

Gladia let the sand slip from her fingers.

She breathed in the air and closed her eyes. She waited in silence for a few minutes.

The voice of the ocean, a timeless whisper, was calling her.

She stood up and took off her shoes, walking closer to the water. When she touched the liquid with her feet, she realized that it was cold and colorless, as his skin had been before going on stage. The skin of …

"Wei, you don't have to do it. I, Mark and others can handle it. Don't be stupid."

"Listen to her, boy," Mark had supported her, chewing on the edge of his cigar. "You look like shit."

"Mom, Dad," Wei had replied, watching both of them impatiently, "I'm as healthy as a crab …"

"… in a California roll," Mark had concluded for him, glaring at the Hyperist.

"Wei, look at yourself, for God's sake! You can't even stand up. You've fallen twice in the last forty-eight hours. You think we've forgotten it? You're exhausted!"

"I didn't fall," Wei had protested. "I was just sniffing the floor while resting my eyes. Don't you ever do that? It's fun. You should try it."

Gladia had raised her arms in frustration. "Some people are immune to good advice," she had said, shaking her head, clearly exasperated.

Mark Strutzenberg had approached Wei. "Listen to the doctor, genius. You look like a twice dead corpse."

Wei had wrinkled his nose and squinted his eyes, pointing at the huge cigar while his tongue hung from his mouth. "Mark, please. I'm trying to breathe."

Gladia had opened her mouth to speak. Wei had waved at her with a raised finger, the gesture he made when he was giving an order or when he considered a discussion closed.

"Don't worry, sugar. I'll be fine."

And he was gone, without another word.

Gladia breathed heavily, fighting back the tears.

She had both feet in the ocean at that point and was slowly getting used to the cold water.

She knelt down to plunge her hands into the water. Once, twice, three times. She looked at them, in silence, with a strange expression on her face.

No matter how many times she washed them, her hands continued to emerge soaked in blood.

It was Wei's blood, while around them other explosions were tearing the room apart, followed by screams, curses and cries for help.

But the rest wasn't important. For her there were only those almond-shaped eyes that had watched her. She could still see those amber eyes, once full of energy though now blank and half-closed… and the cold white hand that had clutched hers.

There had been blood in and out of that broken body.

Two lips had moved. A word had been spoken. Gladia had put Wei's hand on her chest. She hadn't realized that she had been crying.

When those muscular arms had pushed her away, Wei's hand had fallen to the floor with a thud; his lips still.

Gladia wiped her eyes.

She got out of the water quickly. She ran, tripped and fell on the beach. She rolled once, twice then she stopped supine. For a few minutes she did nothing but breathe.

Eventually she sat up, arms wrapped around her knees, forehead resting on her forearms.

In that position, she relived that scene a thousand times. Every time she discovered something new and wondered how she could've prevented it.

One way to save that life.

One way to avoid the death of his dream.

A beep on her arm shook her from her thoughts.

"What is it?" she asked, annoyed. She sniffed.

"Time's up. We have to go."

Gladia didn't answer.

The voice continued, unyielding. "Now! Don't make me say it again."

She pretended not to hear. She closed her eyes and waited till the world ceased exploding before her eyes.

She waited in vain.

When she finally got up, Gladia had run out of tears.

The car was waiting on the side of the road, exactly where she had left it.

A tall man, dressed entirely in white, was waiting with his hands clasped behind his back.

"Get in," he said, looking around.

Gladia still had tears in her eyes.

She cleared her throat and swallowed hard. She removed the last layer of sand from her foot and got into the car.

The man on guard peered around him one last time.

When Gladia was finally in, he moved his wrist toward his mouth.

"Alpha to Commodore. We're leaving."

"Copy that, Alpha. We have you on the screens."

The man got into the car and closed the door.

∞∞∞

"I hope you're satisfied now. That was the stupidest thing you could have done! There, I said it."

Gladia shifted in her seat. She looked uncomfortable.

"I heard you the first time," she said, touching her forehead. "Get over it."

"You just can't take this thing seriously, can you? Don't you realize the danger? Do you even understand what—"

"Goddammit, Leon!" Gladia blurted. "It was his last wish. It's something I had to do. Period."

"Your safety …"

"It's none of my concern. That is your job."

Leon shook his head. "You're not making it easy."

The man stared out the window.

Gladia needed to think, to keep her mind busy. Wei's motionless pale face continued to flash before her eyes. His lips were opening and closing now. He was uttering a word …

Leon interrupted her thoughts. "While you were …" his words drifted off. The man looked at her and continued, in a neutral tone, "I have received some updates."

"What …?" Gladia cleared her throat. Her mouth was dry. She had to drink, but not now. Now was the time for answers.

"Do we know anything else about Nazarov and Trudeau?" she asked.

Leon shook his head. "Our PIs and the police still believe that they are two separate cases of suicide. They've found no evidence—"

"Of course they've found no evidence," Gladia snapped. "If I wanted to kill the brain and the legs of Polaris I wouldn't leave shit behind me, right? Can't they put two and two together? Jesus Christ, what kind of people are running this thing?"

Silence.

Gladia drummed her fingers on her knees.

"What about the autopsies of Shimao and … and Strutzenberg, is there anything new?"

Leon raised a hand. His face became an expressionless mask.

"Yes, Commodore," he was saying, talking on his wrist. "Confirmed, ten twenty-two at the rendezvous."

Leon gave some instructions to the driver, who nodded and decreased the speed of the car.

Gladia waited for him to finish. "You were saying?" said Leon.

"Is there any news from the two autopsies? What killed them?"

"Yes," Leon said, tugging at his thick ginger-colored beard. "All the tests have confirmed the earlier results. We know that they died almost immediately. Same way Wang did."

"They died in exactly the same way?"

"Almost immediate collapse of the internal organs," Leon confirmed.

Gladia ran a hand over her mouth. "And we still have no idea what kind of weapon could have done that?"

Leon laughed a bitter and joyless laugh.

"We're not even able to figure out how the assassins brought those weapons inside, through all the security checks. They're so clueless that someone is talking of ... Dear God, it is ridiculous just thinking about it." He scratched his neck then continued, "Some of them are beginning to talk of some kind of organic weapon."

"What do you mean an organic weapon?" Gladia repeated with her eyes wide open. "What the hell is that supposed to mean?"

"They didn't give me any specifics. Only that, looking at the security recording, it would appear that they shot ... well, using their own bodies."

"What? Is this a joke?"

"If we had a corpse, we could learn more but ..." Leon said no more.

Gladia nodded. She remembered what she had seen on the security recording after the attack. The bodies of the four terrorists had completely liquefied when it was clear that the security was about to overwhelm them.

She had never seen a person melt. She still dreamed the scene every night. But, in her nightmares, it was Wei's body that melted like snow in front of a fireplace.

She shook her head to clear it from her thoughts.

Leon continued to speak. "When and *if* we find out how they brought those weapons into the room, we'll also have to figure out how on earth they penetrated the force field. It was a Lampda Trust protecting you. I can't even begin to imagine what could penetrate that thing."

"So it's confirmed? It wasn't disabled?"

"No. The force field was working properly. It was their damn weapons. Their weapons went through it as if it were butter."

More silence followed.

"Their weapons," Gladia repeated, thoughtfully. "Do we at least know anything more about these people?"

"The main track continues to suggest an extremist Landist faction."

"Is that all?" Gladia looked shocked.

Leon didn't answer.

The woman clasped her hands behind her neck. "You're basically saying that we know what we knew a week ago; nothing more, nothing less?"

Leon crossed his arms. "We're sure of only one thing. These are dangerous people -- someone damn well organized with whom we have never had to deal before. They could be anything. A new group of cyberio, technorists as we've never seen before, unsatisfied Landists, the four goddamned Horsemen of the Apocalypse ..."

"Spare me."

"It's true, we have no clue. They're ghosts in the shadow. The only thing we know is that these guys were able to kill three people in the most heavily guarded building on the planet. They also probably killed Nazarov and Trudeau, too, making it look like suicide."

"No. Not probably," said Gladia, her voice trembling with rage. "They were definitely killed by those bastards. I'm sure of it. I worked with Nazarov and Trudeau for five years. They would never have done something like that, not even ... Not even after what happened inside Infinity."

Leon nodded. "I agree, which brings us back to the original topic."

"Please, don't start that again."

"Gladia, listen. Five of the six people most directly involved in the Polaris project are dead. Dead! Do you understand? That makes you the only one ..."

Leon stopped talking all of a sudden. Gladia looked at him puzzled.

"What?"

"Hush," Leon ordered. "Alpha to Commodore. Alpha to Commodore. Do you read me?"

"Sir," said the car's driver. "We've just lost contact with Commod—"

"Tell me something I don't know, genius," Leon said curtly. "Try to—"

An explosion cut off his words.

The car was hit by a violent shock wave. The driver lost control of the vehicle for a few seconds and nearly ended up off the road.

Another explosion occurred.

Gladia put her hands over her ears and closed her eyes.

The car this time was tossed from side to side.

"Take off! NOW!"

Leon's scream was the last thing she heard before the third explosion hit the car like a giant hammer from the sky.

Gladia lost her hearing while her body surged against the seat belt.

Then the car flew into the air. It turned on itself twice before falling to the ground.

A sharp pain at the base of her stomach and somewhere on her back coursed through her body. Something struck the woman on the head. Suddenly, everything became grey and indistinct. Her eyelids slowly closed and she lost consciousness.

When she opened her eyes again, the world was a strange collection of blurred images, with no sounds and no smells.

She couldn't feel her arms and her legs. She didn't even remember who she was, but she understood that she was moving. Gladia was searching for the door.

She had to get out. Get away. She had to keep breathing.

She never found the door handle, but the door was opened anyway; from the outside.

A hand dragged her away from the back seat.

She couldn't see very well.

Was someone laughing?

Gladia tried to focus on the figure, the human shape before her. That was the only thing she was able to recognize. It was so close ... So close.

Her brain stored the image but couldn't understand or identify it.

It's not possible. I must be crazy, she found herself thinking.

What she thought she saw was an incredibly tall autotron that was looking at her with two small and yellow eyes. Then a voice inside her brain gave her confirmation that that couldn't have been true. Autotrons don't smile.

It was a face, a human face that she had never seen before. An iron-colored face.

Her strength was deserting her. She saw the raised arm of her assailant who was changing, becoming something else. Then she heard another laugh.

What a strange dream, Gladia thought, fascinated by the hazy outline of the figure that loomed before her.

A sudden sound came from her left.

She closed her eyes for a second. The light was too strong.

She opened her eyes again and saw the assailant's arm move away from her face and pointed somewhere else.

Her eyelids closed again. She heard noises. Maybe it was another explosion. Her hearing was coming back, but her vision was weakening.

Her attacker was now on his knees, apparently exhausted. His face was half flesh, half blood. He wasn't smiling anymore.

Then another sound came and the man's body was thrown out of sight.

Bright spots swam across her field of vision. Her eyes were failing her.

Gladia realized that she could no longer breathe but her stubborn heart continued beating.

She forced herself to keep her eyes open, but saw only light; a blinding light, and a hand.

Was she seeing stars in front of her?

Her eyelids closed and she slipped away from the world of sounds and senses.

All that remained was a bunch of confused feelings and memories.

Her mind recalled Wei's last moments.

The Omnilogos' lips had moved. He had whispered a name.

Darkness took over her.

∞∞∞∞∞

Gladia coughed.

It was dark all around.

She opened her eyes. She still didn't see anything.

Something seemed to be hammering on her right temple from inside her skull.

"Welcome back from Wonderland, princess."

The voice made her jump. More than a voice, it sounded like a distant echo. Was she still asleep? Or was she awake?

She couldn't remember anything.

"My ... my eyes." She croaked. She could feel her dry throat as she swallowed hard.

"Yes. A real hassle," said the distant echo. "I fear your sight will not be back for a couple of days. Nothing permanent, don't worry."

The echo was gone. The voice was slowly becoming clearer and more understandable.

"How are you feeling?" the voice asked.

"I ... I don't know. Am I still dreaming?"

"No."

Her sense of smell also was coming back. And in that moment, she would have gladly done without it.

She smelled a strong and unpleasant stench wafting around her. It seemed like a mixture of sweat and dirty underwear.

"What ... what is that stink?"

"Stink?" the voice repeated, surprised. She heard someone breathe in. "I don't smell anything."

I, thought Gladia. Only now did she realize that she wasn't talking to herself. There was someone else with her.

"Who are you?"

Silence.

"A friend," the voice replied.

A pause, then the voice continued, as if it felt compelled to add something more. "An acquired friend, thanks to my relationship with Wei," the voice said. "You see, I was his partner; a special one, like you. I was one of those who were part of his exclusive circle. Our superhero trusted me enough to reveal to me his secret identity. I suppose you know what I'm talking about, hmm?"

The Omnilogos, thought Gladia. The voice was talking about Wei and his secret. So the voice knew?

Wei once confided in her that only a handful of people were aware of that detail.

He never said who the others were.

"A tragic loss," the voice complained, even if it didn't seem particularly distressed.

Now that her hearing was coming back, Gladia knew that the voice had to belong to a man.

She noticed that the stranger was breathing noisily, as if he was fighting for air. Sometimes his breathing seemed like a fast wheezing. Gladia also noted that the man coughed frequently. A couple of times she heard him burp.

"The man is dead," said the voice, "but his ideas persist. And they are stronger than ever. It's the martyrs' legacy." Then, after a long interval, he added, "Stardust to stardust."

Silence.

Gladia was still trying to figure out if her perception was a dream or reality. Without forms, images or colors, it was as if she was living an incredibly vivid dream, full of sounds and smells and other sensations.

Where was she? Why was she on a bed? Why couldn't she see? Why couldn't she remember what …

Then lightning struck her brain and she remembered everything that had happened. Her head almost split in two. It was too much to conceive in such a short time. She gasped, as if she had been underwater for too long.

"God." She coughed. She moved her arm, but discovered that something was attached to her wrist and she started to panic. She tried to get up. "We … we have been attacked. I …"

"Calm down." The stranger forced her to lie down on the bed. Gladia didn't resist. She couldn't. She was too weak.

"You're safe now," said the man.

"Leon?" she asked. Gladia noticed that her hands were trembling. She tried not to shake too much. It was useless. She clenched her jaw and started sweating. Fear and doubt were slowly overcoming numbness and tiredness.

Do you really want to know what happened? she found herself thinking.

The man cleared his throat. "I'm afraid that the driver and Mr. Politis did not survive the attack. As for you, my dear, you've been incredibly lucky. Incredibly. It's a miracle that you're safely here."

Gladia decided that this was an awful nightmare. Other people died. And it was her fault.

All she wanted to do now was to simply sink into darkness. Drift back to sleep where there were no voices, smells or images and, most importantly, where there were neither memories nor pain.

She would wake up in her lab having forgotten everything. None of this could be true.

Her head began to ache, her temples throbbed insistently. A wave of nausea assailed her. She could barely keep from throwing up.

"You have to understand ..." the voice began, but Gladia shook her head.

"No. Leave me alone," she said, her voice was quavering. "I'm tired. I want to sleep."

She didn't care where she was, or with whom she was speaking, or who had attacked her or why she couldn't see. She didn't care. She just wanted to abandon the world of senses yet again. And this time, never to return.

The man made a strange noise with his throat, as if he was about to spit. He seemed to stop at the very last moment, and remained silent.

Long minutes passed. No one moved. Gladia could only hear a faint beeping coming from somewhere over her head.

Then the man said, "Albert Einstein once said that he did not know how the Third World War will be fought."

Gladia said nothing. She was not interested in what the stranger had to say. She just wanted to sleep.

"In silence," the voice continued inexorably, as if responding to a question. "It's a war fought in silence. And it's already begun, though few people know it."

Gladia didn't move. The other didn't seem to notice or even care.

"Sad and ridiculous at the same time, isn't it?" the voice went on, as if he were confessing before a priest, "but horribly true. The corpses of the last week are just some of its first victims. You're very lucky not to be part of the list. Me, you, anyone could be next."

What the man was saying made no sense. Gladia continued to remain still, to breathe quietly and pretend to be asleep. Maybe he would go away. He would leave her alone if she just kept quiet.

"Polaris was one of Wei's projects," the man went on stubbornly. "He had many."

Silence.

Gladia's heart was destroyed and exhausted, but her brain was listening. He had many projects? What projects? Wei had never spoken of this.

"The boy knew what was coming and took his precautions. Our little friend was a cautious person by nature. He liked to keep his eggs, his projects shall I say, in different and separate places, as well as the people who were involved in them. He didn't trust anyone -- maybe especially the people whom he trusted." He chuckled. "A strange guy, our Omnilogos was, don't you agree? Think about the two of us. I don't know anything about your Polaris, apart from what I see with the rest of the public. And you, my dear, don't know anything about my project; the project that he's entrusted me with."

Gladia hated the man for his persistence and his undesired presence. But she was a woman whose job was to hunt down answers and the voice seemed to give her some really interesting ones.

Curiosity got the better of her.

"What project?" Gladia heard herself ask.

The man shifted in his seat. She could swear he was sniggering. "The Ariul project," he said.

A flash exploded in the darkness. Gladia saw Wei's lips move.

It was as if someone had slapped her face. She almost felt the pain caused by the surprise.

Her mind went back to that single word uttered a moment before the end.

"Ariul." Gladia's face glazed with shock. She tried to get up. "Ariul."

"Hmm. You know what I'm talking about?" The voice seemed surprised.

"Before ..." Gladia left the sentence hanging. She swallowed. "It's the last word he said, during the terrorist attack. He ... he said that word. He said Ariul. He looked at me in the eyes and said Ariul ..."

"Really?" The voice no longer seemed surprised. Now it sounded almost pleased, amused even.

"That is strange," the man said. "Well, I guess we'll never find out why."

"I tried ... I tried for days to find out what that meant. But there are too many people with that name. I haven't been able to figure out ... To find ..." She paused. Gladia felt her strength fade away. She forced herself to remain vigilant. She had to know. She had to understand.

"Who ... Who's ... Ariul?"

"Not who," the man corrected her, laughing. "*What* is Ariul?"

"I don't understand."

"Ariul isn't the name of a person. It's a compound word in Korean. It means City of Water."

"City of Water?" Gladia silently repeated the name. No bell rang in her head. The name made no sense.

"Few call it that now," the voice continued. "You see, the name was invented to make it easier to pronounce for you white muzz ... for people like you. Today, the city is known by another name."

"Which name?" Gladia was visibly shaking now. She could feel the cold sweat slide down from her temple. She felt weak, distressed and on the verge of passing out.

She heard a noise coming from somewhere above her head. It sounded like a fast beeping. She heard the man get up from his chair.

"Your bio-values are unstable, my dear. I'm afraid I've overly taken advantage of your strength. I apologize. I only wanted to make sure that there were no permanent damages. Now you need to rest."

"The name, please. I want to know what the name means."

The man seemed to reflect an outrageously long time.

"It won't make any difference for you to know it, sweetie," he said.

He touched her cheek. He had stubby and sweaty fingers.

She heard him leave.

A door opened.

"Please," Gladia pleaded. She felt the tears begin to well behind her eyes. "I need to know."

The man seemed to stop.

Silence.

Finally he said, "Saemangeum City. That's the meaning of the name. That is what's behind Ariul's project."

A pause as long as the eternity of the cosmos followed.

Then the voice concluded, "And right now, princess, you find yourself in it."

EPILOGUE

THE CEMETERY WAS covered by a heavy blanket of fog.

The moon, a silver scythe against the pitch black of the sky, was trying to fight its way through a thin layer of clouds.

The place was quiet and cold. The profiles of the objects were vague, almost indistinguishable. Noises and sounds came from the high trees all around.

An owl opened and closed its wings as it perched on a large branch. The head of the bird snapped to the right and to the left. It cocked its head on one side, with an inquisitive look, while watching the world below its claws.

The bird studied the lone figure in the night.

The stranger was cloaked in a long coat and a hood that hid his face almost entirely. He was staring at a tombstone; a tombstone with a strange shape.

The solid stone seemed to be an extension of the night itself. As black as ink, it had thin scarlet red veins running through it. The base was a cylinder that slowly tapered upwards and then widening again just before the end, forming a sculpture with various points projecting out in all directions. They were the petals of a flower.

The inscription stated:

EVANGELINE LAYIA ELEANOR
2001-2017
Whoever changes one life, changes the whole world

The figure knelt and touched the grave with both hands. It was smooth and cool.

He mumbled something then drew a small container from his pocket. The stranger opened it and studied its contents: a fine white powder. Without hesitation, with one hand he threw the contents into the air.

For a couple of seconds, the light of the moon was able to penetrate the clouds, and the ashes in the air were lit up by a cascade of silvery glow.

Stardust, thought the stranger, looking at the last fragments swallowed up by the night.

"Rest in peace, you two," the figure said, sealing the container.

A gust of wind rustled the hood back revealing his face.

Tiago Silva Abreu Melo looked around.

The silence continued unchallenged.

He shook his head and smiled.

His eyes lifted to the sky, where there were countless stars and just a hint of the moon peeking through a thin layer of clouds.

He put a hand on his forehead and with a wide smile saluted the bright vastness of the firmament.

ACKNOWLEDGMENTS

July 8, 2011. Cape Canaveral's sky was cloudy that day. I was sitting on the edge of the road, chit-chatting with my friends while absently gazing at the Atlantic Ocean just a stone's throw away. The nearest billboard, a few dozen meters on my left, stated: *401 North Cape Canaveral A. F. Station.*

People were gathering on both sides of the road. There were thousands of them and more kept coming. We were waiting for the magic to start, for a countdown to begin. But the truth was that none of us were sure whether or not the Space Shuttle Atlantis would lift off that day.

Previous launches had been cancelled due to similar unstable weather conditions. As astronauts will tell you, a Space Shuttle departure follows ironclad launch criteria: how windy it may be, how much cloud cover, how cold. In other words, there must be acceptable weather conditions for a safe launch.

And I was afraid there would be no launch at all that day. It was likely that they'd postpone it, as had happened many times in the past.

The sky remained stubbornly cloudy. There was no sign of improvement. I kept talking with my friends as the minutes passed and anticipation built up.

I was there that day from a rather fortunate combination of planning and good, ol' luck. I had asked for special permission from my boss to assist Atlantis' departure. In my written request, I had told him I needed the day off so I could tell a great story to my grandchildren: the story of the departure of the last Space Shuttle in mankind's history.

In the end, the launch was delayed. But fortunately for us the Atlantis did lift off that day. When that happened, a burst of joy and energy erupted all around us. Thousands of people cheered and clapped their hands as the Spaceship moved at incredibly high speed, a rocket of light, smoke and colors finding its way through the sky.

It was the first time for me to witness a truly historical event, the kind you read on the first page of the newspapers the day after it happens.

The experience resonated in me much more than I realized while I was standing on the edge of the road, cheering with the crowd.

When the day was over, I found myself looking again at the pictures I had taken, studying every single shot, experiencing one more time that exciting moment. As the hours passed, I noticed that a rather curious image started forming in my mind. It was simple, yet powerful and inspiring at the same time.

I pictured a kid sitting on his father's shoulders who was pointing excitedly at the firing rockets of the Atlantis.

The image was so intense that I thought I must have seen it earlier that day, but I couldn't remember exactly when. I decided I needed to write it down, to keep it as sharp and as real as possible. When I was done, I looked at the few paragraphs and what I had just written with a mixture of curiosity and wonder. I then started asking myself why that kid seemed so excited about the Shuttle's departure. I imagined that the huge Spaceship must have been similar to the biggest firework he'd ever seen. And yet, why was he so taken by that moment? What did it really mean to him? I found myself interested in finding answers to these questions.

At that time, I had no idea I was actually writing the first chapter of this book.

And here I am now, three years from the departure of the Atlantis telling you of that day, of what it meant to me.

To think that this book and all the things that followed are a consequence of that moment amazes me. It makes me think how a person's life can be revolutionized in a matter of seconds.

Of course, Wei sitting on his father's shoulders was only the beginning. This story is not only the outcome of emotions and feelings derived from that episode. It's also a work that required years of research and reading, of asking myself questions for which I had no answers.

Furthermore, *Omnilogos* would not be what it is without the people who helped me shape it and improve it further so that I could deliver it to you as something I could be really proud of.

These are people to whom I owe a debt of gratitude. Without them, this book would likely be a rather flat and boring story; something that most likely would never have "lifted off".

To my father, who convinced me that the book's epilogue had to be rewritten from scratch if I didn't want to completely screw up the entire plot and to my mother, who made me realize how Gladia Egea was a vastly more important character than I'd ever imagined. To my sister, who spotted more grammar mistakes on the original Italian manuscript than all my Betas combined together and to my brother, who commented on the very first draft of this story and gave me incredibly valuable suggestions to make it better.

To Mana Tsuda, who created Wei's first sketch and laid down the foundation of the book cover.

To Benjamin Roque, who turned Mana's beautiful sketch into a powerful book cover.

To my friends Pietro Venditelli and Alessandro Tamagnini, who helped me strengthen the story with their constructive criticism.

To writer Robin Gadsby, who helped me take a critical eye on things, showing me that writing doesn't always need to wear a suit and tie, but it always need to 'behave' smoothly.

To Margaret Marola, for proofreading the first draft of the novel after my translation into English and to Charlotte Gledson and Dr. Richard Lawhern, Ph.D. who edited the revised manuscript and made major improvements to my English grammar and structure.

Omnilogos was my first novel, and I like to think at it as a prologue, a story that introduces a story. Now that the spark has ignited the fire, there is no going back.

A new saga has begun.

Michele Amitrani
October 28, 2015

ABOUT THE AUTHOR

Born in Rome in 1987, Michele Amitrani is a transplanted Roman writer now living in Vancouver, British Columbia. He has grown up writing of falling empires, space battles, mortal betrayals, monumental decisions and everything in between.

He now spends his days daydreaming on park benches, traveling through time and space and, more often than not, writing about impossible but necessary worlds.

Omnilogos is Michele's debut novel and the prologue of an action packed Sci-Fi saga drenched with what some have called the sense of awe typical of Asimov's Foundation series.

A staunch supporter of Self-Publishing, Michele helps other writers to realize the dream of making their works available to the public by sharing tips and resources on how to write, publish and publicize works independently on his website micheleamitrani.com and on his YouTube channel.

When he's not busy chasing dragons or mastering the Force, you can find him at MicheleAmitrani.com or hanging out on Facebook at /MicheleAmitraniAuthor.

DID YOU LIKE THIS BOOK?

For today's indie author, every bit of exposure helps. If you liked Omnilogos Extended Edition, then perhaps you could spare a few minutes to write a review on Amazon or Goodreads or just share a link on Facebook.

Reviews and shares are really important to self-published authors, so if you enjoy *Omnilogos*, let somebody know, so they can enjoy it too.

Thank you for your support!

Can't wait to know what happens next
in Saemangeum City and beyond?

Neither can I!
But I am delighted to present you
with this special preview from

PELARGONIUM

Book Two of The Omnilogos Series

Enjoy!

Reflections on the Water

ARIUL

2039

LENA MARUISHI WOKE up with the feeling of having a giant python entwined around her leg. On the border between sleep and wakefulness, she instinctively grabbed her knee.

Her skin seemed cold and clammy, but there was nothing else out of the ordinary. Her leg was fine.

Lena breathed in and out, over and over, until she felt her heartbeat slowing down. The imaginary pain that apparently had awakened her, turned into a simple side effect of the nightmare.

She cursed through clenched teeth as she shook her head to clear it. She rubbed her eyes and found them wet, swollen with tears. She hastily wiped them with the back of her hand as she let out a yawn, allowing that simple gesture to relax her nerves. Then, she looked slowly around. A flash of sudden awareness reminded her of the confined space in which she found herself.

The interior of the airplane was well illuminated by a familiar quartz-colored light that gave a safe and relaxing look to inside of the fuselage. Lena rubbed her neck and closed her eyes. She curled the corners of her mouth in a silent expression of embarrassment. Inwardly, she hoped that no one was watching her while she was recovering from that stupid nightmare.

A noise to her left suddenly reminded her of the nearby passenger. She turned toward him and studied him for what might have been the hundredth time.

Despite herself, she could not suppress a smile.

She looked at the man as if he was a rare specimen exhibited in a zoo. Watching him gave her the same rush of excitement, the same sense of wonder that watching a totally alien creature moving and breathing in front of her eyes might have aroused. The mere fact of having him close enough that she was able to study everything that made him so exotic, was enough to run a shiver down her spine. It was a tacit confirmation of her whereabouts and, most importantly, of where she was heading to.

The man seemed to be immersed in an apparently impenetrable sleep. The gaping mouth regurgitated dribble and grunts alike. Lena carefully waved a hand in front of the stranger, but nothing happened. She stopped to shake her hand. Closing it in a fist, she pressed it to her cheek, then propped her elbow on her knee as she continued to look at the man, fascinated by the slow but steady rise and fall of his chest.

The passenger provided a show that never bored her. She had spent a good part of their journey watching him with amazement and curiosity, accompanied by the background of his interminable snoring.

Lena's eyes lingered on the stranger's clothes, arranged so as to form different colored layers overlapping each other, making him look like a strange variety of incredibly overgrown caterpillar.

It was the first time in her life that she found herself so close to a Saemagen. Given the fact that soon she would be surrounded by people like him, she might as well get used to them, she thought to herself.

She realized that watching him was a way of reminding herself that it was all true, that she was not dreaming. The thought filled her with a joy that was difficult to describe, like a never-ending rush of expectation and excitement that made her think that anything was possible.

The stranger moved imperceptibly on the seat as he grunted something unintelligible then returned to drool. *Unbelievable*, Lena thought as she was fascinated by the state of semi-hibernation in which the stranger seemed to have sunk. He had done nothing but sleep except for waking up to eat his lunch, only then to return in a blink of an eye to his snoring.

Lena remembered the man as he had been busy fumbling with cutlery, intent on enjoying his quite peculiar meal. *Yes, quite peculiar in-*

deed, she thought.

She swallowed hard and pursed her lips. As she recalled that episode, an unpleasant feeling at the base of her stomach forced her to rub her belly. Was it nausea that she was feeling? Yes, she remembered it all too well. The man had plunged, two fingers into the belly of the huge cockroach served on that strange rust colored leaf, with palpable satisfaction. Lena closed her eyes and saw him again disconnecting with surgical precision, pieces of the abdomen of the enormous insect, craving its meat, putting it into his mouth and chewing with gusto. After finishing his dish, sucking its innards, he had passed to the next insect, repeating the operation.

"Pardon, miss. Are you done with that?"

The high voice made her jump. She whirled toward the aisle and saw the gentle and smiling face of the hostess who was pointing to her lunch tray. She had opted for a more traditional dish of pasta and chicken with vanilla pudding for dessert.

Yet her food had barely been touched. After seeing her traveling companion, the girl had left the contents on the tray largely intact.

"S-sure." Lena cleared her throat, trying to hide her surprise. She smiled thinly, and clumsily handed the tray to the hostess who took it and put it with the others.

"Could you pass me his too, please?" the hostess asked, indicating the tray of the other passenger beside her. The man, deaf to their conversation, continued to drool and grunt undisturbed.

Lena looked at the tray. It was empty, except for a couple of larvae as white as milk, some carrots covered with hot sauce and the three empty shells of the huge cockroaches that had been the main course of his lunch.

Lena swallowed again as she passed the tray to the hostess, who smiled, thanking her before moving to the next passenger.

The girl looked around a few times as she rubbed her bleary eyes and let out another yawn. She had slept about an hour, but it seemed to her that she had just closed her eyes before waking up with a start. She didn't feel rested, but trying to sleep again was impossible, she realized. She could feel the rush of adrenaline, clearly indicated by her unsteadiness, calling her to do something, anything.

She impatiently drummed her fingers on her knee and decided to summon the flight plan to see at what point on the journey they were.

With amazement, she found that the plane was to land at its destination in just over an hour. *How fast is this thing?* she asked herself, surprised. Again, the palpable sense of excitement made her want to run up and down the length of the plane. Were they really so close?

She realized she was shaking when she leaned to resume reading the book that she had left on the shelf in front of her seat. A book she had barely begun.

She checked the flight plan once again. Her eyes were attracted by it as if an inexplicable force pulled her, like a moth attracted by a light. It was not hard to figure out what was causing that wave of nervousness. Her expectations had done nothing but grow, the closer she got to her destination.

Fifty-nine minutes upon arrival.

Fifty-eight minutes.

Lena snorted softly, angry with herself. She had promised herself that she wouldn't count the minutes separating her from the destination. But it was increasingly difficult to keep faith to her resolution.

She shook her head and breathed slowly, a weak attempt at controlling her growing excitement.

Fifty-seven minutes.

She found herself hating her inability to check, or at least hide her nervousness. It made her feel so stupid, so insecure. Was this the image she wanted to give of herself? What would the others think of her?

The passenger on her left continued to snore quietly.

Fifty-five minutes to landing.

Lena clenched her teeth and closed her eyes for a heartbeat. *It's all right*, she said, breathing slowly. *It's not Mars, silly. Calm down.*

Reluctantly, she turned off the flight plan display with a quick wave of her hand.

She took her book, opened it and tried to trade nervousness and concern with feelings more familiar and manageable; at least for a few more minutes.

It was close to thirty minutes from landing, when the airplane began its descent. The voice of the captain interrupted the activities of the passengers with his calm and professional announcement.

Lena snapped her head toward the aisle at the sound of the voice and the book almost fell from her hands.

"Good afternoon." The voice was clear, as if someone was talking only a few inches away. "This is the captain speaking. It's a quarter past two in Saemangeum City and the temperature is thirty degrees Celsius. We should land at Gunsan Airport in about thirty minutes."

The message was repeated in Korean, Mandarin and also in Castilian.

Lena looked to her left but her traveling companion didn't even blink. She considered the possibility of waking him up, to inform him of the imminent landing. But the voice of the captain was replaced by that of the hostess and she turned and paid attention again.

"Ladies and gentlemen, as we begin the descent, please remain seated and allow the seat belts to arrange themselves in landing mode to ensure your protection."

Lena saw the seat belt sneaking quietly from one side of the seat to the other, gently wrapping her hips in a safe and comfortable position. The flight attendant continued her message when all passengers were seated, with their belts secured.

"We also would like to remind you that once we enter Saemangeum City airspace, your appliances will not be able to connect to the traditional Ether. Please consult regulation number 4 issued by the Directorate regarding cybernetic security for further information. Thank you for your cooperation and we apologize for any inconvenience."

Lena completely forgot her intent to wake the adjacent passenger and let her eyes feast on the incredible spectacle of clouds, land and sea that flickered outside her window. A web of roads and bridges began to emerge as they slowly but surely approached their destination.

Now she could almost make out the metropolis that awaited them a few thousand feet below. From that height, it looked like a treasure chest filled with hundreds of incredibly shining jewels. As the plane lost altitude, more details were revealed before her eyes. Eventually, it was impossible to find an area not embellished with silver and platinum colored buildings that reflected the light of the water all around her.

Lena swallowed a couple of times as the airplane landed without noteworthy noise, bumps or shudders. The inertial dampers of the vehicle were the most effective that Lena had ever experienced. If it were not for the view outside, she probably would not have even noticed that the plane was no longer in the air.

The flight attendant spoke again, on behalf of the Ariul Airlines, thanking the passengers for choosing their company and took her leave with a greeting.

Lena waited with the other passengers while the airplane was inserted into its landing berth and the channel connecting the gate was locked to the vehicle. When the usual yellowish light of the aircraft interior was replaced by a blue sky light and the belts were repositioned into the seat armrests, the passengers knew that the landing was complete.

Lena was surprised to see the Saemagen who had accompanied her throughout the journey get up suddenly from his seat, hastily rub his legs and after a quick nod in her direction, take his carry on luggage and walk with the first passengers to the exit.

The girl watched him make his way quickly, passing the people who were just getting up from their seats. She blinked in surprise. She had never seen anyone wake up like that.

Meanwhile the airplane was emptying rapidly. The girl took her small backpack from under the seat and walked with the others toward the exit, while trying to stretch her arms and legs.

Some people lingered to check out whether they left something behind them, but for Lena it was different. She didn't need to look back. All her belongings were inside her small backpack.

Once she was near the exit door, Lena was greeted with wide smiles and deep bows by the airline personnel, their gold and emerald uniforms reflected the bluish light.

Lena smiled as she looked for the last time at the interior of the Ariul Airlines's airplane, trying to take a mental picture of its futuristic design, wide corridors and immaculate seats.

When she finally stepped off the airplane, her brain registered the fact that she was in another place, under another sky, in a new world.

But there was little time to savor the moment, to realize that she had finally reached her destination. Lena was too busy following the trail of people who passed through the tunnel connecting the airplane to the gate inside the airport.

She had spent much of the trip evaluating the other passengers. Most of them, she had soon realized, were tourists or businessmen who had, like her, departed from Los Angeles, but a half-dozen stood out due to their flashy clothes and their strange eating habits. It was the group of Saemagens who had spoken to each other for the entire duration of the trip. The only other Saemagen on board had been the guy sitting next to her. She tried to find the peculiar group and finally spotted them ahead of her.

Unfortunately, she soon lost sight of them. It seemed they were in a hurry and, unlike the other passengers, they were in a familiar environment and knew exactly where to go.

Lena, on the other hand, had not received any specific information about the post-landing, apart from the fact that she needed to reach the border control gates and speak with one of the immigration officers. She decided to stop in front of the first information obelisk conveniently located at the end of the tunnel that connected the airplane to the airport.

She touched the smooth surface of the screen and quickly found what she was looking for.

She nodded, reading the information, then touched the small apparatus in carbon-glass fixed above her temple. In an instant, her oculus expanded to form a viewer. With a gesture, she moved the information she needed from the obelisk to its portable viewer. Almost instantly a cobalt blue line showing her the way appeared on her oculus directly in front of her feet, like an unending arrow, snaking its way along the airport's shiny floor.

Lena followed the trail of light produced by her device.

As she followed the signal, she was aware that her heart was beating faster and faster, even though she was walking at a slow pace. She knew that she could do nothing to control her emotions. She was scared and excited at the same time. After all, she was home; her strange, new home.

Lena had grown up listening to countless stories about Saemangeum City. The world's first zero-impact city always seemed to find its way to the top spot on the news. Obviously she had read everything she could get her hands on, studied maps, watched videos, documentaries and experienced dozens of simulations that abounded on the Ether. She talked to people who had been there for vacation or business trips. She heard rumors and asked questions and advice from anyone who knew more than she did, about the famous City of Water.

Somehow, though, she had never really thought that her turn would come. Her curiosity had been little more than a pastime. She always pictured this place as a destination beyond reach, exotic, even weird, like an everlasting iceberg in the middle of the desert. It was a place created in fabulous stories and alien customs, difficult to imagine and even more difficult to truly understand.

As she followed the blue line showing her path, Lena realized she was experiencing a strange feeling, something she had never experienced before. It was as if she was wearing a skin that was not her own, living someone else's life, a stranger's life that she discovered step by step.

Very slowly, her brain registered the fact that she was a stone's throw away from the place of her dreams.

Lena had a sudden urge to check that all her documents were where she had stowed them. After rummaging through her pocket and grasping her passport with trembling hands, she found herself reluctant to let it go. What would have happened if she had lost it? What would have happened had someone stolen it? Had it fallen out of her pocket? Or had it evaporated away for no particular reason…

She couldn't suppress an embarrassed smile while formulating these silly thoughts. However, her hand remained clasped on her passport.

The blue path took her to an elevator. Once inside it, the main floor button started to pulse with the familiar cobalt blue light confirming her next step. Once she pressed the button, the blue line disappeared from her visor. Lena re-stowed her oculus with a quick wave of her hand.

By the time the doors opened, Lena knew that she had reached her destination.

The Korean Border Service occupied a gigantic hall, clean and bright, illuminated by pearl white light. At that moment the huge space was almost completely empty, except for the people who had disembarked from the airplane a few minutes before.

She allowed most of them to pass by her as she walked deliberately slowly. She was painfully aware that her nervousness was growing exponentially. She shook her head to clear it. This was not a time to be distracted by her silly concerns. Rather it was time to figure out where she should to go next.

Lena looked around and noticed that there were two lines. She glanced at the big screen on her left which displayed: *Korean citizens and residents.*

It was not for her.

She headed toward the other line and counted just half a dozen people waiting in front of her. While she was waiting, holding onto her passport as though her very life depended on it, she glanced at the officers busy scanning and questioning people. She counted six border control officers. Lena evaluated each of them carefully: four women and two men. Three were serving the 'Korean citizens and residents' line. She looked up again at the big screen above her head and was surprised when she found that the screen actually indicated two directions. On the left corner she read: *International arrivals* while on the right corner: *S.C. visa holders and S.C.V. candidates* was displayed.

Only then Lena realized that two border officers were actually working at the 'International arrivals' line, while the last one was busy at the 'S.C. visa holders and S.C.V. candidates'. This last officer was the only one that did not look like a Korean.

Puzzled, Lena looked uncertainly to her left, and then to her right, then again to her left. She savagely chewed her lips as she felt the palms of her hands starting to sweat.

She was not sure where she was supposed to go. Both options meant to her more or less the same thing. She looked at the information obelisk placed near the elevator and for half a heartbeat she thought to go back to ask for directions. *Or is it better to ask someone waiting in line*, she suddenly thought, looking around intently.

"Next in line, please."

Lena looked in front of her but saw nobody. Apparently, *she* was the next in line. The people who were waiting patiently behind began to stare at her, a curious look on their faces. She felt the eyes of the whole room on her.

"Next in line, please."

The girl almost stumbled on the floor. One part of her brain commanded her to take a step forward, while the other part ordered her to go back and ask for information.

"Miss? Is there a problem?"

Shit, Lena thought while somehow her legs moved automatically toward the voice that had called her. Before she knew it, she was facing the officer who served the line: S.C. visa holders and S.C.V. Candidates.

"Passport, please."

Her hand already clung to her passport. She pulled it out of her pocket so quickly that she almost threw it in the officer's face.

She murmured a timid apology that the man didn't even hear, then looked at her shoes with scrupulous attention. After a few seconds, she raised her eyes again. Although she was nervous, she could not help but notice that the border guard was a handsome man in his thirties, with night black skin and big brown eyes.

Lena shifted on her feet uncomfortably, unable to hide her nervousness. "S-sir ... I ... Ah ... I have a question. I was not sure if this was the right line for ..."

"What is the purpose of your visit, Miss Maruishi?" the man asked, while carefully studying the passport.

Lena cleared her throat. "I ... Ah ... I've been selected for a Virtuous Visa by the Saemangeum Directorate, s-sir." Lena immediately thought her answer was too vague. When she opened her mouth to add something else the officer nodded.

"In this case, you are in the right line," the man said. "I will need both your hands, Miss Maruishi. Please place them on the display. Here, if you please."

Lena put both hands on the thin carbon-fiber display that the officer placed in front of her. After a few seconds, a green light began to pulse on the right-hand side of the display.

"Thank you for your cooperation," said the man, taking back the display, folding it and putting it on his desk. "Please proceed straight ahead until you reach that blue terminal over there." He pointed with both hands to the terminal. "Once there, you can follow the directions and head toward the Candidates' Welcome Area. An attaché of the Directorate will be there waiting for you."

Lena nodded, taken off guard. *Is that it?* she silently asked herself. *Are we done?* However hard it was to believe, she was almost disappointed. Without really knowing why, she had expected something completely different, like a scrupulous interview or some kind of elaborate test. She wanted to ask the border officer something, but the man quickly waved a hand and the person behind her came forward.

Before Lena left, however, the border officer surprised her by looking directly into her face with a wide open smile. "Welcome to Saemangeum City, Miss Maruishi," he said. "Make us better."

Made in the USA
Charleston, SC
02 November 2015